For Harambe
Goodnight, sweet prince 🖤

All Saints Hotel and Cocktail Lounge
Nathan Monk
Copyright © 2021 by Nathan Monk
All rights reserved.

FatherNathan@gmail.com
CharityInstitute.com

ISBN-13: 978-0-578-95506-3

Cover design: Copyright © 2021 by Tashina Monk

Printed in the United States of America
First Edition
10 9 8 7 6 5 4 3 2 1

ALL SAINTS HOTEL & COCKTAIL LOUNGE

Nathan Monk

A Novel

Trigger warning:

This story deals with politics, religion, abortion, murder, sex, suicide, racism, transphobia, drug use, collective trauma, and the effects of late stage capitalism on an unsuspecting generation.

Act I

Two Thousand Nine

CHAPTER ONE

CREATION

Do any of us start out as saints or sinners or is it just some accident of circumstance, childhood trauma, and maybe access to healthcare? I don't remember ever wanting to give a shit if I was good or bad. I just wanted to survive the next shift so I could pay my landlord's mortgage. Let's be honest; in the sainthood department, most of the best saints are really just naughty little sinners who are better at public relations than the heretics. Who are the sinners anyway? They are just the ones who the saints burned at the stake before they got a chance to tell the truth or at least their side of the story. When our collective trial by fire began upon being thrust into the world, I don't imagine any of us set out to be anything special. We didn't have a fucking plan. We were just a bunch of scared and overly zealous kids grasping for a future we had all been promised, only to find out when we got there it had been reverse mortgaged so our spawners could go on cruises and never retire, just for fun. We did everything we were told to do.

"Go to college so you don't flip burgers!" our parents would say in liturgical unison.

And all the politicians said, "Amen!" with raging boners over the interest we would be paying until the day we died of a preventable ailment.

In the beginning, we never even questioned why we disparaged the culinary artists who prepared our meals, nor did we anticipate that we would all soon be fighting on the same battlefield together begging for table scraps. Comrades in arms of a war we didn't even start. We were casualties of a massive game of Craps our parents were playing with the economy, betting their odds against our planet, our gains, our jobs, our education, our healthcare, our future. We were bitter millennials long before they even told us we had a title. No, we were just the accidental pregnancies, the third babies, a footnote to Gen X, wearing our siblings' hand-me-down shoes, and being told we would never compare.

This was the decade before Bernie would take all our communal rage and turn the hymns of the Occupation into mantras that felt like an authentic version of the hope and change Obama sold us. Even before we had the vocabulary to define our collective anger, we were itching to march somewhere, anywhere, even if we didn't know what the destination was. We needed a map, but we were too busy taking payday loans to finance abortions while telling ourselves that someday, maybe, it wouldn't feel like we would be bringing their grandkids into what felt like a third-world America. We wanted to die but were too afraid we would survive it and be stuck with the medical bills. Plus, someone needed to live long enough to pay off the good time our predecessors were having. So instead of immediate death, we substituted it with drinking our tips each night and chain smoking as a slow motion suicide.

We would spend our nights holding Council Meetings of the Dredges around the billiards table, hoping for a tomorrow that might turn our small coastal town into one of the metro cities to which we always said we would escape. Could Chicago or Nashville or New York City be hiding our potential in a little box, if only we could get there to find it? Anything other than this tourist trap we called home. Our community was nothing more than a piss-stop on the way from Texas to Disney World. We sucked on the teat of the providence of Interstate placement and just hoped to God that someone would become addicted enough to Grits-A-YaYa to maybe stay an extra night and tip us so we could pay the electric bill.

So we would convene at the only altar we knew, the sanctuary for the sinners, heretics, and concubines of the South; the ragtag band of dishwashers, hotel staffers, and spring break attorneys that lined the bar to drink to another successful day of surviving.

"The best damn thing we can hope for is a hurricane," Billy would grunt once a night as he would pour another round. "That's where the money is. No matter what anyone tells you, our industry is not the beach but Jim Cantore."

Everyone knew everyone. Everyone had fucked everyone. Everyone hated everyone. There was no new money in this town. No escape plan. No ladder reaching up or even down. We just floated en masse at sea level hoping not to drown in sin or bills. The same dollars circulated from the Walmart to the military base to the beach hotels and then back to thongs of the strippers at the Angels Gentlemen's Club, money just passing from hand to hand, neighbor to neighbor. There was no accumulation of wealth or prosperity. Even the rich folks were just poor illusions of having made it when, in reality, they were just little fish who were smart enough to escape the big ponds so they could play sharks in one of poorest puddles in the Union.

We all dreamed, but we knew there was nothing on the other side of any of this for most of us. We had all watched as our friends or enemies would escape, knowing full well that something would draw them back like the tide. Off they would run, only to be dragged by the neck back to the town they thought they were finally free from. We would watch them walk back into the bar like a revolving door with grand stories of lives lived outside of the confines of the grips of their conservative roots. New tales of adventures with new drugs, and new bars, and new bodies that kept them warm for a winter or two before the unceremonious return, just in time for the tent revival and altar call to be washed clean again, before becoming clerks at their dad's best friend's law office.

By nature of my Southern upbringing, I'm inclined to believe in something divine, damning, or at least superstitious. But as I look over the landscape of the destruction that followed us all as a generation, I'm less likely to believe there is any grand design or predestination— unless we truly are all children in the hands of an angry God. Nothing that followed over the last decade makes any sense if there is some creator orchestrating our steps. Why would anyone, divine or otherwise, wish this on anyone? But then I take a step back and realize the plan may not be divine, but it certainly was a plan. We are all just puppets in a masterful show for the entertainment of powerbrokers that will never know our names. We are nothing but broken creatures, ants under the magnifying glass of monsters hiding behind suits—Wall Street and Big Pharma and the Prison Industrial Complex. They somehow figured out a way to make our parents cheer on our destruction instead of our success. We became the suspects, the terrorists living under their new roof, a marauding gang of anti-fascists ready to sell our souls for a couple of social media likes.

Yes, Mom, we did it all for the lolz.

What a laugh riot it has been to live under the highest inflation and lowest economy so we could pay into safety nets that would be consumed before we ever had a chance. We were all giving our lives in some way, over griddles with burger patties, in hallways of our schools to preserve the Second Amendment, or in deserts for you to fill up your SUV. Hell, there wasn't a single one of us that didn't know someone who had fought in Iraq and Afghanistan. They would return through that same revolving door. I sometimes wondered when they would replace the Vietnam vets on the street corners, panhandling on the Panhandle. "Never forget!" Oh, how we would forget their faces soon enough. They would be hidden under scruffy beards and ignored by the VA. Living in a military town, we knew all too well the song and dance. Just another cog in the machine of how our generation was being forgotten before it ever got a chance to begin.

When we weren't being slaughtered in our schools or oil fields, we were the unwilling guinea pigs of technology and possibility. The iPhone was still an infant as we came of age to social media just beginning to move cozily into our beds and bathrooms and relationships. We entered society as we were just moments away from occupying Wall Street and yet a decade away from burning Ferguson to the ground. Stuck somewhere between revolution and a nightcap. Everything filled with a calm rage just before the storm. Each morning waking up and wondering, "Is this the too far? Is this the moment everything changes?" and then ordering another crunch wrap supreme.

This was back when Donald Trump was still just a silly D-list celebrity firing people on television and seemed quite safely far away from being able to fire nuclear missiles.

Here we all sat at our circular table, the vagabond friend group. A collection of leftover misfits from high school with predestined failures to launch because there wasn't any room left for us in the board rooms because our elders where too stubborn to vacate and make way for us. We could bring them coffee, though, at $7.25 an hour before going back to our apartment with six other roommates. That was super cool of them. But here they have no power over us, not in this dimly lit room filled with smoke circulating through the red lights.

Everything felt perfect in these moments of communal solitude. The five of us were more than friends and less than lovers. Tonight, we didn't feel as powerless as the elders told us we were. We felt as if we could take over the entire world or maybe just City Hall. It didn't matter, we had hope. This was the day we would crown our new leader who would carry us into a new horizon. This was Obama's inauguration. Barry came in and took us all by storm with hope. So much hope. Why did everything feel so goddamn hopeless then? Nothing felt like hope when we were still scraping by. At 25 shouldn't I be somewhere else by now? My father owned a home and was well into his second marriage to my mother by this age. Not me, I was scraping by just to not have to move back in with my folks. Only grit kept me living in an 8x10 room downtown with three other people. I felt like I should be worried about having kids or wasn't I still a kid?

It all seemed so disjointed and confusing. In spite of it all, we were swept away in this alluring and seductive idea: hope. Like sailors lured by a siren's song, we came running to the edge of our respective ships and jumped headlong into those waters and swam until our capillaries burst. This tempting serenade of hope and change rang like a promise, a simple promise, and we would sign our fate on a bar napkin, thinking we could make a difference.

So here we were, encircling that table and waiting to savor every moment of this victory. Five friends. One city. And a decision that would change everything.

If I am honest with myself, it all started that night. This was the moment when decisions would be made that would forever change the landscape of everything that would happen. A priest, a hooker, a journalist, a burger flipper, and our resident philosopher all walk into a bar. This was about to be the worst joke ever told and we didn't even know it. Nothing that followed would be funny at all. We just couldn't see it. Only three of us would survive, but we all died that night. There would be no resurrection. No absolution. It all started with the best of intentions. How soon we would find out what happens when mortals charge up Olympus.

Who will absolve our sins? Who will forgive our transgressions? I don't know if there are angels or God. But what I do know is we all found heaven and hell at the All Saints Hotel and Cocktail Lounge.

***

Shane was always the first or last to arrive. He never showed up in the middle. Sometimes he would get there before everyone because he wanted to set the scene. Other times, he would appear last because he had already made a scene somewhere else and needed to re-center himself with a sympathetic audience. He was a candle in the wind and there was no way to hold him down. There would be times when we didn't hear from Shane for a month or two. He would just disappear into the wilderness for a while to commune with the gods and nature and the idea of a woman who would replace for him the need for any other form of sustenance. Then, in an instant, he would reappear again out of nowhere. Our lives would be moving in and out and then he would just be there like Christ in the upper room.

He wrote for the local paper and was constantly certain that today would be the day when they would finally drop the axe on him. There wasn't a single day when he wasn't in some sort of trouble with his editors. See, Shane lived in the future, constantly making plans and sometimes following through with them. His plans' intentions could be gloriously shattered in an instant if something more interesting or beautiful appeared within his line of vision. That's why he missed my birthday last year. Her name was Emma. It was also why he missed New Year's Eve. He was in Egypt. He just disappeared and was gone and then here he was, swearing that he had voted before he left. Talking about how fascinating the world we lived in was. Excited to drink. Excited to party. Excited to be excited.

His hair was long and formed into accidental dreadlocks and he wore a hat that it was rumored he stole from Johnny Depp while visiting a comic convention in LA. He was skinny as a rail and looked always as if he was both coming and going. His style was like a newsboy had been attacked by your grandfather's closet.

When he walked into the bar, our eyes locked. I wasn't exactly sure when the last time I saw him was. He had been gone during NYE and BARE Ball and so it had been at least a month. He sauntered over to where I sat at the table, took me by the hand and lifted me up into a massive hug that defied his frame. He kissed me on the cheek and said, "Let me look at you!" like he was an old man. He cupped my cheeks in his cold hands and smiled even wider.

"Let me buy you a drink!" he shouted, laughing as he took me by the hand to the bar.

We leaned against the bar well waiting for our turn. Billy, the only evening bartender at our little watering hole, looked directly past the line of folks ahead of us and shouted his bartender's greeting.

"Your usual, boys?" He was holding two tall glasses, one in each hand.

"Two!" Shane yelled back.

"What the hell?" Some guy who I had never seen before was at the head of the line and looking for a fight. "Wait your goddamn turn."

Billy grabbed the guy's hand. "You got cash?"

The stranger looked half paralyzed. "No. I … uh … I have a card."

"Yeah, we are cash only." There was a clear get the hell outta here hidden in the fine print of Billy's statement. The guy pulled his jacket down like he was a badass from some teen movie and looked at Shane and me like he was sizing us up.

"Yeah, well, you just don't even matter. You matter at some useless dive bar, that's the only place you will ever matter. My dad—"

"Your dad is the milkman, you spoiled brat!" Billy shouted over the jukebox, and with that our new friend exited the building with a huff and a minor puff.

Billy turned back to us pushing our drinks toward us. "Good to see you, boys!"

"I was here yesterday." I smirked at Billy.

"Yeah, but it's not ever good to see you. It's only good to see the two of you. Where is the rest of the crew?"

"They are on their way." And with that, the conversation had reached its conclusion, so he turned around to write a line under our names on our tab. Shane and I made our way back to our usual table and took a seat.

Shane started to tell me all about Egypt, but it was less about the country or the Pyramids or museums and much more about this woman from Australia he had met name Mia. They found each other on the third night after he arrived. She was far more adventurous than he, which was almost alarming in the magnitude of the statement. The thought of Shane meeting his match enraptured me in the stories he weaved of late nights drinking warm wine along bustling market streets. Then, like all of his other romances, it ended with a plane ticket and a return to home base but never an exchange of email addresses or telephone numbers. Just flashes of continental experiences and memories that would morph into legends. It was always an honor to hear the first iteration of a tale so you could watch it grow from infancy into a full-blown Indiana Jones/erotica novel.

It would be unfair to paint Shane as a Don Juan. He wasn't just out there to seduce people. That wasn't even his intention. He was an explorer of life and all of the parts that make life savory and sweet. He didn't fly to Egypt for sex, he went to live, and it just happens that life often evolves to the bedroom. To him, sex was just an extension of a conversation. Admittedly, he had adopted this philosophy from Joy. She was the one who won the debate back in high school that changed everything for how Shane saw, well, everything. Now he lived life as a spirit experiencing the planet. Not free but free to live. He was trapped by the same things as the rest of us—a job, requirements, clothing, and food. He just chose to experience those trappings in a very different way from the rest of us. He didn't let these things encapsulate him; he made those things work for him. If he had to wear pants they might as well be plaid and if he must go to work then it might as well be the type of place that gave him access to more interesting people. As a journalist, he was allowed to ask and provoke and probe to his heart's delight.

I would be lying if I said that he hadn't slept with a lot of people. That was a very true statement. Some of them were famous and some of them served him drinks in Burma. He would start those conversations and ask the right questions and unwrap people so completely that often the natural conclusion would be that, once they were already this naked, they might as well consummate the experience. To him, the package a person was wrapped in didn't matter. He wouldn't fall for their gender or appearance but their mind. The fluidity of his romantic encounters was the benchmark of his ideology that the human experience is not defined by our limited understanding of social constructs.

It was so good to hear his voice again. I could stay there listening to his stories for hours. He didn't talk like other people. It wasn't just him regurgitating experiences. He wove the tales together by asking you a series of questions. You became part of the experience.

"Did you know that Egypt fell under Roman occupation?"

"Since we are on the subject of sex, are you seeing anyone?"

"Have you ever truly felt so completely satisfied by a meal that you could be content never to eat again, everything else would be consuming ash in comparison?"

And then, somehow, organically, he would tie that all back around to his story, his adventure, without it ever feeling narcissistic. You were fully engaged in the experience with him and him with you.

He suddenly stopped just to say, "I love you. You know that?"

"I know, man. I love you too." And he would take my hand again. He touched everyone. He was complete with everyone. And the worst part about it all was he really, really meant it. There was not a single bit of pretense or bullshit in any action that he took, except that promise that he would pay for the drinks. He would absolutely leave me with the tab tonight.

"Hello, boys."

We both turned toward the familiar raspy voice. There she was, our Joy. I hadn't seen her since BARE Ball. She was lovely as ever, but it also felt different to think that today. See, the ball was an annual NYE celebration for those of us who worked in the service industry. It was a massive event. One of the nightclubs in town hosted it. It was the only night of the year that they were ever closed to the public. On that night, everyone would file in like we were the talk of the town. We would rent tuxedos or buy dresses. It was an open bar and they always had an amazing spread with hummus and shrimp as big as your hand and a massive roast. We would eat and drink until midnight, some seven days after the actual turn of the New Year, and it would now be our turn to count down and make promises we wouldn't keep. It was our turn to be served. They would replay the ball dropping at Times Square and we would all pretend like we hadn't seen it yet. And then we would continue to drink all the way up until 2:00 AM and then order a cab and make our way back to All Saints to drink until last call.

It didn't matter that this routine never changed. It always felt new and full of possibility.

But as we raged into 2009, it seemed different. The Bush error was over and change was coming. We were a bunch of blue dots in a massive sea of red. Joy and I had volunteered for Obama's campaign all summer long. We made calls and took signs to people's houses. It was lovely and you couldn't help but feel electrified by the possibility that everything would now be different. Our country would soon be so different. The tide had finally turned and this young Black senator from Chicago had finally shattered the glass ceiling. We would finally see a Black man hold the highest office in the land. It seemed like we would be putting a period at the end of the sentence of racism that had held our country hostage for so long.

We couldn't have imaged then that, right here in our home state, just a few hours away, a young Black kid would be walking home with Skittles and a soda and would be gunned down; that this wound we thought was being healed would be exposed as not just a scar but as a gaping hole that had never even been sutured. We had all been living a big lie. We were fooling ourselves.

It certainly didn't feel that way as we arrived with our signs under our arms, placing them in neighbors' rights of way.

I also don't think I was expecting to see Joy the way I did that night. She wore a gold glittering dress that fit around her as if it had always been part of her form. It was built around her and she was made for it. We stood there watching the ball drop fully unaware of all the chaos that waited ahead of us and believing that hope and change were just two weeks away from transforming all the injustices into a river of justice that would flow down even into these swampy waters of the bayous around this little Southern town.

Five.

Four.

Three.

Two.

She looked at me and smiled. I don't think we had ever been this close to each other on fake NYE. She was always with someone. I didn't think she was there with me, but there we were together. Were we there together? I don't think I knew that. I mean I had picked her up and we had been hanging out the entire night. I hadn't asked her to come with me and she hadn't asked me. There we were, shoulder to shoulder, watching and counting and now looking at each other. And before I could say, "ONE!" the ball had dropped and her lips were pressed against mine and mine hers. We stayed there like that for maybe an eternity or possibly only a second. She pulled away leaving most of her red lipstick on me and she smiled.

"Happy New Year, Leo."

There she was standing in front of me now and I realized that we hadn't said a word to each other since the ball. I had failed to mention any of this to Shane as we discussed all his adventures and mine. I guess I was still processing it all.

"Hi! Hi!" I said. Shane shot me a curious glance. That is the problem with having a friend who is a professional linguist. He notices every nuance. The other problem with your friend being a reporter is, well, he doesn't mind asking the hard questions. As a matter of fact, he is very, very good at asking all the questions. I could see out of the corner of my eye as those questions were being tabulated in a list inside Shane's brain. With each numeration his smirk grew just a fraction of skin until it was a full-blown presumptive grin.

"Holy shit!" Shane exclaimed. He looked back and forth between the two of us. "Did you two fuck? You did. Well, I'll be damned. Just one little trip across the sea and you miss all the good shit."

"No," Joy quickly interrupted.

I also had a no I was trying to get out but it had a question mark at the end of it. Because of two reasons, I was pretty sure she was lying but I was also not completely sure she was lying. See, I couldn't really remember a whole lot of that night. I remembered waking up at her house and I remember that I wasn't wearing anything. But she was gone. We hadn't spoken since. I wasn't sure if I had been the world's biggest dick and had just totally blown off one of my closet friends like I was a cool kid one-night stand. Maybe she was avoiding me. There was no real way to know for certain without communication and we weren't doing that either. I suppose it was also possible that she took me back to her place; that I had thrown up on nearly everything and she washed my clothes. I mean, yes, my clothing was washed in the morning and folded waiting at the end of her bed. So yeah, I didn't know. I was more eagerly awaiting the answers than Shane was.

"No?" Shane said with the appropriate question mark I was hoping to muster.

"No," Joy said with absolute certainty. Then she mussed my hair. "We made love. Leo is way too sweet to fuck anyone. He was just so tender and loving I was afraid he would make a proper Southern woman out of me, so I ran for the hills and hid until I heard that the expat had reemerged stateside."

I looked up at her with curiosity and she looked back at me with complete deadpan. I couldn't tell if she was telling the truth or just telling Shane, in her way, that it was none of his business. I was pretty sure that it was my business though. I just didn't know how to, exactly, ask the question.

Before I could find my feet again to say anything, Joy yelled out across the room, "Nicholas!" A large figure dressed entirely in black moved across the floor toward us. He was a massively tall man. He towered above all of us at 6'4" and this combined with his jet-black hair, just like Joy's, made him an impressive specimen. He would have been the Panhandle's most eligible bachelor if he weren't married to Jesus. Whatever hope we had of completing this conversation was dead on arrival now that Nick was here, not just because Nicholas was a priest but also because he was Joy's older brother. Both of those identity markers made him the outcast of the group because he was completely uninterested in conversations about sex, decadence, or shenanigans. He was a few years our senior, but we were also some of the only people that Father Nick could be his real self around. He just didn't want us to be our real selves around him. We were his reprieve, but it was not reciprocal, we had to be on our best Sunday morning behavior ... most of the time. Sometimes we could get him to drop the pretense, not just because Joy was family but because we had all grown up with him. We had watched him go off to prom the saintly son of the DeLuna family and return no longer a blessed virgin.

We also had all seen him that entire next day wallowing in guilt before he disappeared inside of himself and eventually into the Church in order to repent for his sins. He was a very conflicted man. He wanted to be both pious and a peer. He just didn't fit in anywhere. I think we all knew he was going to have to make a choice at some point. I just didn't know which way he was going to choose. Shane used to say that Nick ran into the Church in order to get away from the shame of being human. "The problem, Nicky, is that your brain, brawn, and balls are attached. You can't run from them."

"Shane," Nicholas said without much emotion as he approached our table.

"Nicky," Shane said back in response.

Shane was a long fallen away Catholic. All of us supported Nick when he decided to go to seminary. We even got in line with calling him Father in public, even Joy. All of us except for Shane. No, he hated the idea. Shane used to buy weed for Nick and they were way closer than the rest of us, even Joy. All the way up until that night of Nick's senior prom and that was it. Their friendship was over and Shane never quite recovered from it. That next day, as Nicholas set there in those pews of the church down the street, he swore to God that if He could make this guilt go away he would give everything he had left to God.

He made good on that promise.

I don't know a whole lot about the Bible, but my mom's favorite verse was, "Your sins will find you out." She used to shout that at Republicans when she was watching her nightly news shows. Your sins will find you out.

For Nicholas, that sin was Clementine.

The girl from the prom wasn't just some random crush. Nick didn't really have those. He was scared to death of women and himself. He knew he had a responsibility to either get married, have lots of babies and a good job or become a priest. In an attempt to appease his parents, he found a date for prom and that was Clementine, Joy's best friend in the whole world. She was thrilled to go with him. Clementine despised almost every man in the world except for Nicholas. I think she was in love with the both of them, but Nick was just perfect in her eyes. In his eyes, she was an easy way to get his parents off his back. An annoying friend of his little sister's but she would do. It was an easy fix. His parents' approval meant everything to him. He was built out of baseball and science camp. He was all American but also brilliant. That's a rare and dangerous combination. He probably could have easily been a senator or president. Instead, he chose to put a collar around his neck. I don't think I knew at the time what a political move that was.

Clementine always felt like she didn't fit in and wasn't as pretty as the other girls. She was taller than most and the shape of her body was proportionate to her size but just larger than the other girls at school. Nick was so tall that the two of them made sense next to each other. That didn't stop people from being cruel. The night at prom, as they danced at the school, some guy leaned over and asked Nick how he felt dancing with a whale. Clementine ran out of the room and Nick followed. It was just like a movie. Sixpence played in the background or some such shit, I'm sure.

He found her crying on the concrete stairs that led out of the gym. He told her how beautiful she was and how perfect her dress looked on her. He brushed the tears from her eyes and then her hair behind her ears. They kissed. Then the someday priest and the future plus-size nude model would lose their imaginary construct of innocence to each other in the backseat of his mother's sedan in the school parking lot. Something that he would always be reminded of. Something that would always haunt her because now she felt she couldn't ever admit to the person she truly loved more than anyone else in the world that she did, in fact, love her. Not now that she had lost her virginity to her brother.

That was all then and this was, of course, now. They grew up to be the polar opposites of each other. Our Father Nick found a way to be full of piety and wash away his self-imposed sins. Clementine learned to express herself in a way that allowed her to feel as beautiful as she was. Every time she arrived, she completed our little circle. Tonight was no different. And yet, tonight was completely different.

Tonight, we gathered around our usual table. A circle of friends, all of us intertwined and full of love for one another.

If there is a God and if He would be willing to grant me a wish like a genie, I would go back to that night and tackle us all. I would engulf us all in bubble wrap and never let a single one of them out of my sight again. But it didn't feel like I was bludgeoning any of them to death in that moment. It didn't feel like I was shoving pills down their throat until they would softly slip away. I didn't know I was killing them. Killing us. I just thought we were high on possibility and hopeful that soon this recession would be over and we would finally be able to be adults. The television clicked on as Billy nodded to us to look up at the screen.

He walked out on the stage and placed his hand on the Bible and said, "I, Barrack Hussain Obama, do solemnly swear that I will faithfully execute the office of president of the United States, and will to the best of my ability preserve, protect and defend the Constitution of the United States. So help me God."

CHAPTER TWO

THE BAR

We called it "our bar" as if we had stock in it. This space was an odd neutral zone with an ever-revolving cast of characters. There was only one harsh divide: the day timers and the night crowd. The staff started their shift at 6:00 PM every evening. The day timers had Ethel to pour their drinks for the last fifty-eight years. A picture of her lying stretched out in lingerie and her long legs extending nearly the length of the bar hung above the cash register. Ethel was as much the bar as any other fixture in it. She was a Southern transplant having divorced her husband in Nevada after one horrific year of marriage. She drove east until her car broke down right off the interstate. She rented a room at the All Saints Hotel and found her way to the bar for a drink and a smoke.

She never left.

I'm not sure she ever tired of telling the story. I had heard her recount it to newspapers and magazines and strangers from all around the world that stumbled into the All Saints. She would point to that picture above the cash register and smile. She used to lift her leg up to the bar and touch her toes with a laugh. "I still got it!" Then she would get to her favorite part of the story, the one where she told her husband to shove it up his tush and walked out. She never looked back. Then she would say, "I guess back then you were just your man. You were Mrs. Smith and nothing else. Just always walking around in that shadow. I hated the shade."

The patrons aged along with her and new young guns like us would slowly trickle in and find our space. Every Sunday morning she would make a large batch of food. Fried chicken and collard greens. BBQ and cornbread. Heaping pots of chili. She would set it out on a small buffet that remained hidden the rest of the week. She used to charge five dollars a plate until they made it illegal to sell food at places that allowed smoking. She was forced to make a choice: follow the law and end the tradition of a home-cooked meal on Sundays or disrupt the regulars by finally getting with the times and banning smoking. But in a little underbelly place like this there is always a third option. Bend the rules.

Ethel now set up a small tip jar next to the food and it was all on the honor system.

This little hole in the wall bar was held together with aging bricks and had passed hands between half a dozen owners over the years. It changed nothing. Sometimes the hotel patrons would complain about the noise or an occasional bar fight. Ethel may have well been the last person who stayed at the hotel to ever drink at the bar. Occasionally, tourists would wander in and quickly leave. This wasn't for people who wanted to see the beach or have a bushwhacker with little umbrellas in them. No, this was for us townies. The bar was full of odd duck retirees and self-made hundred-thousandaires. The middle people who had enough not to have to go to the office tomorrow but never made enough to matter to the fancy business folks who ate at the fancy steak houses downtown and would never be accused of being alcoholics since they drank bottles of wine instead of heavy-poured cocktails.

During the evening, right around 8:00 PM, the crowd shifted from the day timers over to the night crowd. At first, it would be young professionals, lawyers and paralegals and nurses. Slowly, they would all go home before 11:00 PM so they could go to work the next morning bright and early, hoping to make their way to being the middle people themselves someday. Finally, the real night crowd would arrive. My people. The wait staff from the local beach restaurants and swanky downtown restaurants. The folks peddling drugs would arrive shortly after, selling lines of energy in the bathroom. A couple of dollars so you could beat your body into submission to stay awake another hour just to let some serotonin drip down the back of your throat.

If Cheers had a Cousin Eddy … that was the All Saints.

The carpet on the floor had long been beaten down by a thousand shuffling feet digging in their bad decisions, ash, and spilled memories. One million particles of cheese puffs and chicken grease held it altogether. The large wooden entrance door had come from a closed down Episcopal Church that had been rebuilt on the other side of town. The rumor is the original owner bought the old door for ten dollars and never bothered to take the church sign off of it. The hotel was built for sailors and transient businessmen. It wasn't ever something pretty to look at. The rest of the town was building up around it, but the All Saints was a rustic bygone of a time when sensibility was more important than fashion. Retired church doors, dark red lights, barstools made by hand from an old sailor, nothing changed. In the hands of someone else, this place could be a museum, but we didn't want it. No, all night and day we spent serving the tourists seeking stories of nostalgia and salt water. They traveled to relive their military days or to take their kids to see the mouse and we were a good enough stop as any. We would serve their greasy kids hamburgers and chicken tenders because they were too picky to enjoy some of the best seafood the South had to offer. When we arrived inside these hallowed halls, we were ready to abandon that life and were content to enjoy it right here in this little never-changing diamond in the rough.

Right beyond the towering doors there was a small hallway that led you to one of two choices. You could go left to the pool room, with its two billiard tables and an ever-changing rotation of pinball machines. Stadium seating lined the walls with old metal movie chairs so you could sit and watch games as you waited your turn at the tables. Maybe tonight would be your night to finally beat the mentors. They were the men who looked like day timers but had the spirit of the night crowd. They would run the tables with their handlebar mustaches and thick Southern drawls while drinking their whiskeys and lamenting the days of drinking moonshine under the stars. Two signs hung in the room, "No Cigars!" and "No Gambling." One sign was always used to put cigars out on and the other was used as a tally for bets.

If illegal betting on a billiards game wasn't quite your speed, the other option was to go to the right of the entrance where you are greeted by a long, windowless room. This space was full of circular tables where faces were hidden by those dark red lights and halos of smoke. The bar itself was long and slender dark wood with maroon buffers held down by brass pins. The walls were speckled with random art from local artists, flea markets, and patrons. There was the occasional newspaper clipping from the local rag mentioning the bar or obituaries of regulars, lasting memorials to the forgettable salt of the earth that made this town turn.

That bar was the closest to an altar many of us had been to in a long time. These cocktails and stale pretzels made for many a last supper as we drank our sins away, confessing our wrongs and insubordinations and one-night stands to Ethel or Billy as they doled out yet another round of absolution for the road.

I loved this bar.

***

The inauguration had long passed by the time we had all made our way around our large table in the center of the bar. Billy had promised he would record it for us. Just like NYE, and everything else in life, we would experience this too after we had already waited on those who were privileged enough to enjoy life in real time. The whole of the swearing in took less than a minute. Chief Justice John Roberts stumbled on the words and then Obama stumbled right back and thus began the presidency that was supposed to save us all.

Billy had taped the entire thing for us. In this way, our little bar felt far more like home than any of our houses ever did. These bartenders treated us with a type of tenderness and familial quality that I don't ever remember getting from my parents. We were the last of the latchkey kids. A generation born into the dawn of a technology boom none of us were prepared for. It was far less cool than the *Jetsons* and would get us just shy of 1984. We grew up in a totally different America than even our siblings were going to see. We were sitting on the threshold of a collective cultural change and I suppose it all changed April 20th, 1999. That was the last day I suppose any of us were innocent.

My mother had picked me up from school early that day because I had a dentist appointment. Afterward, she took me to the ice cream shop. I never saw the irony in parents always choosing to get their kids sweets as a reward for having to go to the dentist, but there we were. We sat in the parking lot for a moment listening to the radio. The song came to a sudden stop and there was a momentary silence. I remember my mom and I both looking at the radio waiting for calamity or maybe wondering if it had broken. No newsfeed popping up to tell us what today's worries would be. No alerts on our phones. We weren't plugged into the Matrix just yet. Then a news reporter came on to break the silence.

"Earlier today, there was a shooting at Columbine High School outside of Denver, Colorado."

My mom immediately shifted the radio to a news station. I listened, numb, as the broadcasters explained the chaos in non-regional dialects, ice cream melting down the cone and running through my fingers. I thought of those kids, running down hallways and lying scared, hiding under the tables in the library. All I could see were the faces of Joy and Shane and Clementine watching black leather boots pacing back and forth as their cheeks lay against the industrial carpet.

"I want to go back to school!" I shouted.

"Calm down," my mother responded.

"I need to check on my friends."

"Your friends are fine. This is states away. I checked you out for the day. We are going home. They will call you when they get home."

Home. Isn't that a place where you are supposed to feel part of a family? Somewhere you are supposed to feel safe. Our house was not a home. I don't know if any of my friends had a home. No, we lived in constant fear of overstepping our welcome at our parents' houses. Clementine hid herself deep inside the closet at her house afraid to come out and show who she really was, love who she truly loved, in the way she loved them. No, she didn't feel like she was home. She knew that to express herself truly would mean she would be sent to the streets. No, none of us had homes. My mother didn't attempt to assuage my fears or help me feel safe in this moment of desperation. We were accessories and tax breaks. Just little fleshy social contracts, not children, not cherished, and constantly reminded of what a burden we were. Everything we did we were reminded of the price tag that went along with it.

"Don't you know how much those braces cost me every month?"

"You think it's cheap to feed you?"

"Just you turning sixteen has caused my insurance to go up triple!"

I waited by my phone for hours with nothing. My brother and I got into a huge fight because I wouldn't let him sign on to AOL. He wanted to Instant Message with some friends from a chatroom he was a part of. My mom at least agreed with me on this. I waited and waited.

Finally, I got a call from Shane.

"Dude, you are so lucky you weren't at school today."

"What happened?"

"It was fucked. The whole day was fucked. The guys from the audio/visual department came running down the hallways with TVs. They rushed them into the rooms. Soon, everyone was just kind of in a panic. All the girls were crying. The buses were held up for like an hour. Parents started showing up like crazy checking their kids out of school. I know Joy and Nicky left early. I haven't seen Clementine. It was just wild, bro."

After that, everything changed. We all went from being kids to being suspects. Shane and I got kicked out of the mall that Christmas for wearing trench coats. The mall cops followed us around for like fifteen minutes and then approached us. They made us go into this little room and asked us a lot of questions. They told us we couldn't wear them at the mall. They asked us if we were shoplifting. They searched us for guns. Our schools had banned wearing them too. Everyone was different there too. The month after the Columbine shooting, our school got a bomb threat. A few weeks after that, our school started having metal detectors and cops. Clementine got busted for having weed in her locker because a drug dog was brought in. She got suspended for the rest of the year and had to homeschool. She was banned from all school functions indefinitely.

It seemed that just around the time that everything started to feel normal again, here came the AV nerds running down the hallways again. Senior year began with the towers falling. It was all too much. It felt like the world was falling apart and we were just collateral damage in some game grown-ups were playing. A war began and it seemed like half the guys from my graduating class joined the military. They drove around in trucks with "Infidel" written in white letters across their windows. We now had an enemy at home and an enemy abroad. If you were different, if you didn't look like Leave it to Beaver, you were a suspect. The Muslim kids and the Black kids and the queer kids and the alternative kids; we were a walking perp line.

My parents never did seem to understand what it felt like to be going through all of this. Living in a world where we couldn't text our friends and ask if they were alright. Living without control. Watching as our friends went to go fight an invisible enemy called terrorism.

Our friends dying outside of oil fields protecting special interests. None of it made sense. Just a few years ago, we were all suspects, potential school shooters, having to go through metal detectors to make sure we weren't armed and then straight out of high school they handed all our friends guns and sent them halfway across the world to die in order to get gas prices back down below two dollars.

That was all a decade ago. We felt that fear melt off our shoulders as the hands of hope and change were placed on that old leather Bible and he swore that he would protect us all. We looked up at that screen, our bar daddy Billy smiling at the screen along with the rest of his misfit children. It was a beautiful minute and thirty-eight seconds of our lives. As soon as it was over, a voice yelled from the back of the bar.

"Yo! Billy! Turn the jukebox back on, man. I paid for like seven fucking songs."

Billy looked at us with a shrug and said, "Hope and change, kids. Just not tonight."

He lifted up the remote control and flipped the mute button. We looked at the television and listened as "Womanizer" began playing on the new digital Jukebox that had just been installed. The year before, we had a regular jukebox that used CDs; now we had to listen to whatever Top Twenty garbage this idiot put on. It was an odd soundtrack to watch the president shake hands to, but it was still beautiful nonetheless.

The most beautiful day of our lives.

"You know this won't change anything, right?" Nicholas chimed in.

He was the only one of us who was skeptical of all this change that was coming. It made sense; the Catholic Church had been pretty vocal against the incoming president. He was a baby killer and a socialist and was going to ruin our country. In many ways, Nick didn't seem like the status quo Catholic his parents were. He could be fun and he was different, but underneath that collar was just a man who had a responsibility to his constituents. And there was a bit more ambition about him these days than there used to be.

"The fuck you talking about, Nicky?" Shane jumped in.

Nick sighed. "Listen, I get the appeal. I really do. But let's be honest, what change can he really bring about anyways? The presidency is more a symbol than a reality. He will be no different than the rest, just another politician with promises bigger than their ability."

"Yeah, what are you doing, other than giving people free wine and cookies?" Shane quipped.

Nicholas looked visibly annoyed. He wasn't particularly uptight, but Eucharistic humor seemed to always be a line in the sand of what he didn't find funny and Shane knew it. And so, of course, it was his favorite line to cross at any opportunity he could find.

"I'm just saying, politics is local."

"Yeah, so I will restate my question... What are you doing?" Shane dug his heels in.

"I do what I can, when I can, Shane." You could hear the piety leaking out between Nick's teeth. He had shifted into his Father Nicholas character. We always hated this bit because sometimes he would get stuck in this mode and couldn't shift out of it. Then the whole night would be ruined. "I care about my community. I do whatever I am able. We do a drive at our church every month for the local soup kitchen and rescue mission. Those are the things that really make a difference."

"Bullshit." Shane cut him off. "That is a Band-Aid! Those things don't really help. They just give people another day. It doesn't actually address the problems. People need jobs. They need housing."

The way these two would argue it was like a divorced couple, they never actually got anywhere. Each would just dig in deeper at every jab. They would just fight around the hurt they both felt at how much the other had changed since high school, never addressing the real issues of how much they wished things were how they used to be and neither one willing to make the concessions necessary for them to make the jump back into friendship. And we were always just stuck somewhere in the unfriendly fire. Occasionally, one of us would be dumb enough to try to interject and would then end up catching a stray bullet to the chest.

"Could you two just fuck already and get it over with!" Joy mused.

The sudden silence was deafening as Clementine and I tried not to laugh. Nick and Joy shared a momentary glare at each other. Shane leaned into Nick with a big smile. "I'm game if you are, big boy." I'm pretty sure Shane meant it too. He never discriminated against any lover. And then Nicholas went on about how inappropriate Joy's comment was for the better part of ten minutes. It seemed he did get stuck in Father Nicholas gear and couldn't shift. He was somewhere going off about the inappropriateness of even the appearance of homosexual overtures towards a member of the clergy. We were about five seconds from a full-on debate about "lifestyles."

Before things got too heated, Clementine innocently threw in her own thought. She rarely ever got political. I suppose for her, so much of her life was already a statement as it was. She didn't really want to spend her evenings freely exchanging ideas or justifying her existence.

"What can we do then?" she gently interrupted.

It was a simple question, on the surface. I suppose it's the question we were all really asking. What could we do to make real change? I mean we voted. We canvassed. Nick was doing the best of what he thought he could do by using his position to give into the community. We all knew there was more we could do. But what? None of us had any real power or influence. Shane basically wrote fluff for the newspaper that never really amounted to much more than local gossip. Whatever stories he did write about local government his editor neutered and neutralized until the stories didn't have any teeth left. Nick was the most established of us all and he was still nothing more than a glorified deacon. He was an associate pastor at a medium-sized parish. He was light-years away from ever having any legitimate power. I made sandwiches at a locally owned restaurant. Joy was still in college, after her gap year accidentally turned into two. Clementine was an aspiring plus-size model who did more work for free than she ever got paid for.

"What can we do then?" This question Clementine had asked lingered above our heads thicker than the smoke that was dancing between the lights that dimly lit our faces as we ruminated on this query.

I'm not sure what came over me. Maybe it was having just come down off the mountain of volunteering for the presidential campaign. It could have even been the testosterone pulsing through my veins as I wondered what had really happened between Joy and me the other night at the ball. Whatever it might have been, it would soon seal all of our fates in ways that would bring salvation to some and damnation to others. I was loading a gun and placing it in the center of our table for an unwitting game of Russian roulette with the words that flowed out of my face like an accident.

"Let's do it," I said.

"Do what?" Joy asked.

"Let's do it! We can change this town. I mean, not that they would admit it, but both Nick and Shane are right. We have to make a change right here on the local level. There aren't enough rooms at the shelter. There isn't enough food at the soup kitchen. Those things really are just putting a finger in the dam of the problems we all see happening. And we can't expect the president to do it all. Even if he followed through with every single promise he made, well, it would take decades for that stuff to trickle down here to the South. Hell, I learned about how many major bills don't even go into effect until after a president leaves office anyway. So let's do it. Let's change right here, right now."

"What do you have in mind there, buddy?" Shane asked with a smirk.

"I don't know, man. You hate your job, right?"

"I resent that. I love my job! It's just an abusive relationship and it doesn't love me back."

"Right!" I said, almost jumping to my feet as if a magical dry erase board was going to appear behind me. "You're always saying that your editor is holding you back. You've got stories to tell. So let's tell them. Let's expose all the problems we see. We could actually make a real difference. Every single one of us has access in different ways. Hell, even at my job I hear things all the time.

Council members and lawyers and rich people are always in and out of the restaurant. Having meetings. Making deals and plans. I hear shit. I know some waitresses who have heard some real shit. Let's start our own paper. Online. Let's blow the lid off of all this bullshit. Who knows! One of us might even run for City Council."

"Ha!" Nicholas couldn't contain himself. "Y'all are going to get me defrocked. I'm out."

"Why is that?" Joy looked sternly at her brother.

"Listen, this is a great thing and all. But let's be honest, what difference can it really make?"

Shane looked at Nick with a momentary tenderness. "Come on, you were just saying politics is local. You can't tell me you don't want to see some change too. A little bit of hope. Isn't that your whole gimmick anyway? We don't even have to use our real names."

"Okay," Nick said.

"Okay, okay," Shane said in surprise. "Billy! We need another round, a pen, and some napkins."

We spent the rest of that evening drinking to our good health and writing. We wrote out ideas and a mission statement. Right there on rum-stained napkins, a new idea was birthed and possibilities bled onto the rough paper. We wrote down the names of the frequent offenders, the sheriff and millionaires and hotel owners and restaurateurs. Hell, Nick even wrote down the bishop's name. It was clear that we were about to do something. Change something. Maybe it would amount to nothing, but in that moment, right there, we thought we were akin to the founders, young and ambitious, shouting out possibilities to Thomas Jefferson as he quickly made notations in the margins of what would become a declaration of war.

Was this what freedom really felt like?

That's how I felt in that moment: free. I was free to hope. Free to dream. Free to dare. The audacity of it all was thrilling. Joy leaned over and reached out her hand toward mine. She gingerly took the pen from my hand and grabbed a fresh napkin. She covered it with her forearm as she wrote manically for a few moments.

She placed the pen down. Slowly, she turned the paper around towards all of us as we read the words. It suddenly all felt very, very real. Without anyone even asking, we each signed the bottom of the paper before us. Our individual John Hancocks sealing our fates and futures. And as our different signatures were etched out on the damp napkin, I knew we weren't going to change the world. That was exactly the point! We weren't going to worry about the world today. Just our little slice of that world that we could actually do something about. Just a little bit of a tear swelled up in my throat as I read those words:

Panhandle Free Press

We were about to burn this motherfucker to the ground. Right after another round.

CHAPTER THREE

THE STATESMEN LOUNGE

One summer, the five of us drove to Nashville to see a show. We had stayed out especially late the evening before we were set to return. Joy had a special knack for saying, "We won't stay out late, it's just that we have to see the city (person, place, thing, body of water, whatever we were doing at the time) one more time." The results were always the same. We would go back out, leaving later than expected because something set us off track, and just right around midnight it would be 7:00 AM.

All of us had to be back at work/school/the parish that next day and it was a solid seven-hour drive back. We decided the best thing to do was take shifts. Everyone was sleeping in a pile of human in the back seat and Clementine was keeping me awake riding shotgun.

If you've never had the privilege of driving through the smoky mountains, you need to bucket list that shit. Now, up North you'll find lakes and stuff called "Blue Mountain Lake" or some such thing. You'll arrive thinking that you'll find some lake that is either extremely blue or a mountain that is at least. After a few moments of bewilderment at the lack of blue, you might ask someone why it's called Blue Lake Mountain and get an answer like, "Back during the Revolutionary War, a kid found a little blue rock here." That's not how things are in the South. If something is called Neon Creek you better get ready for the entire thing to make you feel like you are swimming in toxic sludge. If something is called Gator Rock it looks like an alligator. We sort of cut to the chase like that. So when we say that the mountains smoke, we mean it. This particular morning, the fog was rolling off the hills and mountains so thick it was covering everything.

The eerie silence was cut with the knife of Clementine's voice, "What in the actual fucking fuck is that!"

She was pointing over into a hollow just to the east side of the car. Part of me wanted to slam on the breaks to make sure my eyes weren't deceiving me. The other part wanted to run away as fast as I could. The other three in the back jumped up.

"Pull over!" Joy screamed.

The ridges on the side of the highway made a sound like a classic horror film as we came to an abrupt stop.

Across the highway, in the stillness and silence of the fog, we could see hundreds of figures marching around in the mist. We exited the vehicle in silent disbelief as these specters made their ghoulish journey towards each other. The sun finally came out over the ridge and we could see the blue and gray of their uniforms become more distinct. No one wanted to admit what we were seeing, but none of us could look away. A flash of light crashed across the skyline as we saw a cannon explode and then the soldiers picked up pace toward one another, finally clashing in an epic battle. Guns blazed and bayonets glistened in the morning's new sun. As the fog continued to disappear we could see crowds behind them wearing modern clothing.

We weren't seeing ghosts of the past caught in an unending battle but men reenacting the sins of their great-grandfathers. Sons of the Confederacy and the Union would meet on these bitter battlefields each year to rematch in an eternal dance that always rushed to the same conclusion. They would debate battles and strategies and body counts but never substance; the Lost Cause delusion continuing to infect the consciousness of the American South in an attempt to rewrite the well-documented reality of their engrained feelings of supremacy.

We watched as the Battle flag was lowered and a white flag of surrender was raised in its place. With solemnity we all gathered back into the car, none of us ready to admit we all thought we had seen ghosts, our ancestors falling again on the same battlefields for all eternity never quite reaching the right conclusion.

Some of the dirtiest holes in American history were dug with rusty shovels by folks who couldn't afford land of their own. These tunnels of oppression were designed by men of affluence but their crimes were carried out by the hands of poor farmers. The cycle of oppression continues because the powerbrokers convinced poor people that other poor people were trying to steal their cookie.

We purchased freedom of speech and freedom from religion, with the blood of enslaved people. The rich and powerful were not soaking these fields and deserts with their own blood. No, they were paying paupers pennies to subjugate their neighbors. So we collectively watered the land with Native tears as we displaced them from their homes to make way for a fantasy of a Western frontier. We bleached out Black blood from cotton in order to build the fabric of this country. We crossed over centennials before we even acknowledged who was a human or worthy of owning lands or their own personhood, the intent of freedom and its ability to extend to all humankind never fully seeing the light of day. Here's a crumb, now we are going to go pick on the next person for a while.

How do you legislate a philosophy? Pen to paper is one thing, but ideas to reality, filtered through hundreds of thousands of brains with their hatred and fears and bigotry and love and need and want … how does it keep everyone free? And where does your freedom begin and mine end? Who decides, who picks, who lives, who dies? So we rebranded slavery in a more palatable form. We renamed plantations prisons and slaves prisoners. We justified their lack of freedom as repaying a debt to society. How can you owe a debt to a society you've given everything to and yet it hasn't even chosen to see you as a human? The relaunch of slavery worked perfectly, it was repackaged, and an "under new management" sign was placed out front. The Northern states were still able to blame their Southern siblings, while building a plantation by any other name on Riker's Island, nodding in approval as society replaced the lynching noose with a needle and a gas chamber.

As the decades moved on, the South became saddled with its nearly singular identity: a racist third-world country living at the bottom half of the United States. Forgotten, of course, is that the South is the most diverse composition in the entire country. More Black, brown, and LGTBQ+ folks live in the South than anywhere else in America. Yet, we remain a punch line of Southern twang and hillbillies so that America never has to collectively address that the blood of enslaved people and the genocide of Natives fertilized every crop and dug every road from sea to shining sea. It just becomes easier never to address our collective and universal sin when you can point your fingers southward and say, "Look at those backwoods rednecks" while your knee is on the throat of a Black man in Minneapolis.

Fortunately, the rest of the Union is able to forget their hatred of the South long enough each year as they flood our beaches and national forests. No, they are fully ready to urinate their way down Bourbon Street and yeehaw down Broadway in Nashville flashing their gift shop Stetson knockoffs atop a hay-filled ride past the tourist traps.

Summer break, the great equalizer of these United States.

When you visited our town, there were three places you were told that you "have to go to!"

1. The Beach
2. The Bushwhacker
3. The Pub

This was essentially the basis of our entire economy. We lived in paradise, but it came with a price. The other tier of what kept us afloat was the military base and gentrification. In order to reach the beach, you had to jump off the interstate and drive through our small downtown corridor. The streets were laced with brick buildings and wrought iron fixtures. The architecture was a blend of Spanish, French, and pre-colonial works of art. It was Bourbon Street's third cousin. An almost success of Americana that had become forgotten to time, disrepair, and the Lost Cause antebellum mythos. However, a renaissance was upon us, and soon shops were transforming into boutiques and old salons into breweries. Before this restoration movement happened, there existed a large pool hall, a sports bar, an upscale steak house, and a massive nightclub that was held together by the young military recruits wishing to forget for a night the dangers that lay ahead of them.

A small handful of venture capitalists began to invest in the corridor hoping to transform it from a pass through and into a destination within a destination.

With the sudden uptick in growth of downtown some fundamental changes began to set in. For decades, downtown was the cheapest and most efficient place to live for struggling college students and the working poor, and it had been the longtime residence of the communities of color that were left to pick up the pieces of the suburban white flight exodus. Now the immense growth of downtown was causing another demand: housing.

Not housing for those of us who were eking out a meager living. No, downtown was now chic. Logically, the best thing to do was to begin tearing down the historic homes and neighborhoods surrounding the spiderweb of old brick roads leading into the working-class houses and replace them with storied condos and townhomes. The area was soon flooded with land-grabbers who were still able to get loans in our post-recession economy. They began buying up homes from families and widows who were on the razor's edge of foreclosure. When cash wasn't enough to displace families or people living on the streets, the rebranded deputized slave catchers were dispatched to round up the undesirables and evict the stubborn. The whites wanted to reinstate their dominance in the areas they had abandoned. Anyone who didn't fit the demographics the establishment wanted to attract to their new downtown would be placed on the chain gangs to clean up debris around the interstates they once slept under and bulldoze the houses they once called home. The very reasons that gave downtown its charm and culture were being leveled to make room for progress and neighborhood associations.

The tidal wave of change was crushing everyone and everything around us. Tourism had completely crashed as a result of the recession. It seemed like a strange juxtaposition; we were all working hand-to-mouth to keep roofs over our heads and yet there was so much growth and construction happening all around us. It almost felt like all these folks knew something that we didn't; that they had been let in on a secret and we were sitting on the outside looking in wondering where they were getting all this money and opportunity from. It's almost as if the old money dividends were empowering the same families to rebuild the South in a reimagined narrative. How were we supposed to fight or compete when gas prices were hovering somewhere around four dollars a gallon and everything else spiked as a result? Transportation came to what felt like a screeching halt brought on by a catastrophic blowout. It was as if every dad in America was standing on the side of the highway looking at their busted tires and wondering how they were going to get these lug nuts off since it seemed that the only people who actually had tire irons were those racing by in luxury vehicles with roadside assistance on speed dial on their car phones.

But I digress.

As downtown was busy trying to make itself a thing, there existed the three established brands.

1. The Beach
2. The Bushwhacker
3. The Pub

It was hard not to become cynical in those times. It was hard not to be cynical before those times. But it was nearly impossible to be cynical when you stood there at the edge with the salt water rushing over your feet, the sand dancing between your toes. The emerald waters and white sands glistened like a precious cut stone imbedded into a platinum setting lying precariously on the soft skin of Golden Era starlet. The Gulf of Mexico could heal you in ways that no medicine could. This salt could reach down deep into your soul and cleanse every part of you, flushing out the deepest infection. Whatever anxieties and fears you might have, it could all be washed away in the secular baptism of these waters. The beauty of being surrounded by what seemed like an uncut emerald engulfed in a blanket of diamond dust was dwarfed only by the majesty of the violent glory of the night. When the sun would disappear across the horizon in a sharp flash of orange and deep blue, darkness would enshrine the entirety of the world as you could see it. The heat would remain as a thick and salty film soaking every inch of you. The dampness of it all would drip through your clothing working in unison with the gulf to beckon you to remove your clothing and dance within her watery mouth. The waves would crash invisibly upon the sand until your eyes would finally adjust enough to see the phosphorescence twirl around in the frothy edges of the curves of the waves seductively moving like a forbidden lover. Would you dare to strip away these sweaty fabrics imprisoning your body and take your chances with lurking creatures and the unforgiving liquid mammoth before you?

Just like our little bar, the tourists often missed the real beauty of this home of ours. No, as we would dance naked under the stars and play with the spirits of the gulf, they would hide from the spray of the sirens luring them to live. They would place silk Jimmy Buffet Hawaiian shirts and cargo shorts over their burnt bodies and hide away in the cinderblock buildings with crude murals painted by local former bank managers turned artistes à la retirement. The Bushwhacker was filled with these margarita enthusiasts who were about to convert into believers of the real beverage of the beach dweller: the bushwhacker. This was the namesake of the beverage that had been rumored to have originated right here within the blenders of this very establishment. A chocolate-y pseudo milkshake mixed with coconut rum, kahlúa, and creme de cacao. It was the sensuous and darker bedfellow of the Piña Colada. It was this drink that entranced the passerby into a devotee.

Then there was my home: The Pub.

Unlike All Saints, The Pub was a space for locals and tourists alike. It was one of the original bars in town. It was perfectly situated in between the beach and downtown. It was literally one of the first places you would see upon exiting the interstate. It was the perfect piece of real estate. The building had slowly evolved into an Anglo-Celtic wonderland, a far stretch from the small watering hole it was at its inception. The building had grown around this little space, now engulfed with large wooden doors and stained-glass windows imported from exotic lands like Sussex and Notting Hill. It was equipped with a small gift shop selling rosaries and claddagh rings and cookbooks. The centerpiece of the bar would lead you to a labyrinth of tunneling hallways that would usher you to different types of debauchery.

There was a large dining hall full of noisy families and their children. The hostess would strategically place birthday parties and family reunions in this room. Tucked far away from the obnoxiously jubilant types was a wine cellar. This cool dark room was made up of antique wine barrels and rustic stonework. A fireplace sat neatly against the wall encrusted with grape carvings and a winding stairway up to the private reserve of collector wines hidden behind bulletproof glass. But if one were to take a running jig out of this room, down the hall, and across the bar lay another room entirely. Placed between the bar and the brewery was a raucous music hall with the world's second smallest stage where a rosy-cheeked man would stand to sing dirty limericks and cover songs from around the globe. He was as integral a piece of this place as each brick and beam. McDougal would sit there at his bar stool upon the stage and play his guitar and hum notes through his harmonica and the patrons would be whisked away to another time. Another place. It was a full vacation encapsulated into a misshapen building along the Florida Panhandle.

The only thing that held all these mismatched rooms and themes together were the dollar bills placed along every flat surface. Each one was inscribed with birthday wishes, proposals, anniversaries, well-wishes, and little children's scribbled attempts at signatures. Each dollar melted into the next acting as a patchwork quilt of memories of regulars and hopeful new traditions of families who were finally taking that vacation they kept saying they would.

Now, if I took you by the hand and walked you back away from the brewery and the music hall and past the bar and down the hall and the dollar bills and we stopped just before we reached the kitchen there would be a small unimpressive door nearly hidden by green bills. A small plaque sat upon that door with a large single key lock and engraved there upon the bronzed centerpiece of this door was a young gentlemen with a top hat and a tuxedo. Written above this figure's frame in Gaelic-inspired letters were the words: The Statesmen Lounge.

You wouldn't see the room if you were tourists. Not unless you mistook it for the bathroom or maybe if you were a drunk regular looking for an exit after last call. Otherwise, it was unassuming and easily dismissed. But behind this door lay a mirrored replica of the bar. With the exception that each booth had dark red curtains that could be closed for privacy. This room had its own staff and its own cook and menu. No one knew how one received membership. Every person who had ever run for city council or mayor or sheriff or the utilities board would be summoned to this room. The members would all gather there, holding their beer steins with their names etched upon them, and drink to their good health and question the candidates. Someone would emerge victorious.

This was the democracy of a small town. Pints for ballot boxes.

I had been preparing the steaks and Reuben sandwiches and potatoes at this place since the summer before I started college. I spent more time inside its walls than I did within my own apartment downtown. Whatever downfall the rest of the world was feeling as a result of the recession, it seemed The Pub was immune. We were busy every night. That didn't mean the staff wasn't suffering. Yes, people showed up to eat, drink, and be merry. That didn't mean they were as willing to leave an adequate tip. No, this was a time of cutting corners without depriving yourself of luxuries. So we were all doing double the work at half the pay.

Even after all these years, I didn't have access to The Lounge. Only the most notorious staff members had this privilege. That doesn't mean you didn't hear things. You certainly did! Some of the folks thought that their secrets began their safekeeping the moment they walked through the door of the main establishment. But the staff that worked within The Lounge didn't know the suffering the rest of us did. No, these patrons learned long ago that the easiest way to keep a secret buried was money. Not a few singles placed upon a wall with promises of fidelity. They tipped well enough to ensure that those waitresses and cooks would never want to lose that position. If you made your way up to Lounge staff, you were set. These staffers owned homes and paid off cars. There were people who retired on this job. If you worked at The Pub, your dream was to one day prove yourself worthy enough, or just dumb lucky enough, to be moved to Lounge staff.

The way people spoke about it, it was like an unorganized secret society, which probably made it worse in a million ways. I wondered sometimes if every town had something like this. Even if it wasn't a secret room hidden inside a pub, it was tables around the mayor's residence or just a corner spot at a local coffee shop or the parish hall of a church. There were probably a million little deal-making spots scattered all across the nation. If politics was local, as Nick had said, then this was ground zero and I had everything but access.

***

The weird thing about having your entire life destroyed before your very eyes is that it doesn't feel very impressive or all that deconstructive in the moment. You don't really know what is happening until you take a look back behind you and realize all the wreckage and are able to see clearly that you could have changed everything if you had just gone right instead of left. If you had just slowed down. If you had just spent that extra money to get your brakes checked. Hindsight is a cruel mistress. She will crawl into your bed uninvited and whisper sweet guilt into your ears. It was the same thing with our town that was happening within our own lives. Except that the benchmarks were easier to notice. We would physically watch as old schools were turned into shopping centers and breweries and townhomes. It didn't seem like a lot and then, next thing you knew, everything had been flattened. Just enough of the scraps of it were being left behind to give it the façade of it being the same place. This little slice of America was eroding into worship of the god of progresses and consumerism with little concern for the locals. They can always import bodies as easily as beer. As the landscape was being demolished, scrapped, and burned, so were our spirits. They always say, "If smoking did on the outside what it does on the inside everyone would quit." I wonder if that is true for gentrification. If the human spirit was visible from the outside, if all our brokenness and sadness and pain was easily seen, could people be more empathetic?

No, they'd just make everyone wear bags over their heads.

The night of the inauguration we had all felt like the world was at our fingertips. It had been more than a month and the best we had to show for our spirited evening was that Clementine had taken up a collection amongst us to buy the domain name for the paper. Shane had fallen into the arms of someone. If this was going to work then we needed to make sure that all the pieces were in place for when our mad genius was ready to take a wrecking ball to the ivory towers that our local kings had built for themselves. It was our responsibility to build the infrastructure so that once this paper was ready to get off the ground, whenever Shane decided to appear again, we were ready to take action.

I knew what needed to be done: Joy.

Well, you know what I mean. I needed to get Joy involved in a more central way. She was always the brains of the operation anyway. Ever since high school she had been orchestrating us into calamity or imminence. She was our matchmaker-mother-mentor. I'd never been 100% sure she wasn't an old wise forest witch who had come down into the little city to teach us a better way.

My leg began to buzz. I reached into my pocket. It was Joy calling. *Witch,* I thought.

"Speak of the devil…"

"…and she shall appear?" She responded on the other end.

"What's going on?" I asked coolly.

"I was just driving by City Hall and thinking."

"Yeah?"

"I was just thinking it's still standing. I thought we were going to 'burn this motherfucker down' and I understand you are too big of a pussy to have meant that anything more than metaphorically, but it is also still standing metaphorically."

"Rome wasn't destroyed in a day?"

"Yes, it was."

I looked around me. I was stuck between the dumpster and grease pit at The Pub. I was about to be late for my shift. I sucked in the better part of a cigarette and then just exploded my thoughts in a moment of brevity.

"Listen. Meet me at the All Saints tonight."

"What for? Another round of bullshit and zero follow through?"

"It's only been a month."

"I wasn't talking about the paper."

My heart sank deep into the souls of my feet. This was the closest thing she had done to actually addressing what happened at BARE Ball and the morning after and her joke to Shane that was suddenly feeling much less like a joke. Was this really happening? And why was it already February? *Fuck, Leo, get your shit together.*

"Yeah, okay. So all the more reason for us to get together tonight."

"Okay. I'll be there."

I disappeared into the back bowels of The Pub. For hours I would stand there on my aching feet, still crushing my own heart in them, as I shifted back and forth on the balls slicing onions and rushing back and forth between the grill and tossing salads. These minutes melted into hours and every few moments the manager would pop into the kitchen and cut someone. Waitresses made their way in and out to the lockers picking up their items and leaving. Staff was dropping like flies. It must have been a slow night. It never felt slow on the grill. Flipping this burger, checking the temp on the steaks, rushing to grab the potatoes. A well-choreographed routine. I flowed in and out of the kitchen. I would spill gravy and wipe it up with my Bachelor's degree. I was beholden to someone else to shout out my name so that I could rush home, try to get the stink of onions and grease off me enough to run down the street and open the old church door and finally be free. Free to drink, free to dance, free to love. Giving that building ten hours a day just so I could enjoy three.

The manager popped his head in. "Leo! What are you doing?"

Just living the American dream, goddamn.

Chapter Four

To Be or Not

There are really only two types of people in the world. Yes, there are variances of personality types and motivations. People are profoundly diversified. But life really comes down to the two major types of folks: those who do and those who say they will but never do. The world is full of dreamers whose ideas, inventions, art, books, philosophies, and aspirations will die along with them. In many ways, life is found in the doing, not just the imagining. That isn't to say that imagination and dreamers aren't important. Of course they are! But so many of us stay somewhere stagnated in our hopes and we never take the time to get up off the couch to actually try to actualize our dreams into reality.

Tomorrow.

Next year.

After school.

After the kids move out.

After retirement.

And then, "We are gathered here to remember the life of…"

I was one of those people. Just waiting for something to happen to me. I'm not sure what I was expecting, that someone would just randomly walk up to me and say, "Hey pal, listen, you look like the kinda fella who's got ideas. Big aspirations! I can see it right through these walls as you flip meat. You are just the kinda kid we want to invest in." And then I would remove my apron and it would whimsically fall to the floor in slow motion. Monologue would begin to play over the scene as I spoke about how this is exactly what I had been waiting for; that the moment had finally arrived. I wanted the reward without the work. I was investing my time into surviving instead of taking decisive action toward my future.

Taking on the challenge of this paper was the first time in my life that I had made a decisive action. What I was quickly realizing was that making one decision wasn't going to be enough to get us where we needed to go. Not enough to get me where I needed to be. My whole life had been a massive calendar of indecision. I went alone to prom. I applied late to college and didn't get the choice of the litter. I took electives before finally deciding on political science.

Political fucking science.

I went into nearly $40,000 dollars in debt. One of the most expensive single sheets of toilet paper I ever purchased. Every single day my debt doubled as my inability to find a career became an echo ringing in my ears.

In my imagination, finding a career after college would have been similar to my fantasy about someone rushing into the kitchen and declaring I was the fella they had been looking for. No, careers don't grow on trees like they did for my parents. My parents were from a generation that refused to retire. They waited to have us, told us to go to college, start a life, and by the time we were finally here in that mythical future they promised existed, houses required a $40,000-dollar down payment. How strange that before I was ever worth a penny I could get a loan to get an education but now I was working 40+ hours a week and I couldn't afford to get a loan to buy a house, a car, or start a business. So I flipped burgers, the one thing I was promised I would never do if I just put in the hours, went to class, and walked out in a cap and gown.

By this age my father had already paid for his college education in full. A feat he loved to remind me he did while working a part-time job at a convenience station pumping gas and topping off fluids nights and weekends. By my age my father had purchased a starter home and was married to my mother. They honeymooned for a month across Europe before he started a job at the Postal Service. His life had stable roots before he hit thirty. I was scary close to being a real grown-up and I owned nothing. I had nothing.

My parents still took me out to dinner for my birthday.

I lived in a four-bedroom house with five guys. Even with cutting every corner imaginable there didn't seem to be any level of future out there beyond this. This cycle that turned us out on the other end as what? I'm not sure what happened. Honest to God, I was a bit surprised to be alive. Frankly, as a teenager I never imagined I would make it this far. I'm not sure what that feeling was or where it came from. Maybe we would all be raptured or the world would end in a massive nuclear blast or Y2K. I never could see life beyond high school and then, without warning or fanfare, we were thrust into a world that didn't want us. Wasn't prepared for us. And certainly wasn't built for us.

So who was to blame for our collective lack of ambition and ability to succeed? It's hard to be motivated to try to win a game that was already rigged from the start. Nepotism secured a bright future for a select few and then rest of us were given the honor of bussing their tables until Jesus returned. Do not pass go, do not collect $200, and there is no reason to go to jail because a cop will shoot you with your hands raised. No, they never taught us about qualified immunity in the game of life or that monopolies would dictate our every move. We grew up with war overseas, war in the streets, war in our schools, war on the drugs that we used to escape, war at home, and war in our minds. We saw a lot of battles and few wins. They never let us run free when we were kids, what made us think they would allow us freedom to be adults? No, we were an entire generation birthed from broken condoms and cocaine-infused orgies funded by the abundance of the '80s. One massive accidental pregnancy. And what shall we name it? It's a boy! It's a girl! Pink and blue. No room for any other colors of the rainbow. Congratulations, Greatest Generation, meet your grandkids, the Millennials!

***

I placed my drink atop the small circular table that was in the far right corner of the barroom next to a knock-off free-standing Tiffany lamp. During the winter, this was where they would drag out the ratty second-hand Christmas tree to spruce up the joint. When the whole friend group wasn't showing up, this was my favorite place to sit alone. It was quiet and away. Plus, it had a perfect view of the door. You could sit there and watch the world. People coming and people going, each one making their way up to the bar to tell their stories to Billy as the words would dance around the circles of smoke making their way into his ears. There was nothing he didn't know about any of us. As best I could tell, our secrets were more secure with him than the Pope. I never once heard him speak ill of a regular. Not even those who made their way onto the banned list or walked out on tabs.

"Everyone's got a story. That means everyone's got a fuck-up or ten." He would chuckle. "Way I see it is, no matter what a person does, there's a direction they are going in and sometimes you are the destination. Sometimes you are just in the way. Either way, it's none of your damn business."

The closest I ever remember Billy almost talking shit was one night when I was maybe just twenty-one. I had recently stumbled upon the bar. I was a newbie. He poured me extra strong drinks, the ones the All Saint was notorious for, all night long. There was this girl who kept making eyeballs at me from across the room where she sat adjacent to me on the twin side of the bar. My dumb ass didn't notice. She eventually scooted her way down the bar to me and we talked and shared a cigarette and a kiss. Though I was too dense to see it, she gave me every opportunity to invite her back to my place or to receive an invitation to hers. I just kept on talking until she said her cab was going to be there any moment. Shortly after she left, I realized she had left her glasses there on the barstool next to me.

I quickly grabbed them and looked toward the door. As I rushed forward I realized I wasn't moving. I could feel something constricting my throat like a boa. Then, as I gasped for air, I realized Billy had grabbed the back of my collar. I reversed ever so slightly and he released his grip.

"You seem like a nice kid, kid." He didn't even look up from the glass he was polishing, like he knew he was violating his own ethics code. "Don't do it. She'll come back tomorrow and get those. Don't you chase that woman. She'll eat you alive and spit you out and there will be nothing left of you but bones. She's the Jägermonster. Beware, boy."

I perched back down on the cushioned barstool and made a sheepish smile channeling my best Indiana Jones. Billy looked up from his glass-polishing extravaganza for a momentary reassuring nod and that was that. My salvation purchased at the expense of him breaking his ideology, just a bit.

That experience was basically a metaphor for my love life. Another area marked by inaction and indecision. But on this night I was sitting here at my little corner table, watching that door with wistful anticipation for her to finally walk through it. Maybe tonight I would finally break through, like I had with the paper, and express myself in a way that made some semblance of sense. I began to worry that maybe she had already arrived and left. I hadn't actually set a time with her. I did get off of work relatively late. Maybe she wasn't going to come at all. The bar was nearly empty and it started to feel a bit awkward me sitting all the way over there by myself and then I heard the door creak. I looked up and there was a bright shining face smiling at me.

Clementine.

She took off her coat and made her way to me. She motioned toward one of the two empty chairs at the tiny table. I nodded back and said something like, "Take a seat." At least I wasn't alone.

"What's got you in the corner, baby?" She loved to call people baby.

"I was … well … I thought Joy was coming out tonight. We were supposed to meet up."

"Am I interrupting?" Clementine looked uncomfortable, like she was suddenly a nuisance.

"No … no, you are fine. I'm glad not to be alone."

Just then we both looked across the room as we heard the familiar song of the door opening. There she was. Her long dark brown hair framing the knee-length red coat she wore, hands in the pockets, and a cigarette dancing neatly at the end of her lips. I suppose if I was a smarter man, someone more in tune with my own emotions much less anyone else's, I would have seen that Clementine was looking at Joy with the same fear and anticipation I was. But I didn't notice. I watched as Joy noticed the two of us and walked on over toward our table. She took a brief intermission, just long enough to snag her beer from the bar, with a wink at Billy.

It became increasingly clear that Clementine was here to stay. Our third wheel was only going to prevent Joy and me from having about half of the conversations I wanted to have tonight. Of course, it would be the conversation that was most at the forefront of my mind. The one I really wanted to be having. As much as I loved Clementine, and undoubtedly anything that was said would eventually find its way back to her, I wasn't interested in Joy and I discussing what had really happened at BARE Ball being a group effort.

Within a few minutes it was down to business. Yes, the paper was also suffering from an undefined relationship status. For what it was worth, as flabbergasted as I was with my inability to have the conversation I was hoping to have, Clementine had done something actually kind of brilliant. While she was waiting for us to decide on exactly what direction we would go with the *Panhandle Free Press*, she had built a skeleton site with a logo and a small question bar in the middle above it reading, "Have a scoop? A story we should tell? Questions you want answered? Drop them here."

"So, I took this site and dropped it into reddit in a Panhandle subcategory. We've gotten hundreds of responses." She leaned over to her backpack and pulled out a stack of printed out pages. "Some of these are silly, I guess. People wanted to know about roads that haven't been built or parks that are in disrepair."

"That's good stuff too," Joy said.

"Sure, sure. But there is more stuff here. Deeper stuff."

Joy took the pages from Clementine and began to devour them. We sat there in an aroused silence. There was that feeling again! That feeling that we might be on to something. I leaned over to Clementine while Joy was engulfed in her reading.

"That was really brilliant. Brilliant," I encouraged her.

"Thanks." She smiled.

"Holy fuck." Joy broke the silence.

"What!" Clementine and I said in unison.

"It looks like one of the councilmen has been having an open-secret love … triangle? Square? What do you call it when it's two couples?" Joy asked, genuinely inquisitive and remarkably devoid of judgment.

"Two couples doing what?" I asked, totally lost.

"Fucking," Joy said. "I guess it's swinging. I don't know. Either way, this is some pretty scandalous shit in here. But we can't print that."

"Why?" I was shocked; this was the best stuff we had come across so far. We didn't even know what direction we wanted to go in with this thing, but a councilman and his wife having a swinging relationship with another couple was pretty lucrative storytelling. That would be the story that could put us on the map. That's why people want to read papers anyway. This was a win/win as far as I was concerned.

"We can't print this." Joy looked at me sternly. "It's none of our business. It's no one's business what other people do in their bedroom. A decade from now, you just wait, relationships will look very different than this heterosexual … centered? I don't know. Whatever this normal is, it's breaking down. If we are going to break down this town and build something better in its place, we can't do things the way they have always been done. If you go after someone's personal sex life and act like its wrong just because it's different from yours, what makes you any different than one of those street preachers? This is just fluff. It's sexy and salacious for sure. But is it valuable? No. Does it change how someone can govern depending on whose toes he's sucking?"

"I could have gone without that image." But she made a good point. This was the type of filth the local paper printed as sordid Southern tales during election season. This was just mudslinging. There was no value in it, even if it might have instantly made us a household name. We had to be different than whatever existed currently.

"You can't build a brighter future on the same broken foundation," Joy said with a bit of a self-assured smirk. "And you can quote me on that!"

She gave me a replica of the wink she gave to Billy, except she gave my knee a little rub with a nudge. Jesus, I am pathetic. Friends should be able to touch friends without the other constantly reading into it. Yet, here I was dying slowly on the inside wanting to know if this was just friendly banter or a potential proposal of marriage, sex, and babies. I jolted myself out of my disassociated delusion and snapped back to focusing on Clementine.

"So what else you got, Clementine?" I asked.

"There is a lot in there," she said. "And I agree with Joy, I wouldn't want someone outing me against my will. I don't think we should focus on things like this. I want us to be ethical and ideological about our responses to the problems in the community. This country has a long history of discrediting people based upon who they love or who they sleep with. Just look at Alexander Hamilton!"

"Who?" I had no idea who that was.

"Hamilton!" Clementine laughed at me. "The Founding Father? He wrote all of George Washington's speeches and half of the Federalist Papers."

I just stared at her and so she decided to go on.

"You've got to be kidding me. You are such a dolt. He invented Wall Street and shit like that. He had an affair and it cost him the presidency."

"Yeah, no clue. I think you are about the only person in the world who gives a shit about that. But your point is taken. Let's steer clear about that stuff and—"

Before I could finish my sentence, the door of the bar slammed open. I guess it had started raining at some point because the wind was really having it and Shane was standing in the gaping hole of the threshold soaking wet. He looked like Dick Tracy or maybe Inspector Gadget. He was wearing a brown fedora and a tan London Fog trench coat. It had a massive badge on it with red lettering that read, "PRESS." I sometimes think he got off on being a literal stereotype, he looked like he was a playing a character of a reporter. I bet he has at least twice walked into his editor's office and smashed his fist against her desk and yelled, "Listen here, you gotta print it! It's the truth, goddamnit. Isn't that what we got into this business for? The truth, I tell you! Come on, chief, you gotta let me do it, see. The integrity of the Constitution, freedom of the press, it hinges on moments like this!"

He flashed his leopard print thrift store find umbrella splashing it toward the pool room. Some of the patrons grumbled and he ran toward the table.

"They are all in bed with each other!" he yelled at us, gulping my drink.

"We know," Joy said.

"Every last one of them!"

"We know," Clementine echoed.

"Fuckaggeddon! The lot of them!" he cried.

"We know!" we all said in unison.

"Wait, what?" Shane looked confused after he finally decided to join the conversation instead of being theatrical. Joy handed him the piece of paper about the councilman. He took a moment to peruse it with a genuinely inquiring face and then shoved it back at her.

"Shit. That's hot. I would watch the hell out of that. But no! Not literally in bed with each other. I mean, I've got the story. Murder. Mayhem. The mayor. The sheriff. The bishop... They are all in on it. I've got 'the story'!" And with that he turned around to Billy. "Another round for us all! And, uh, put it on Leo's tab... Thanks, buddy!"

With that, the thunder clapped as if God was on Shane's side about the theatrics and the lights flickered for a moment. Shane lit a cigarette as the dim contours of his face were made visible in the dark. "Do I have a story for you, chief!"

CHAPTER FIVE

WHAT HAD HAPPENED

Our senior year was weird. The Twin Towers had fallen. Some of our friends were already signing up to join the military before they even graduated. They would walk down to receive their diploma and hoped they lived long enough to go to college. It seemed odd to prepare for celebration and war all in the same timeline. I guess humans have always struggled with this juxtaposition, love and death. There were also little wars raging in the microcosm of our lives. Clementine was banned from going to prom after her yearlong suspension from school. She also already had a complicated relationship with the whole concept of prom. It was just two years before when she had gone to the dance with Nick and everything that happened there and after was already staining the event for her. We were trying to see if there was a way that we could maybe petition the school to overturn their decision. It didn't seem right if it wasn't all of us. At first, she protested and said that she didn't need to go. It wasn't important. She had already been. We should all just go.

"It's antiquated, really," she said with a forced smile. "It's not like I can take who I really want to anyway. I promise you don't need me."

That wasn't going to happen!

Fortunately, we had an alternative option, aptly named: The Alternative Prom. Down by the train tracks, pretty close to what was currently still the "wrong side of town" there was a small defunct shopping center. It was quite literally on the wrong side of the tracks. The train tracks ran directly in front of it. Across the tracks were the Convention Center and a fancy pants hotel. Just like the All Saints, it had a bar attached to it, except this was somewhere where important people drank important drinks and discussed important things. Of course, we were what felt like a millennia away from even knowing the All Saints existed. But just a few feet away from the chandeliers and burgundy hallways of the towering hotel was another place altogether. This little shopping center had been rented out to a small coffee shop called Picasso's. It stood directly next to an always closed storefront in the same center that was full of dusty prosthetic limbs. It had a sign on the door indicating that it was a legitimate business, but we never saw anyone go in or out.

We didn't know at the time that this little spot was a training wheel for the All Saints. It was where we would learn to let our emotions out over a drink and build the idea of community. Most weekends we spent here with each other, sitting on the second-hand pleather couches and spending our parents' money that they gave us so we would get lost for a night.

During prom season they would throw a special event for all of us misfits who didn't quite fit in anywhere. We fit in here. Even though they didn't sell food, the owner would make a massive vegan spread for the event. It was twenty bucks a ticket and it included everything. They even had a live band. We decided that this was how we would spend our prom weekend. We even rented one of those rooms across the street at the fancy hotel on my father's credit card. I knew I would eventually get caught and be in a ton of trouble. But it was worth it. A small price to pay for an absolutely perfect night.

Joy and Clementine went together. I went alone. Shane brought some girl from Catholic High and Nick was off at seminary, which was probably for the best.

The irony that Clementine had been the prom date for both of the DeLuna siblings was lost on none of us. She had already turned one into a priest the last time.

So we waited on pins and needles to see what was going to happen to Joy! I couldn't quite see her dressed in a habit. Even though she did somehow embody the spirit of Maria from *Sound of Music* she never quite fit. She was always everywhere. You could never hold her down.

Joy decided to wear a tuxedo complete with bowtie and Clementine wore a beautiful dress. I would be lying if I said they didn't look actually kind of perfect together. They danced and they kissed and later that night Shane and his date took the master bedroom and I spent the night watching reruns of *Cheers* on the couch. Around 3:00 AM Clementine and Joy showed up, drunk and giggling and saying they couldn't go home.

They never said where they went. They never said what they did. But I guess they both would have said it was none of anyone's business.

***

When I was little, my mom used to say to me, "This isn't for little ears. This is grown-up stuff," and usher me off to the other room. I would sit in my room, ear pressed against the door hoping to catch just a glimpse of this grown-up stuff that they would soon be having a conversation about. I could never quite make it out. I never got any of the details. I sometimes wonder if things would have gone down differently if they had let me in on some of that grown-up stuff. Our grandparents saw some shit. They worked really hard to make sure that their kids wouldn't experience the pain they did. Our parents mimicked this behavior but I don't think that the intention was the same.

In this moment, as Shane sat there, soaked to the bone, telling his story, I kind of wished my mom would run in and say, "This is grown-up stuff," and send me to my bedroom. With every new layer of his tale, my stomach turned. I knew he was right. I knew it all made sense. But I just wanted to tackle him, to tell him to shut up. I wanted to shove the entire thing back into the can with the other worms. There was no hope of that. As he unloaded onto us he was nothing but smiles, giddy like this was the moment he had been born for. Joy, Clementine, and I sat there horrified. Now, in Shane's defense, I don't believe he was joyous about what he was telling us by any stretch of the imagination. I am absolutely certain that under there he was absolutely mortified about what he was telling us. He had just already gone through that process as he discovered what he was now unraveling.

Shock.

Surprise.

Scandal.

Horror.

Denial.

Fact-Checking.

Acceptance.

Now it was time to tell the story and that, for him, was what he lived for. Above everything else he was as a person, a storyteller was the top of the list. From birth he told stories and with such flair; he spent much more time with adults than he did with youngsters as a general rule. We were his only real friends his age growing up and even then he would let us have it sometimes, spouting off things like, "You guys are so juvenile in your thinking!" If he had ever had the chance, he would have dated the teacher, not for the bragging rights but just to be with someone he felt held his same level of intellect.

Shane knew everyone in town. He had a routine. He would smoke cigars with the real estate brokers on Tuesday and then he would spend his afternoons playing cards with the old men at the barbershop. Wednesdays, he would thrift all day. He would sometimes take a different cast of characters with him as he searched for buried treasures. Thursday nights he always had dinner in the park with some of the guys living on the streets. He mostly kept his weekends free to do whatever floated his fancy as he powered through a whirlwind of adventures bouncing to breweries and eating dinners with politicians that always turned into an interview. His editor would frequently accuse Shane of being loose with facts, but he always argued that he caught people in the moments where they were being loose with the truth. Mondays were Dungeons and Dragons day. He would sometimes skip out of work early just to play a good campaign.

You couldn't go anywhere in town without someone stopping him to swap stories and hugs and greetings and a little bit of, "How's your mamma and them?"

He was the superlative journalist because, even though he truly enjoyed these people's company, he would never have a problem writing a story about any one of them. For Shane there were no sacred cows.

Though he loved almost everyone, there were three people he hated: the mayor, the sheriff, and the bishop. He hated those three with such an unapologetic bias that his editor wouldn't let him write about them anymore. So it did bring forward a bit of a cause for pause when he had come forward to finger these three at the scene of a crime so big, so intertwined, and so utterly damning. However, as he weaved the story together before us like a patchwork quilt of lies and trickery, it became unambiguously clear that we had stumbled across something extraordinarily evil.

"Y'all, my editor would never, not in a million years, allow me or anyone at the paper to run this story. This is it! This is what we've been waiting for!" Shane wiped the sweat from his brow with an embroidered handkerchief he was told to keep after a meeting with some big shot attorney. It had the attorney's initials on it. He loved that thing.

What Shane laid out before us was such a sordid Southern tale of corruption and diabolical deception that not even Mark Twain could have devised a more crooked cast of characters. This scheme was beyond the pale of human decency. It was hard for our minds to truly accept what was being said, and yet, nothing else made more sense than what we were being told.

There was much that needed to be discovered and untangled and verified, but essentially what Shane had unearthed while at his regular gig at the established paper would, in fact, bring this little town to its knees. In essence, this is what he disclosed to us that night:

There was a five-acre parcel of land that had gone into possession by the city because of a tax default. The original owner had died and no next of kin ever came forward to claim the land or pay the taxes on it. The parcel lay there vacant for the better part of a decade. Four times a year, the city would go and clean up the property, mow the lawn, and then attach the expense to the tax bill. Eventually, the property went up for auction.

A small endowment program within the diocese had been set up for them to purchase real properties and other assets in order to secure wealth for the diocese to continue to function. The bishop directly oversaw that endowment fund as the president of its board of directors. He saw this piece of property was for sale; its prime location was near the water, it was right downtown and one of the few remaining large plots of land still available. However, it was undesirable for two reasons. There was a house directly in the center of the property that had long been taken over by squatters. They had the utilities turned on in their names and there was a small possibility that they might have the ability to put forward a squatters' rights proposal if the property was developed.

The second issue was that it was adjacent to a small project development apartment. It had originally been operated by HUD directly. However, after a large divestment program within HUD, the property had been given over directly to the city to operate. The thirty-seven residential apartments were now owned by the city and the residents were all HUD recipients. The city had long neglected repairing the property but couldn't find a good way to force the eviction of those who lived there. They simply didn't want to deal with the scandal.

According to Shane, the bishop had reached out to the mayor in order to secure that the vacant parcel would not be overly advertised as coming up for auction. This would secure that they would not have anyone else bidding on the property and they could acquire it at a bottom-dollar price, essentially securing the property for only the cost of the back payments of the taxes owed to the city.

This took place without a hitch and the diocese was now the owner of five acres of prime real estate for fractions of a penny on the dollar. In order for them to bring the value of the property up they would need to develop the land and build a condo complex on the property. No bank would go for this investment until the issues of the squatters and the adjacent project housing were resolved.

The mayor devised a plan that would kill two birds with one stone. All he would need was for the sheriff to play along, which he was more than obliged to do. This was the very type of Wyatt Earp shit that he lived for.

One afternoon, the sheriff met with a local judge at The Statesmen Lounge and explained that he believed that the squatter house was being operated by a dangerous drug dealer. He believed that a stockpile of illegal weapons, cash, and drugs were stored within the building. He further claimed, falsely, that this house was providing all the drugs to the project housing directly behind it. He explained to the judge that they were low on evidence but high on certainty. Over dinner he was able to secure a guarantee of a search warrant.

This Unholy Trinity was fully aware that if the resident of the property were to speak, the jig would be up. So they had to secure his silence. The sheriff hand selected a rookie deputy who had a reputation of being trigger happy and already had three formal complaints against him. Before the raid on the house, the sheriff spoke to the team that would be conducting the raid. He told them in no uncertain terms how dangerous this would be.

"Make no mistake, boys, this is the type of thing we get into law enforcement for. This is a once-in-a-lifetime moment to really get a genuine bad guy. But be aware, you are walking right into the depths of hell and there is no telling what you might find. You will be in danger and you need to be on high alert. Anything could happen. Be vigilant. Be ready. Be mindful. Let's pray…"

And as the sheriff prayed for the safety of his troops, that young rookie deputy with the trigger finger had his heart racing up into his throat. He made a decision right then and there that he wasn't going to die. So when they knocked on the door, and then knocked the door in, and that old man was sitting there on his couch and stood up with his cane, the deputy was absolutely certain it was a shotgun. Without saying a word, he unloaded an entire clip into the old man.

No more witnesses.

A seasoned deputy who gladly worked at the pleasure of the sheriff took charge. He placed everything necessary inside, including a list of individuals who were clients of this supposed drug lord. The names, in alphabetical order, were the residents of the project housing. So when the story broke, people demanded the arrest, conviction, and eviction of all the residents of the property.

Now that everyone was gone, the mayor was able to finally send in the inspectors and condemn the property. The property was razed over a weekend and since the workers were already there taking down the government-owned property, the mayor was able to throw in tearing down the house in the middle of the property now owned by the diocese at no charge to them. A beautiful act of charity on behalf of the city.

"And just last week, this…" Shane laid on the table a copy of the local paper with the bishop, the sheriff, and the mayor with golden shovels and construction hats breaking ground on the newly minted Sunbright Townhomes development. It was the perfect crime. Everyone believed that these three beacons of morality and virtue were keeping the town safe with swift justice: law and order.

Now the diocese would sell these townhomes off one by one and increase their endowment a hundredfold. The sheriff had an amazing win, just in time for re-election. And the mayor had finally swept away the last little bit of blight as he prepared to roll out the red carpet down Main Street to declare the official renaissance of downtown. Everything was perfect. Everything was clean. They had overlooked nothing except…

"McKenzie!" Shane declared with enthusiasm.

"The waitress at The Pub?" I asked, shocked.

"Yeah, we dated a little in high school. And last week." Shane smiled. "See, she's heard some shit waitressing back there at the ol' Statesmen. But this took the cake for her. This was the bridge too far. So when the gang from hell met there to discuss, and brag a little, about what they had pulled off, she heard it all. Or damn near enough of it, enough to piece most of it together. So she called me. That's why I've been MIA for the last couple of weeks. I've been following every lead, dotting every I and crossing my heart a fucking lot."

Clementine looked concerned. "How do we know it's all true?"

"We don't yet. There are a lot of holes. We are going to have to do a lot of digging." Shane looked suddenly determined. No more laughs, just fully engaged in the task at hand.

"What do we do next?" Joy asked.

Shane gave her a solid look in the eyes and put both of his hands on the table, leaning in with a whisper and a glimmer in his eye. "We order another round, we fuck our lovers, and then kiss our mothers goodbye, because we are going deep into the lion's den. This is the type of story people live for. This is the type of story people die for. This is how folks win Pulitzers." He paused. "Y'all, if we do this right, nothing is ever going to be the same again."

Joy set there uneasy and then finally said what we all knew, what we all hoped we wouldn't have to face but had no choice. "We have to tell Nick."

Chapter Six

In Nomine Patris

We all filed into the cathedral looking like a band of ragamuffins. Joy sat near the front with her parents in the third row. The first two rows were filled with dozens of priests all wearing the same white robes. The place smelled sweet, a mixture of beeswax, incense, and aged wood. Shane, Clementine, and I found our way to a mostly empty pew toward the center of the building. Shane suddenly stopped in front of us, his knee hitting the floor and crossed himself. It seemed compulsory, like he didn't even mean to do it.

"Genuflection," he said with a shrug, as if thoat word meant anything to either one of us.

I had grown up Methodist and really only attended church for the big things: Christmas, Easter, weddings, funerals, etc. I'm not even sure what religion Clementine's

89

family was. I don't know that our friend group would have ever much discussed issues of faith, minus existential issues of what happens when we die, if it weren't for Nick. His decision to go full throttle into his Catholic guilt by way of becoming a priest over losing his virginity sort of transformed the trajectory of our friend group. He always seemed to be living somewhere on the outside of our reality. It was as if he had one foot in Heaven but liked to come and get dirty in Hell with us heathens from time to time.

I suppose Nick and Joy were two different sides of the same coin. Their ultra-conservative Catholic upbringing caused him to run from his own urges and into the safety of celibacy. His little sister, on the other hand, cleansed herself of her guilt by way of adapting a philosophy wholly different than that of her right-wing-leaning parents. She proposed that sex was nothing more than a full-body handshake and that no one should ever be ashamed of who they are, who they sleep with, or what they do behind closed doors.

High school was absolutely miserable for her. Because of her wildly unorthodox views on human sexuality, she received unending advances. Guys at school mistook her desire to unwrap why we tick as being synonymous with promiscuity. If it was, well, I wouldn't know. The only boys who ever bragged about sleeping with Joy were guys who were lying because they knew they would be believed. She never described herself as bisexual but I also don't think she ever wanted to be constrained to any sort of label. She also never batted a lash at the proposal by Clementine to attend the alt-prom together. It's what she wanted to do, it's who she decided to go with, and she felt zero need to explain herself to anyone.

This was such a contrast to her brother's experience of attending prom just a few years before. He instantly felt the need to tell someone what he had done: the family priest.

The DeLuna siblings were exactly the same except that they were completely different. I don't know another way to describe it. Their motivations were identical but their actions were a stark contrast to how people can view the world and respond to their surroundings.

For Joy, she found kindreds once she finally made it to college. People who understood the language she was speaking and were less inclined to shame or exploit her ideologies on sexuality and how humans engage, and disengage, from the activities of intimacy. As each day moved along for her during higher education, her brother paralleled his own advancement stepping further and further away from the ideologies she was creating. She made steps towards dismantling the ideals of patriarchy. He danced closer and closer to giving up the carnal pleasures of life in exchange for the highest level of patriarchal office that existed, the originals boys' club: the priesthood.

So here we three sat, looking back and forth between Joy and Nick. I wondered what he was thinking just then, just moments away from becoming a priest. Did he feel powerful? Humbled? It was kind of like the college graduation that the rest of us were waiting for, except that he had the promise of a future on the other side of this. I sometimes wonder if Nick just figured out how to beat this rigged game we were all playing. We didn't know it at the time, but the economy was about to bottom out, our futures were about to crash and burn, and these college degrees we were missing life for would be useless. We would be working menial jobs for the rest of our lives just to pay off the interest. We were running toward a finish line that kept moving further and further away. The only liturgy we would soon learn was, "We are all one paycheck away from homelessness," and all God's people would say, "Just leaving the dream!" No, Nick beat the system; for the rest of his life he would know what the rest of his life would look like. No more worrying about where he would lay his head or what to eat or if he would find the love of his life. Nope, that had all been decided for him.

"What an idiot," Shane whispered in my ear. "I know I haven't been the best friend to him these last couple of years, but I wish I could have talked him out of this. Opened his eyes to how silly this all is."

"We are here to show support," Clementine whispered back, which indicated that Shane wasn't being as quiet as he thought.

"Yeah." His head lowered as if he was in prayer. "Maybe one day he will see how corrupt this whole beast is. Until then, I guess he's Daddy Nick now."

***

Reality is a dangerous thing. Our dreams can take us anywhere, to places we hope to go, or place us with people we wish to see. But some fantasies can be grossly horrific once they jump over the threshold into reality. For Shane, he had always hoped to open Nick's eyes to what he felt was a fundamentally corrupt institution. Shane's parents were more passively devoted Catholics than the DeLuna family. Shane and Nick had served together as altar servers at the same church. They both clearly walked away with very different understandings of the level of reverence the Church deserved. But as much as Shane despised the Magisterium, he loved the man. Even after their falling out, Shane never stopped truly caring for Nick, even if he couldn't stand looking at him for more than a few seconds.

It was the kind of heartbreak that people assume is exclusive to romantic love. After watching their breakup, I'm not sure there is really much of a difference between lovers or friends going their separate ways. They shared every bit as much intimacy, if not more, as lovers minus the physical consummation.

Years ago, at Nick's ordination, Shane had told me he wished he had a way to show him how corrupt the beast was. Now, given the opportunity, you could see the butterflies rustling under his skin, deep down in his gut, and churning his stomach. It was like finding out that the husband of the woman he loved had been cheating on her. Sure, telling her would likely end the relationship, but it wouldn't bring them any closer. It would likely widen the wedge.

We all offered to be the one to talk to Nick. Even Clementine said she would do it. But Shane was resolute in his determination that it had to be him.

"I am the one who found it all. I'm the one who has to tell him. It's my responsibility. He is my friend and I care about him too much to take the coward's way out," Shane said with absolute determination.

It was the first time that he had referred to Nick as a friend since high school. There was zero doubt he felt it. His voice was so full of loving empathy there was no way anyone would be able to doubt the genuineness of his intent. What we should do and what we do as people, however, are very different things. There was no way to tell how Nick would react to this damning news.

After we all had our impromptu editorial meeting the night before, Joy had promised she would get Nick to the All Saints that next night so that Shane could unload the news onto him. When Nick finally did arrive, the rest of us got up to leave the two former friends to engage in what would be, undoubtedly, the most difficult conversation they would ever have, especially since it was being done on an already shattered foundation. This would either further break them or be the event that would finally bond them back together. With Nicholas DeLuna, there was absolutely no telling which way it would go.

As we all stood up Nick greeted each of us, minus Shane, who remained seated. Nick had that same familiar sweet smell on him as the cathedral did that day of his ordination: beeswax and incense and old wood. The scent cut through the fog of cigarette smoke and stale beer molding in the dusty carpets. A small waft of redemption within this den of sin.

The girls and I made our way back toward the far end of the bar where two twin dart boards sat against a forgotten wall. We had decided earlier not to adiós ourselves to the pool room because we couldn't see anything from there. Should things go not so well, we wanted to be close by. No matter where we stood, we would not be able to hear a thing. The rustling of feet and the orchestration of the jukebox and the flirtations of old men bellied up to the bar would drown out any sound those two would make between each other.

"Hey, Billy." I waited for him to turn around. "Can we have the darts?"

He handed us a chipped drinking glass full of multicolored darts in varying levels of disrepair. We each picked through the selection, checking their tips and balancing their weight in the palms of our hands. We collected quarters between the three of us and dropped them slowly into the machine, finally selecting a round of Cricket.

There is no worse kind of staring than when you are absolutely not supposed to be staring. Just the intention not to look almost compels your brain to shift your eyes in the direction of the forbidden fruit. Once you make the initial trespass, it becomes all the more difficult not to take another glance. All three of us participated in this little dance. Occasionally, one or another of us would call out the offender's name letting them know that it was now their turn to throw the darts. We were all relatively good sports at the game but none of us were doing rather well tonight. No, our minds were somewhere else, far away, in the direct opposite corner of the room, at that small round table with the faux Tiffany lamp, wishing desperately to be a fly on that wall.

"I wonder where in the story he is," Clementine wondered aloud.

Nick was just sitting there stoically. It was hard to tell which persona he was wearing tonight; in this moment, as he looked motionless at Shane, he was a still as the statues to which he prayed. I just hoped he was as good a listener as them.

We all knew what Nick was hearing. We also knew how hard it was to hear. It would be different for him than it was for us. Our repulsion was out of our concern for our fellow human beings. None of that disgust came from being surprised to hear that any of these people were corrupt. Our collective belief in the goodwill of our government officials or religious leaders had long been shattered and chipped away at long ago. Not for Nick though. None of us were having any heroes knocked from pedestals over this situation, except for Nick. We just felt a deep compassion for those who had been harmed in the process of this poisoned mission. I suppose we didn't even think of Nick as being a cog in the same machine, that he too was being harmed by all this in some way, that he was still a victim, of sorts, of this institution. Yes, he had joined its little army, but he was still just a foot soldier, not a general. Not yet, anyway. Nick was being rocked to his core, even if it didn't show on his stone-like face in that moment. We had all discussed the night before the great danger that we would be putting this story in if we told Nick. Surprisingly, it was Joy who led the charge of possibly not even telling him.

"Listen, I love my brother. But he will crush this thing before it even gets out the gate. He is many wonderful things, but he is, above everything else, an ideologue." She looked almost ashamed of herself for saying, "This story is too big for us to fuck it up, even if that means lying to Nick."

Clementine agreed. "We all care for Nick in our ways. I just don't know. He is a purist for sure; I don't know how he could take it. He could go straight to the bishop for all we know. It seems too risky. If Joy is alright with it, I'm alright with it."

Honestly, I had always been sort of indifferent to Nick. It's not that I didn't care, I'm sure I did. He was always around, lurking in the shadows of our existence growing up, and now it was the same thing, just always sort of around. So if something happened to him I'm sure I would miss him in that way you miss your toaster oven when it goes on the fritz and you have to replace it with something. Shane and Joy and Clementine were like my real family and Nick sort of felt like a cousin who lived on the other side of the country. Sure, he was your family and you were supposed to love him, but also, like, if he died what would it really change about your life? I'm pretty sure he felt very similarly about me. As a result, I was far less concerned about the possibility of all this information hurting his feelings or anything. Though I did think they were right that he could rat us all out and kill this thing before it ever had a chance to happen. I was also keenly aware that even though it wouldn't really affect me, it would have very real-life consequences for Joy, which was something I cared a lot about.

"No," Shane interrupted calmly. "We have to tell him. If we do not, and this story breaks, he will never trust any of us again. Even if we are risking everything, it doesn't matter, we have to do the right thing and tell him. If the tables were turned, I would want each of you and him to do the same thing for me."

As we all looked across the room at them, us three collectively staring, we were no longer ashamed to look because they were so engulfed in their conversations they didn't even know we existed. I don't even think they were in the same room as us anymore. They were somewhere else, far, far away in some metaphysical conference. So we continued our rotation of throwing our darts in a triangle of distraction, Clementine, Me, Joy, over and over again, momentarily glancing back over at Nick then to Shane and then continuing our rotation again.

I wondered if the story had taken this long when Shane told us the first time because it seemed like they had been over there for an eternity or more. Then, abruptly, they were both up on their feet and stood across from each other. They embraced and just held each other for a while.

Bull's-eye.

They walked together toward us and we shuffled around as if all we had been doing was playing darts and completely ignoring them the whole time. We tried to feign a conversation, but it failed miserably.

Nick broke our awkwardness. "Okay. This is obviously not what I wanted to hear tonight. But the Bible is full of betrayals, right?"

We all sort of shrugged and nodded, not really sure where he was going with this.

"So as true as that is," he continued, "we have no choice but to do the right thing. I'm going to want to see a lot of evidence. The smoking gun, so to speak. But if we can tangibly put all these pieces together then we have a story. It's a story we have to tell."

"I'm proud of you, Nick"—Joy gave him a big hug— "really, really proud of you."

"If nothing, I am just always seeking truth, even when it leads me into uncomfortable places. So let's go find the truth."

We took up residence back at our big round table. There we were, a ragtag group of weirdos and misfits ready to take on the establishment. It felt important but it also just felt natural. That night, we talked about a lot of things. We discussed so much more than just our impending date with destiny and launching the paper with one of the most scandalous stories this town had ever heard. Somehow, we evolved past all that and into fun stories about our times together, our hopes for the future, what this could all mean. We looked out across the table at one another and we were just five friends passionately in love with each other and ready to take on whatever the world had in store for us. We seemed young and invincible but also watched in our minds' eye as we aged right before our eyes. We could see grandkids and homes and even Nick as a future bishop. The whole world lay before us, a future for the taking. For the first time in maybe ever, I saw myself in the future and we were all there together.

If we can endure this then nothing can tear us apart, I thought.

Chapter Seven

First Comes Love

My grandmother always said, "You never know what you are going to do until you do it." I remember always thinking that was a weird phrase. I felt like I never did anything without thinking about it from a million different directions. How would my actions affect other people? What would happen if I went? What would happen if I stayed? There were always so many variables. I was a crippling ball of indecision. The whole concept of making a choice is our greatest freedom, but it can also be my biggest prison.

Our little friend group was scattered to the winds during college. Nicholas left first, being a few years our senior. He had ventured off to New Orleans for seminary. It seemed a bit humorous that he had gone to a city so notorious for its sin and degradation. New Orleans is where the rest of us would run to blow off steam; it's where Nicholas went to go get holy. Even though it was only a three-hour drive away from home, we rarely saw him. He was busy building a new coalition of friends. They called themselves the men in black, I shit you not.

For the rest of us, we were in our sophomore year and as displaced as could be. Clementine went to NYU and was excelling at life. For her, she escaped the South and was exploring all the things that the East Coast had to offer, plays and boutiques and acceptance for just being herself. The rest of us stayed in-state in an attempt to keep our tuition fees lower. But we still were displaced from each other. Shane went to the University of Central Florida and was studying journalism whereas Joy was experiencing her own freedom in Tallahassee. Even though she abhorred sports, she loved the atmosphere of going to the football games and meeting people outside of what her normal had been her entire life.

As for me, my inability to make a choice left me with no choice at all and so I was stuck at my hometown community college and doing the best I could. But choices were piling in on me nonetheless. Pick a class. Pick a major. Pick a part-time job. Should it be a full-time job? I wasn't quite failing, but I was surely floundering.

We all did our best to stay in communication in the ways we could. Some weekends we would travel to see each other. Probably one of my biggest regrets is that we never made it all the way up to visit Clementine in New York. We kept planning to and it just seemed so far. Holidays would come and go and we would see each other on Christmas and NYE and I would have Joy all to myself on Easter.

Because her brother was in seminary, he was the star of the show on Easter weekend visits. No one in her family was interested in hearing her talk about her feminist lit classes or how she just wrote a philosophy paper on the mating rituals of the bonobos and how they lived in sexually progressive communities and that the evolution of humans meant that we were only socially and not biologically monogamous. No, all the aunts and uncles and family friends wanted to fawn over Deacon Nicholas and how he would soon be turned into the walking hands of God. The dichotomy of their two viewpoints was growing a wider wedge in their family with each passing year. Nicholas was preparing to tell people they were going to Hell for thinking about masturbating and then Joy over here was considering becoming a sexologist. As far as the family was concerned you had Saint Nicholas, Jr. and the Whore of Babylon all under one roof.

Shane and Clementine didn't make the trip home for Easter. I would make the best of it and take the weekend off from work at The Pub, the job I had finally landed on.

We would go out to the beach and walk around taking photos of one another at the old fort ruins. We would go to a concert. Just do anything other than let her focus on the fact that she was second string.

It was actually Joy and I who were the explorers who stumbled across the All Saints. I suppose that is how it became our bar, our home, our refuge. Even though we shared it with the others, we always knew it was ours first and foremost.

One unimportant night my phone rang. I flipped it open; my front display was cracked and just glowed green with little oil slick smears where the lettering display used to show. I answered into the void without knowing who it might be.

It was Joy.

I listened silently as she told me about a boy. She wasn't really sure why she hadn't mentioned him before, she said. It was a throwaway line. I listened as she explained this life she was living, disjointed from home. He was suddenly everything until he wasn't. They met at a football game. Oh, how he wasn't her type, of course. They became inseparable for over a month. But when you are young, a month doesn't move at the same pace grown-ups live in. When you're an adult, a month doesn't seem like enough time to accomplish a project at the office. When you are young, you could build an empire, conquer a small country, begin a revolution, or fall deeply and madly in love in one news cycle. Through muffled sobs, she told me how he had changed everything she thought. All of these ideologies she had been building had been thrown out the window and suddenly, whimsically, magically, she was in love. Truly, madly, deeply. She had suddenly wanted to commit to a "forever person" and he was supposed to be it. The girl who never believed in monogamy or in singularity wanted to become a Mrs. Jock-Idiot-Weekends on the Cape, Esquire.

The problem with Joy abandoning her theory on the inability for humans to maintain fidelity is that as soon as she wanted that Disney Princess life, he became her human trial for her thesis on non-monogamy.

My heart raced in an anger I didn't know I could feel. This guy basically plucked her out of a crowd, pulled out the big guns to woo her, and then as soon as she had let all her defenses down, he was gone. He cheated and justified and then just said, "Fuck it, bro." That was that. But not really. His stain was going to potentially be a bit more long lasting.

"Leo, I trusted him. We were together and exclusive and I don't know what I was thinking but we just sort of stopped using protection."

"K," I said, waiting for the other shoe to drop.

"I'm an idiot and my parents are going to kill me or I'm going to go to hell if… I don't know what to do, Leo.

I don't! I have to make a choice. I mean I've made my choice. I just need a partner in crime. I can't go alone and I don't trust anyone here, not like that. Can you come with me?"

***

Winter was the dead season. There were a few festivals and such in the fall, but it was all mostly just attended by locals. The tourists would leave us from October until spring break. That was the official kick-off of busy season and that is when life would suddenly become a non-stop rollercoaster of picking up shifts, staying late hours, and doing our damnedest to stay alive. Some nights would become so wildly packed that I would be certain the fire marshal would barge in at any moment and shut us down. It was all over town and the beach, everything was slammed.

For those of us who worked in the service industry, we had to learn to plan and save some of our earnings during the summer rush so we could make it through the bleak months of the winter. That is the struggle of living in a town that only matters seven months out of the year.

Joy was now bartending at one of the long strings of tiki hut bars along the beach and loving life. It gave her the ability to basically party with new people every single night and get paid to do it. It was far less fun for me back in the kitchen at The Pub. We got all the business and none of the fun. It was just a constant scream fest of fast-flying orders and returns and steaks that were undercooked but now overcooked; throwing another hot potato, catching a bag of buns flying through the air, and my feet moving from aching pain to numbness.

Before we got slammed with life, we worked hard to build the back end of the website getting ready to launch. Nearly every night, some arrangement of the friend group would gather together at the All Saints. We were becoming a real paper, minus the print edition or an actual office or staff or pay or readership or advertising. We would take up residence at our favorite table and have our editorial meetings over a drink or ten.

It was Shane and Clementine who had come up with a brilliant plan for the launch. They decided to break the story up into a ten-part series. The plan was to begin with articles that were subtler. We wouldn't actually name any of the people involved. Just vague insinuations about conspiracy and scandal about "a housing development" and leave it at that.

Shane said, "This is the best way to begin gauging public interest and response. It is also a wonderful way to smoke out potential leads. People oftentimes come forward when a story like this starts moving out, they help fill in the gaps we are missing. Hell, the nervousness can sometimes make the bad guys out themselves."

When I was away from work, I never thought about the grill. I didn't worry if a steak was being burnt or a hamburger undercooked. Once I walked away, I was away. That's what a job is, I guess. I didn't have any personal responsibility or ownership in it. This wasn't a career, it was just a job. It paid the bills, most of the time, and so it just existed as a functional setting in my mind. Working there was like eating, breathing, or shitting, you had to do it and your body did it without you having to request it to do so. It was purely perfunctory. So I was able to turn it off as soon as I walked away. That was certainly not how I felt now that the paper was happening. It's all I could think about. When I was at home, at work; hell, it was all I could think about even when I was right there in the moment. My mind would drift away into the future and wonder about the possibilities of what might be on the other side of all of this.

Today was especially important.

Tonight, as Nicholas was in his parsonage saying his evening prayers and I was standing wiping grease from my brow and Joy was slinging drinks for horny spring breakers, Shane was finishing some edits and Clementine was writing the last lines of code. At any moment, without fanfare, Clementine would push a button and our fates would be sealed. The story would be out there in the universe and what the universe chose to do with it would be up to it. We didn't even have to worry about the whole universe! We just needed to make this small geographical area of the universe give a shit. Three hundred thousand people in the county. Just a ten percent viewership was only 30,000. How hard could it be to get a small football stadium's worth of people to give a shit?

We were fucked. It felt amazing.

After the dinner rush, I walked outside for a smoke break. I flipped open my phone and there was a text from Shane that read: *We are live.*

My heart leapt and sank like a runway elevator. There we were, on the horizon of either something or nothing. The hours crept by slowly as I waited for it to finally be time for me to get off work. We had all planned to meet as soon as we could at the All Saints to drink to our impending success or doom. In my mind, everyone else was going to be there before me. The anticipation was slowing time down.

The manager walked into the kitchen. "Who wants cut?" he yelled, and I had my apron off before anyone else could say yes. I ran out the door and to my car. I wasn't even going to go home to take a shower or change. I was still in my ugly black kitchen shoes. The excitement was too much to handle.

When I arrived, there was Joy, sitting by herself at the end of the bar. I made my way past Billy who had my drink waiting for me. I looked behind me for a moment, confused as to where everyone else was. I sat down next to Joy.

"I guess we are the first!" she said. "I bet Shane and Clementine are still at her place making little changes or something. I'm not sure why Nick isn't here yet."

It was rare for us to be alone like this. Even though the back of my mind was still very excited about the paper and seeing everyone, it was good for it to be just the two of us. We were sitting very close to where we sat that first night we walked into this second home.

"I guess he would be about four," Joy suddenly said.

"What? Who?"

"My son."

I guess whenever I thought back on that day, when she called me and I came to be with her, I always thought of it in that self-aggrandizing knight in shining armor kind of way. I couldn't have imagined Joy giving it all up and becoming a mom. As far as I was concerned about the matter, she made a mistake, she corrected course, end of story. When I thought of that day sometimes, I thought about how I dropped her back off at her apartment and I slept in my car, just in case she needed me. The next morning, I showed up with movies and popcorn and ice cream. We sat on the couch and I stayed until after she took her second pill. She had just gotten a positive test. If it had been six weeks I would have been surprised. It was nothing. A period party. I never told a soul and neither had she. We really never talked about it. So to me it was just being a friend and doing what friends do.

This was the first time she acknowledged it like this.

On the surface, I guess someone would say this looked like regret, but it wasn't, not if you knew Joy. That's not what it sounded like at all. It was a simple reflection on life. She always thought of the possibilities. What if we went up instead of down, left instead of right? But not in the way that I did. I would become crippled by choice and just decide to do neither until the water rose so high I had to swim my way out in whatever direction was left. She wanted to go left and right, up and down. Her only regrets in life were the times she couldn't do it all. I suppose if Joy could, she would have split herself in half and one part of her would have ventured forth into parenthood and the other part would have gone to college. One Joy would have faced the realities of parenthood and diapers and college funds. The other Joy would stay up late and debate over a beer until the sun rose. In her perfect world, there would be thousands of Joys living all the different opportunities and adventures and mistakes all at once so that she could experience the deliciousness of life from a million different cups.

"You know it was a boy?" was the only thing I could think to say to break the silence.

"No." She laughed. "There would have been no way to tell something like that. I just always assumed that would be my luck. I would have been stuck with a permanent miniature version of Lucas."

I felt completely unprepared for this conversation. What could I have possibly said? This was something I could not imagine, having to make a choice like that, college or kid, career or motherhood. Jesus, I just couldn't imagine. And how profoundly unfair. Somewhere in this world, Lucas is walking around unaffected. No harm done for him. This wouldn't stop him from running for politics or getting a job or publishing a paper. For Joy? It would hover over her forever. Just a choice. People make hundreds of them a day. Even though the only people who knew about her choice were her, me, the doctor, and Jesus, there was always that persisting fear I guess that someone could find out. That someone would have an opinion, think less of her, politicize her personhood.

Somewhere in the world Lucas is running around, free from worry, thanks to a choice that fell solely on Joy. He was set free and didn't even care about the burden that she alone would carry. I bet he would turn around and vote against her right to do it, just so he could have a lower marginal tax rate. He would benefit from abortion and yet restrict access to it. What a world guys like him live in.

"I don't regret it." She looked positive about that and I believed her. "I am not saying, 'he would be four' like I am missing out on a birthday party or something, just more of a realization that I would be responsible for a tiny human right now. I wouldn't be sitting here, excited about the future of what we are doing. I wouldn't have just had the most amazing night at work and then be here with you. I would be rushing off to relieve a baby sitter. And there are people who want that or love it now even if they didn't want it. I'm just saying... I'm glad you were with me then and I am glad we are here now."

I lifted my drink. "To good choices."

"To good choices," Joy echoed as we tapped our glasses together and then tapped them against the bar and took a big gulp of possibility together.

CHAPTER EIGHT

WITH A WHIMPER...

For as long as I can remember I spent every single summer at my grandmother's house. She lived in north Alabama and so it was a solid four-hour drive to go see her. She lived on a six-acre farm house that was surrounded by other farms whose acreage dwarfed her parcel by comparison. Large flowing fields with grazing cattle and horses; there were miles of corn and peaches. We would spend Saturdays going to the farmers' markets and buying fresh cheeses, butter, produce, candles, and honeycomb. Sometimes we would buy pies from the Mennonite women in their bonnets and dresses. Sunday mornings I would wake up early and watch movies she had video-taped for me on television. I would have to get up and manually fast-forward past the commercials.

Sometimes I would stay for three weeks, but some summers I was there for at least a month. Even though I missed my friends, I certainly loved the quiet. My grandfather's old study had been turned into a guest room and so it felt like my own special place whenever I came to visit. We would sit on the front porch and watch the fireflies and shuck corn.

Titanic had just been released that winter and we all went to see it a million times. Something about it captured our spirit of love and adventure like no other movie had. I don't know what it was exactly, but we just couldn't get enough. We were a bunch of teenagers walking around breaking our own hearts over and over again. It was perfect and beautiful.

Right before I left that summer to be with my grandmother, Joy and I went to go see *Titanic* together … alone. We played video games at the arcade while we waited for the next showing. We ordered a big bucket of popcorn and a soda to share. With just the two of us there, I blushed in the darkened theatre as Rose slipped her robe off to be drawn like one of the French girls.

I reached for a handful of popcorn and Joy's hand was inside the tub. We both jolted our digits back away from each other and she laughed. We didn't hold hands. We didn't kiss. We just sat there and watched the ship sink over and over again. It seemed like such a metaphor for our own lives; the rich elites of the world promising safety and security but then it was all a ruse. Nothing was safe, nothing was secure, and the whole system was set up for failure. It had weak points that no one even knew to look out for and there weren't enough rafts for everyone. The unsinkable ship was damaged by a simple little dent. The poor began to drown first, of course, and the waters rushed through the cabins as the musicians distracted us with a little entertainment. Sure you are dying, slowly, but did you catch *Saturday Night Live* yesterday?

After the movie we walked around the lobby, trying to avoid needing to go home. Our parents would be by to pick us up soon enough, but for just a few moments we wanted to enjoy our freedom.

"Let's take a photo!" Joy said, taking me by the hand.

"Oh, man I hate those things."

She pulled me insistently. "It'll be something to remember me by, while you are gone."

We piled into the small booth and pulled back the curtain. I placed a dollar into the machine and we waited. The first photo took us by surprise and we looked like a bunch of goofs. The second photo Joy yelled, "Silly!" And we made faces and then she yelled, "Vogue," and we made our best fancy faces, sucking in our cheeks. Then she took my cheeks into the palm of her hands and tilted my head toward her. "Kiss me."

We kissed there in the photo booth for maybe thirty seconds. I could feel the blood boiling within me. I felt like I was going to die but in the best way possible.

We jumped out of the booth and the machine spit out two copies of our photos. I reached for them and Joy slapped my hand way.

"You have to let them dry, silly! Otherwise, when you fold them, they will stick together and they will be ruined. You've got to be patient with things sometimes. It can't happen all at once. The waiting, the planning, the hoping, the anticipation, that's what makes life worth it! Anticipation is almost orgasmic."

I had never heard a girl use that word before and my fourteen-year-old head almost exploded. I thought I was going to pass out. Then she leaned over and grabbed the images and she placed one in her purse. She pulled out a pink gel pen in the same action and then signed it with, "Don't forget about me, stupid. Joy xoxo." And then she kissed underneath it leaving a big lipstick stain in the shape of her mouth.

My mom pulled up.

"I … uh … I gotta go. See you later."

"Later, alligator." She waved me out the door.

All summer long, I kept that photo in my chain wallet and would pull it out each night. I called into the local radio station and asked them to play "My Heart Will Go

On." I loved it most when they played the version that had words from the movie in it.

"You jump, I jump." I would say along, staring at our faces against each other.

That was one long summer.

***

The website was now live, but we had one big problem. See, none of us wanted the website to be linked back to us. Clementine had worked really hard to make sure that everything about the website concealed our identities. That also meant we were afraid to be the first ones to share it on social media. Shane couldn't share it for fear that it could be linked back to him and cause him to lose his job at the big paper. Nicholas had the same issue. Even though the initial article didn't directly implicate the bishop, future articles would and it could come back to bite him later. We were sort of stuck. In order for this to have any impact, it needed to be read, but no one knew that the damn thing existed and none of us wanted to incriminate ourselves as the originators of the content. So what to do?

Clementine created a burner email account and a fake account on Reddit. She dropped the link into a sub-reddit for the Panhandle. This was the only plan we had at this point. Now it was a waiting game.

Joy and I sat at the bar waiting for everyone else to show up. I had been in a state of anticipation for this moment for all us to be together after the launch and now I almost wished I had just waited it out at work. Not because I didn't enjoy Joy's company, I did, but it almost seemed more miserable the two of us just sitting there now in this silence, drinking another drink, smoking another cigarette, and just wondering what was going to happen next.

I felt a sudden smacking pain surge up my shoulders.

"We did it!" Shane yelled into my ear.

"Fucking shit!" I jumped out of my chair, almost toppling over. "Did what?"

"Clementine is a fucking marketing genius. It's out there, man, it's all out there." Shane was beaming.

Joy and I both looked at Clementine as she sheepishly smiled, unused to all these compliments. She was holding her laptop under her arm like it was the nuclear football. She motioned for us to move to our table and we all made our way over there, grabbing another drink and waiting to find out what was going to happen next. Hell, we wanted to know what was happening at all!

Once we were all situated, Clementine let us in. "I shared it to reddit and, at first, nothing really happened at all. Then I just started to get an insane about of re-blogs and notifications. About twenty different people started asking a bunch of questions and Shane and I worked hard to make sure we answered them without showing our full hand. Pretty soon, it was up to over a hundred questions and comments."

"Tell them the best part!" Shane pointed at her computer like it stored all the answers. "Tell 'em the best fucking part!"

"Well, as of when we were leaving my house, the article had been viewed almost five thousand times. It's hard to tell by the analytics on the blog but"—Clementine looked proud of herself in the least arrogant way a person possibly could—"it looks like it's being shared a lot too."

Just then, Nick showed up. He sat down and Shane got up to grab him a drink. We went back over everything with him. He looked surprised and maybe a little nervous. It was really hard to read him sometimes.

"So, it's happening, then," he deadpanned.

We spent the night in cautious optimism. That night, we closed the bar down. There was a lot to celebrate but also a lot to plan. How fast did we want to roll out the rest of the story? Shane suggested that we needed to let the momentum build just a while before dropping the next bit. He cautioned that we shouldn't wait too long, though, and let people lose interest. We were making a plan.

The next couple of days were touch and go. Sometimes we would get another little surge in views and then nothing. Shane finally decided that it was time for us to release the second part of the series. It didn't give much more detail; that wasn't the point, he explained. The goal was to try and goad just a bit. To get them sweating.

The headline read: Did the Mayor Know about Plan to Under Sell Property?

It was just a question. A simple yes or no would have sufficed. The second part of our step deep into the woods of journalism was about to thrust us into another round of uncertainty. Even though a ton of folks had viewed the blog by this point, ranking in at about 36,000 reads, not as many had signed up for our email list as we had hoped. Would the same plan for distribution work a second time?

That week came and went without much fanfare at all. By the weekend, we were beginning to wonder if this was really going to be worth it.

Saturday night, I got a text from Clementine. It read, "Important meeting. Tonight, 1:00 AM. All Saints. I am sending this to everyone."

When I got off of work, I went home to change and take a shower. I didn't know what to expect from Clementine's text. She was a little jumpy and so it could be either an end-of-the-world emergency or our stats might have dropped by a fraction of a percent. Either one of those could have been equally an emergency to her.

I lay down in the shower to feel the hot water flowing over my aching back. I passed out until I was suddenly awakened by the violent splash of cold water.

"Jesus," I said, jumping to my feet and nearly falling out of the shower trying to escape the ice-cold water. "Fuck this water heater."

When I finally arrived at the All Saints, everyone was already there. I was probably about twenty minutes late. Everyone turned, looking at me disappointed. Unlike Shane, who would gladly tell the same story a million times, Clementine was more orderly. She was sitting there neatly with a few printouts, her laptop, and a pen and pad open to keep notes. When I sat down, she immediately began.

"Now that we are all here—" she shot me a look "—we have a lead and a problem."

She passed out all the printouts to everyone. It was an email from an anonymous sender. They claimed to work in the mayor's office and said they wanted to meet with us.

To whom it may concern,

I am an employee of the mayor's office. I have information that could be pivotal to the continuation of you discovering the truth. It seems like you are close to the truth, but you are still really far away from what actually happened. I can help. But I want to meet in person. I need to know that you are real and that you are a friend, not just someone who is trying to get people to come forward.

The choice is yours. I can be found at this email address for the next 24 hours.

I hope you listen.

Yes, the mayor knew. He so much more than knew.

The problem was what if he was doing the same thing? What if we were being tricked into coming out of hiding? That was my big concern. It seemed like that made the most sense to me. Even this person mentioning their fears seemed like a great way to lower someone's defenses. I wasn't so sure. It just didn't make sense.

"Shane," Nick said, breaking the silence, "you are the expert here, what do you think? What would you do if this happened at work?"

"Listen, I've had to deal with this kind of thing in the past. Typically, the folks are legit. But it's also a really big risk. The biggest risk being that you potentially expose yourself for information that we already have. The good news is that it means we can corroborate the story the more witnesses we have. It's a really tough call."

Nick gave a nodding approval and then looked at Joy. "And you?"

"I'm not opposed to meeting with them." She looked kind of excited about it. "On the other hand, I agree with Shane that we could show our cards before we've even gotten to anything meaty. What if it's a trap? What if it isn't but we still learn nothing? It seems like a lot of risk and potentially very little return."

You could always tell their dad was a banker. Whenever the DeLunas got nervous they would always start speaking in economic terminology.

"I think it's too risky," I interjected. "I mean this whole thing is just getting started and I know we would love to see it just take off and us get to where we want to be, but we have to be honest that it might take time. If we run after every single lead or drop everything like this, we risk killing it before it gets started. Someone said to me, 'You've got to be patient with things sometimes. It can't happen all at once.' And I think that was really good advice then and I think it's good now. Anticipation can be—"

"Orgasmic." Joy smiled.

"Yeah, orgasmic," I said.

We all agreed to let the 24-hour deadline expire. We weren't ready to put our collective balls on the chopping block just yet. We were still just infants at this and we had already likely bitten off more than we could chew. With that decision under the bridge, we agreed to meet back in a couple of days after the third article hit. This was going to mention the suspected murder of the squatter on the property. The hope was, I guess, that if that was what this individual wanted to tell us, we would go ahead and expose it. If they were on our side, they might congratulate anonymously. If they were a foe, I guess we hoped that we just dodged a bullet. Or who knows! Maybe they would come back and tell us there was more that we weren't seeing and we would re-evaluate then.

With that, everyone departed. There was school and jobs and life that still needed to be attended to. It's not like this was putting food on our tables.

I closed out my tab and talked with Billy about some TV show he was hooked on. Billy suddenly pointed over at our table and there were someone's keys. I picked them up, gave a wave to our Patron Saint of Intoxication, and walked out the door. Joy was standing by her car, fumbling through her purse, desperately trying to find her keys. I walked over toward her.

"You missing something?"

"Yeah, I must have left them inside."

I twirled them on their pink key ring at the end of my finger. She grabbed them from me.

"You are such a goof." And then she looked at her feet for a minute and back at me. "You had a pretty good memory for that quote."

"You too. I mean you remembered what I was talking about."

"It was kind of the perfect kiss, huh?" She looked right into my eyes so deeply I almost felt uncomfortable being seen so much.

"Yeah, my first."

"Really? No shit. I didn't know."

"You know, you really broke my heart that summer when I got back. You were off with Jacob by the time I returned. I thought we were going to run away on a cruise ship and drown together or something when I got back."

"Damn, I really missed out on an opportunity for romance." She reached back into her purse and pulled out a small folded piece of paper. "I've still got them, you know."

I looked again. It was our photos. I reached into my pocket and pulled out my wallet, it still had a hole in it on the corner where my chain used to be. I opened it to reveal that I still had my original set of photos too. Joy looked almost shocked. We held the photos together and laughed. She took me by the hand and we just leaned against the side of her car and talked about that night and that summer away and how she actually ended up going steady with Jacob for almost a year until his dad got deployed and they had to move to California.

"Come on, get in." She opened the door to her car. "You've been about as patient as any man could be. I have been too, you know. It's not like I didn't want you. I just wasn't ready for us. I had a lot of things I wanted to feel and discover first. I probably still do. But I'm ready now to try if you are, patient man."

Anticipation, orgasmic.

CHAPTER NINE

...AND A BANG

By the end of high school we had lost three kids in our district to overdoses, four to drunk driving accidents, and nine had committed suicide. Two of the suicides were at my school. I didn't know either of them. The rumors circulated a lot and it was hard to distinguish the myths from reality. But the best I could tell from it all is that it was a boyfriend and girlfriend or more accurately an ex-boyfriend and ex-girlfriend. They had broken up and the guy didn't take it very well so he had started some nasty rumors about her and even showed around a nude Polaroid photo she had given him. Someone photocopied it and it circulated around school for a bit.

According to the paper, her parents found her in her car parked in their garage. The ex-boyfriend wasn't allowed at the funeral. The guilt etched away at him over time and right before graduation, he took his dad's old police department issued .38 Special. They found him lying on her grave with a note that said, "I'm sorry."

The truth is I didn't know anyone my age who hadn't tried to die, wanted to die, or wished they could die. The whole world was changing around us into an increasingly dark and dismal place. We watched the towers fall. I remember watching that video of the guy who jumped playing in a loop in my brain. I used to wonder what he was thinking as he fell. Was he scared? Did he regret it? Was he thinking about emails he forgot to respond to?

I wondered how long it felt like.

Then we watched as a war began and I started to think about how scared all those kids over there felt. I mean we had one attack on one day and we were terrified. In retaliation, we bombed towns and villages and buildings and hospitals and schools. I sometimes wondered who the real terrorists were. Most of all, I thought about how much none of us on the ground are responsible, not here in America and not over there in Afghanistan. Or was it Iraq? Maybe it was Syria now. All of us just civilian casualties of a war we didn't want, a war we didn't start, and everyone just really afraid of what might happen next.

Clementine used to wear long-sleeved shirts and jeans, even in the dead hot of summer, to cover the scars she would draw into her arms and legs. We were too scared to tell the grown-ups but not sure of what to do. Honestly, it seemed safer to just try to shower her in love and support than it did to take the chances of letting an adult know what was happening. They always overreacted and made it about them:

"Haven't I done enough for you?"

"You really hate life this much?"

"How hard can high school really be?"

"Just wait until you have real problems!"

My parents were furious with me for going to an anti-war protest. Dad railed on about how I could jeopardize his job, Mom's job. He asked me if I was a communist. Did I support terrorists? Did I hate my country? All the guys my age were signing up for the military; maybe he just raised a coward.

"I could die out there, Dad! And for what? Cheaper gas prices?"

He didn't even look up from watching Bill O'Reilly. "I would rather a dead son than a communist son. A coward son. Better to be dead than anti-American."

There were a million things I could have said to him. I should have told him that protesting was also very American. That expressing freedom of speech was American. That disagreeing with your government was truly American. That wanting people not to starve was American. That not being the world police was American.

Those were all things I could have said. Should have said. I was just finishing my sophomore year at college; I didn't even hear the insults about my lack of patriotism. All I heard was that my father wished I was dead.

Later that night, I sat on a park bench downtown. It was completely dead, other than one random dude who was sleeping outside under newspapers. He was surrounded by beer bottles. I could see camo pants peeking out underneath his blanket of yesterday's news. I walked over to see the small cardboard sign that lay next to him: US VET. ANYTHING HELPS. GOD BLESS!

Here was this guy who served his country, and now he was sleeping outside, drunk to numb the pain. I walked back over to my bench.

"This guy's sleeping outside, nowhere to go, and I am the un-American one for asking why?" I said out loud, to no one in particular.

I reached into my pocket and pulled out an old Swiss Army knife my grandpa had gotten for me. I carried it with me everywhere. Slowly, I pressed the blade up against my wrist. I pressed as hard as I could and nothing happened. The blade was too dull. I gave it another shot and still nothing. After a few minutes of shock, I walked back over to my car and opened the back. There was an unopened set of kitchen knives my mom had gotten me, I guess in hopes that I would eventually need them. I stood there for the better part of six minutes with my hand still on the trunk door, just leaning in on it and staring down at the knives.

Maybe my dad was right, I might be a coward. Too afraid to kill myself. That's what he wanted, right? He would have preferred a dead son to whatever I was. Then it dawned on me I should probably stay alive. I couldn't change anything dead. I threw the pocket knife into the back of the trunk and slammed it shut. In that moment of clarity I realized what I was going to do with the rest of my life. I wasn't going to kill myself; I was going to major in political science instead.

***

There are few things as disorienting as waking up in a space that isn't your own. The sudden need to pee jolted me awake. It took my brain a moment to process a number of rapid-fire thoughts that pulsated through my mind like a log jam. *Where am I? Who is this next to me? Why am I naked? What is that noise?* But almost as quickly as I thought them I began to answer them. *I am at Joy's house. That is Joy. And you are naked because you just had some of the most intimate and beautiful and meaningful sex you have ever had in your entire life. And that noise is your head ringing from shock.*

You need coffee, homie.

We had been seeing each other for over a month now and I wasn't sure that anyone in the friend group knew it yet. We weren't being affectionate in public or trying to be showy. That one night leaving the All Saints turned into a weekend of not leaving the bed. We watched movies and told stories and I cooked dinner in her grandmother's hand-me-down cast iron, wearing only an apron and socks. We ordered Chinese take-out and pizza and popped popcorn and watched *Titanic* for the five hundredth time.

That first weekend together felt like we were making up for lost time. We compiled innumerable missed opportunities and almost dates into just a few storied hours. I had to go to work that next day and as I was leaving she looked up at me from bed and smiled saying, "I'll see you when you get back." With that she rolled over and took a nap.

Sex is so different in the movies. Everyone curls up under the blankets, covering themselves from the cameras, hoping to keep their film within an appropriate rating. Real sex is nothing like that. Maybe it just wasn't like that with Joy. I had certainly had movie sex before. Hidden and secret and lacking in reality. Sex that was fueled by alcohol and dispassionate disappointment. Sex for the sake of functionality or loneliness. Sex just because we were horny and why not.

Joy had always talked about how sex was just another form of human communication, the extension of a conversation that can no longer be expressed with words.

That is certainly how this felt. We were continuing a conversation that started in middle school and we just never completed it. All of our previous dialogue seemed to end with a parentheses or an ellipsis. This didn't feel like a period at the end of a sentence but the beginning paragraph to a novel. Everything else had been the prologue and we were now ready to enter into the bulk of the story.

I didn't move in with her or anything. But it sort of felt like that sometimes. Part of that was because I lived in an apartment with five guys and she had her own space. It was a small one-bedroom apartment attached to a large house near downtown. The bathroom was in the bedroom and then there was a kitchen that had the only regress, a singular wooden door with a stained glass window. It was small and cozy and perfect. It was filled with relics and photos from adventures and mementos from travels. It almost looked like one of those altars in the shops along Bourbon Street, just a mismatched collection of coins and trinkets from everything and everyone that mattered to her. Even the dust that collected on everything held memories of people who had visited for the day or spent the night with her. Our skin and hair and breath were placed upon this altar to be worshiped and remembered and to become part of a long string of stories to cherish forever and ever, amen.

In spite of the fact that the flower of our romance was finally able to blossom, the world still turned, problems still existed, and so did responsibility. The paper was now collecting a small but intentional readership. We were publishing articles outside of just the big scoop. Everyone was finding their balance and style. Clementine had opened up usernames for each of us so we could all sign into the editorial portal and publish our work. Even Nicholas was getting into it. He was writing about things he could never say from his position within the Church. I don't think we had intended to have an opinion piece, but that's where Nick found his niche. He would write about philosophy, religion, and faith. His style was so different from the pompous sermons he would give from the pulpit. He wasn't promoting his absolutist thinking. This was giving him space to ask questions and pose problems. He devoured the comments, even the negative ones, with such fervor.

The big paper had even written article about us. It wasn't a positive one. It accused us of being intentionally salacious and promoting ideas without proof. One quote that especially stuck out was, "This paper, if one could dignify it with such a noble word, is a prime example of everything wrong with journalism in the age of the internet. Any idiot with a keyboard can espouse something, true or false, and do so with the luxury of anonymity, thus thrusting aside the responsibility that comes with being a real journalist: accountability."

However, it was an absolute fact that someone had been killed in a raid on the not-so-vacant house that was momentarily owned by the diocese. It might not have been a fact that the sheriff or the mayor or the bishop wanted publicized. It was true nonetheless. We simply raised the specter that it was possible that this shooting might be a bit more intentional than was originally presented. The individual that was killed had no previous drug charges. He had some vagrancy misdemeanors, trespassing infractions, and things like this. All of which seemed to end after he moved into the vacant house on the abandoned property. He had a job as a dish washer at one of the local restaurants where he was loved and revered. We said as much in our article, quoting co-workers and family. This guy's entire life had turned around when he got into this place he called home.

I think what really rubbed them is how we personalized this man who died at the end of a trigger-happy police officer's gun.

His name was Bobby McDonald.

When he was first killed and the story broke in the big paper, they made it seem like he was some drug kingpin. That he was intentionally corrupting the project housing directly behind his borrowed home. The reality that we painted was much different. He was a veteran with PTSD who had fallen off the radar for years. When he finally returned back to his country, he had nowhere to call home. He lived on the streets and at the mission. He did everything he could to survive and then one especially cold night he broke into this property and no one cared. They didn't care for a week, which turned into a month and became years. He turned the water on and then the electric. He did repairs and painted and patched the roof.

Hell, if we did this with every single vacant and abandoned property in America we could likely turn this whole thing around. But stealing vacant property was a privilege of the rich, not the impoverished.

The paper and City Hall were trying to smoke us out. Our series on the scandal was rapidly coming to a close and we were putting all the pieces together. We had yet to provide the evidence, which had now become quite substantial, that proved without a doubt that the three superpowers in our community were in league with each other and had all colluded to commit the (almost) perfect crime.

We had it all, not just suspicion but also the smoking gun.

The friend group started meeting nightly at the All Saints to discuss our next moves. We plotted over pool. We made decisions over darts. We storyboarded over shots. It was perfect. We were receiving countless emails a day with story suggestions and we even had a column just devoted to responding to emails. We were engaging with people in a way that the local paper couldn't even imagine. We had a Twitter account and other social platforms. We were democratizing the news. Instead of telling people what they should think, we were listening to our readership and answering them, telling the stories they wanted to hear, even if sometimes we weren't providing the answers they hoped to have.

Tonight, editorial responsibilities were not what Shane wanted to discuss.

When I rounded the corner of the door and into the bar, I was yanked by the arm into the men's restroom. There was Shane, looking sleuth-y as ever. He had a cigarette hanging from his mouth and a glass of scotch, half consumed, in his left hand. The condensation dripped from the side of his glass. It was full-on summer and no amount of air conditioning could adequately fight this heat and humidity. Nowhere was as hot in the All Saints as the bathroom. Here we stood, sweaty and trying not to die from the dense ammonia smell of the urinals.

"I've got a hunch on a story." Shane grinned.

"Awesome! What's it about?"

"Sex, lies, deception, long lost lovers … shit like that."

I shook my head. "We agreed we weren't doing those types of stories."

"I know."

"So we aren't doing them."

"I know."

Curiosity got the better of me. "Who is it?"

"You, you lying sack of horse shit! How long have you been fucking Joy and not telling me?" He was in a full guffaw at this point. Highly amused with himself.

"No comment."

"Is it serious?"

"No comment."

"You aren't going to give me anything?"

"I said, 'No comment.'"

"You realize that I would consider this an admission of guilt by literally anyone else? So I'm going to assume y'all are married and going to have a trillion children. Or that she is just using you for your body. The jury is still out."

"She's not using me for my body." I rolled my eyes.

"So you are admitting she's had your body…" I'll give him this; Shane was good at his job.

"Listen," I said, a bit more sternly than I intended, "it's only been going on a month or so. We haven't had any of those types of conversations. So I am not going to define it in any terms. I'm just happy to be with her, when I am."

"You love her," he said seriously right back at me.

"Yeah, of course I do. But it's not the 'in love' kind of love, you know. Just, I love her."

"Good, because she loves you. So it's done. I'll see you at the wedding."

Some guy walked into the bathroom. By this point Shane and I were so close we looked like we were about to kiss. The women's restroom shared a direct wall with the men's and so neither of us wanted to risk anyone over on the girls' side hearing us. So we were sort of whisper talking right into each other's ears. When this random dude saw it, he looked awkward and put his hands up walking backwards.

"Don't be a dweeb. Just pee," Shane barked at him then kissed me on the cheek while making eye contact with the intruder and we exited the bathroom.

We made our way to our usual table to take a seat with the others. Shane took me by the arm again before we reached our destination. He leaned in against my ear and said, "I'm really, really happy for you. I'm happy for both of you. I've been waiting for this for y'all for a long time. It's perfect. I can't imagine something making me happier than the two of you finally realizing you love each other." And he kissed me on the other cheek. "I love you, man."

When we got to the table, we plotted, Clementine took notes, and Joy was rubbing her foot up the inside part of my pants at the ankle as I slowly died inside hoping that Nick wasn't glaring at me. This was basically my perfect life. I couldn't imagine anything better.

"Alright y'all," Shane interjected, "I've got some friends in town for the weekend. A couple of brothers I used to know back in the day. They are weirdos but genius guys. They used to be informants for me back in the day before they skipped out of town for a while. They are basically informational mercenaries. They used to do some big dirty work for the mayor before he was the mayor and maybe a little bit afterward. They are swinging through town for a couple of days and so they are going to stay at my place. I'll probably go dark for a bit. We will hit the town, maybe the casinos over in Biloxi, the usual shit. They might be able to help me fill in the last little bits of info before we go live with the big one. Maybe this is part of a series of wrongs. We might just be scratching the tippiest top of the iceberg here. If we are, these guys would know."

Clementine was unusually drunk that evening. Joy took her home with her and that meant I was banished back to my smelly apartment with my repugnant roommates. This feeling I was feeling, this longing to be with her, this feeling of missing something, it was something I had never felt before. Was I becoming … clingy? No, that wasn't the word.

Fuck. I'm in love.

Chapter Ten

NARC

Most weekends during college I would go downtown at the corner of Main Street and meet up with the Veterans for Peace for an anti-war protest. It was awe-inspiring watching all these guys get screamed at for hours. My job was to videotape. I'm not exactly sure how I got nominated for this position other than that I was the youngest one there and I guess they assumed that meant I knew something about technology. I absolutely did not. I was horrible at recording stuff. They wanted someone who could be there in case anything went down.

Guys in pickup trucks would drive by and scream one of three different accusations:

Communist!

Fascist!

Socialist!

It was pretty amusing when they would mix them up too. One guy spouted off all three in one brief sentence, "Y'all are just a bunch of fucking America-hating fascists; you want to turn us into a communist country and make us all into socialist puppets. Fuck you, assholes!" So eloquent.

One of the guys I met out there, Henry, was quite the fascinating character. He was probably only 5'6" and he had a sturdy beer gut and receding hairline. He covered it with a baseball cap with dozens of insignias and pins he had collected over the years. Most of them were military in nature but there was also some from presidential elections for Green Party members and a blue ACLU emblem. He always took the hat off in between thoughts to wipe his forehead.

On a particularly sweltering summer day, he took his hat off for a good pat down of his head and then looked at me solemnly. "You know, when jerks happen, when they yell stuff at us, it just reinforces my belief that they think the only good soldier is a dead solider. A living soldier is an inconvenience, we've got opinions. When we die out there on some foreign soil, they put up plaques of us and say, 'God bless our veterans,' but when we make it back, when we live, we are a problem. Yeah, we come back with broken backs and PTSD. All we want is to save the next generation from the same fate."

Learning from those old guys really helped form my political opinions. There was so much I didn't know. I probably learned more sitting at their feet, like my own personal Platos, than I did in any of my political science classes. They are who taught me about predatory recruitment; that they send folks in to promise a better tomorrow to high schoolers in rural areas and inner cities. They give bonuses and fail to mention that they will barely cover their uniform costs. It's part of the school-to-prison pipeline. They basically act as a last-ditch effort to "save" these kids and promise them the world. Just so long as they live long enough to see it.

"They offer them everything," Henry would rail, "cars, women, money, and education. Millionaires sending poor kids off to die so they can sell weapons and gasoline. Just a bunch of pawns in a chess game that started the day they built Wall Street."

It was strange how some of the politics of these guys didn't sound all that different from the rednecks who blasted their horns. They were all looking toward Washington, D.C. as this massive machine that needed to be retooled. Sure, they disagreed on a large number of important topics, but there was a lot that they probably agreed on too. The most important being that they wanted a better America, they just disagreed on which way we needed to go to get there: right or left.

So every single Saturday morning we stood there on the corner to wave our flags and banners and homemade signs. Then one Saturday there were big signs from the city on all the light posts and parking meters. "NO PARKING ALONG MAIN STREET FROM 6:00 AM to 5:00 PM SATURDAY FOR FARMERS' MARKET."

Henry patted me on the back. "Don't worry, kid. Just another war we gotta fight. We're used to it."

***

At about mid-afternoon I got a text from Joy: She's gone, come on over.

I responded with: Getting ready for work. Tonight?

When I got to The Pub, it was packed. Summer was quickly coming to a close. Soon, everyone would be called back to school and work. The slow winding down would move from rushing to a drizzle and then a drip. Once winter rolled in, the locals would magically reappear to enjoy everything they had loaned out to our visitors. Sure, a few of the tourists would hang around late into fall. The money would move slower in unison with the drooping palm trees and the wide open lanes on the bridges leading out to the gulf.

All night I waited for Joy to respond to my text. I burned three people's meals because I was distracted. This is what it means to be a total fucking mess. That is what I was: a complete mess. I needed to cool my jets and quick before I freaked the girl out and she kicked me to the curb for being a needy ... uh ... whatever I was.

Suddenly, my phone began to vibrate in my pocket. I yelled out that I was taking a smoke break and abdicated my duties. It wasn't Joy. It was a missed call from Shane. I called him back.

"Thanks for calling me back." His voice sounded kind of hoarse like he had been yelling or crying.

"Yeah, buddy. What's up? You okay?"

"I got fired."

"What?"

"I got called into a meeting today with my editor. The HR director was there too. They put a bunch of printouts of the *Panhandle Free Press* in front of me. They asked if it was me writing this stuff. What's most ironic is that none of them were my articles. I said no, which was true, and they said it seemed like my style. Apparently, while I was in there they had one of my co-workers clear my desk."

"Holy shit. I'm so sorry. Fuck."

"Yeah, fuck. I think it's my fault too. I had left something open on my computer. Not my work computer, my personal laptop, but I left it on my desk. It was a couple of weeks back and when I got I home, I realized and ran straight back to the office. When I got there, this one guy who hates my guts was kind of lurking around my desk."

"Shit man, this blows. Listen, I'll be off of work in an hour. Meet me at the All Saints and let's talk this out."

"Okay, you are buying."

"Yeah, yeah. Absolutely."

The second I hung up the phone a text came through.

Joy: Meet me here when you are done.

Me: Change of plans. Shane got fired. All hands on deck at the All Saints.

Joy: Fuck. See you there.

When I arrived, Shane was already a couple in. Logically, he had put them on my tab. Billy confirmed with me when I got there that it was alright. Once, Shane had run up over a hundred bucks on my tab and Billy almost rung my neck. So we both learned to check with each other from then on out. Shane had gone to college for this shit and I was making more than him at my shitty job. At this point he would have his student loans paid off sometime around 2075.

He was sitting with Joy and Clementine. He looked completely broken. As much as the big paper drove him crazy, he was working his dream job. The paper was everything to him. He poured everything into it and probably would have run into the burning building to save the presses if given the chance. But that didn't matter to the powers that be. He was out. The heat had really been turned up on our little experiment and this was the first consequence.

We did our typical dance of making our way to our table. Shane just looked so utterly defeated. He had the face I would imagine someone has when they walk in on the love of their life fucking another person. It just gutted him completely. He was slumped over on the table and nursing his drink. Everyone else just sat with him quietly, smoking cigarettes, drinking, and looking at one another hoping that one of the others would have some clue what to do.

"Fuck it," he sniffled out. "Fuck it and fuck them. But if they know it's me, it's just a matter of time until they link it back to all of us. Y'all are basically all I talk about. I don't even have a picture of my mom on my desk, but I have ones of all of us. From spring break in Cancun and Alternative Prom and the silly one we took the night we decided to start the paper."

The truth is what did any of us have to lose? Joy was still finishing up school. She had taken that gap year (or two) after the dodged pregnancy bullet and decided to transfer back here. But she was just working odd jobs and stuff and her bartending gig on the beach would wrap up soon. Clementine worked for herself. She ran a plus-sized porn site and did some modeling. I had The Pub. The only other person who had something to worry about was Nick.

"Who knows?" I said. "I mean after we drop the big story next week, anything could happen, right? I mean you could get picked up by a big paper. There is a lot on the horizon."

"You are right." Shane kind of smiled for the first time all night. "And I've got a couple of side gigs doing a bit of editing and what not. I've got some collectibles I could sell at the house to get me through."

"Darts?" I asked.

"Yeah, fuck it!" Shane threw his hands up. "Seriously, fuck it."

We played a couple of rounds of darts and just laughed. The truth was Shane was right. What the fuck could he do? At this point, the only option was to trudge forward and hope that all of this was worth it. It didn't make any sense to stop now. I guess that's the thing that people just fail to understand about totally dismantling someone's life; they are going to go in one of two directions, they might totally bottom out and fall into the pits of despair … but they might just ascend. Every part of Shane's countenance that night made it very clear which direction he intended to go: straight up to the clouds.

After about two hours, Shane, still laughing, said, "Listen, y'all. This was great. You are the best friends a guy could ask for. But I gotta get back to the brothers."

"They are still staying with you?" Clementine asked.

"Yeah, it's been a bit longer than I expected too. But they've actually helped a lot. I'm so close to ready to launch this story. They just had a bit of trouble out on the West Coast and needed to come back through this way to let it cool down a bit."

We all went our separate ways, or at least gave the appearance of doing so. A few minutes after Joy arrived back home, I pulled up. I walked straight in through the door and set some Whataburger I had picked up on the table.

"What the hell do you think you are doing?"

I froze in an absolute panic.

"Nothing," was the best defense I could come up with.

"No, you are doing more than just nothing. Look at you! Just walking into my house, uninvited, like you own the goddamn place..."

I thought I was going to pass out.

"...being the absolute perfect man on the planet. Whataburger after midnight. You really know how to get a girl going."

We went to her room and turned on the TV. There is truly nothing like greasy food after a long day of working and drinking. I dreaded getting older and all of this catching up to me. But the weird thing is, for the first time ever, I was imagining getting older, there being a world out there beyond this, and even a small part of me was starting to wonder if Joy would be in that world with me. I was trying my hardest not to get ahead of myself, but it all just felt right.

Then it happened. Shane went AWOL. The biggest problem with Shane is that there was no holding him down. If I hadn't been so distracted with being in love and shit, I probably would have predicted it. This was the longest that Shane had stuck around in a long time. I think the only thing that was holding him down was the two papers. That was just too much excitement for him. But the one thing he hated more than feeling trapped was feeling sad. He fucking hated feeling sad. Losing that job was a whole lot of sad.

So he disappeared. It could be a week, a month, or even more before he would decide to pop up. I had seventeen different phone numbers for Shane in my cell. I should have deleted them because it made it really confusing, but it also helped me keep count. Every time he got like this, every time someone broke his heart big time or he lost a job or maybe he just wanted to feel alive, he would just be gone. I should have seen it coming that night. He was trying his damnedest to reframe and just make this his happy. This was just too big a punch to the gut.

So he would toss his phone into the gulf and take his beat-up little VW van and disappear into whatever adventure he needed to find in order to feel alive again. And as soon as he was alive again, he would reappear. He would just pop up and act like this was totally normal. We would bounce back. We would publish his final bit of work on the big scandal and expose these bastards who got him fired. It would be the perfect revenge.

Now we just had to sit around and wait for him to pop back up ... whenever that might be.

CHAPTER ELEVEN

FALLOUT

The first memory I can recall of life is my mother taking me to the store on her bicycle. I was sitting in an upright seat on the back. I was probably only three years old or so. The sky was clear and the street lights were scarce. I watched as the large neon white moon hovered above my head. I stared in wonder at the beautiful orb that seemed to be staring back at me. Everything was silent with the exception of the spokes flashing forward and the hot breath of my mother as she steered us onward.

I was stricken with a sudden sense of panic as I realized the moon was following us. No matter how hard my mother peddled or how many turns we took, there was the massive moon in hot pursuit. I watched its steady chase where it seemed neither to be gaining on us nor falling behind.

"Mommy!" I shouted. She came to a screeching halt, which was not what I wanted. "The moon is chasing us!"

"You scared me, Leo!"

"I'm sorry, Mommy. I'm scared too. Is the moon going to get us?" I earnestly inquired.

My mom paused in a way that my now adult mind assumes was an attempt not to laugh at me, "No, baby, the moon isn't going to get us. It's very, very far away. And it isn't following us. It is right where it's supposed to be. It just looks like it is following us. It's an illusion."

I blinked at her with uncertainty of her scientific credentials. She turned around and looked at me gently. Her chest rose with a big sigh as she soaked in this moment of motherhood and put her cold hand against my flushed warm cheeks.

"I will never let anything hurt you. Never."

With that simple promise, I took my mother at her word. That was all I needed, in that moment, to know that the world was going to be secure and that I would be shielded from all harm. That is what I believed and, at that time, nothing could have convinced me otherwise. My mommy wasn't a princess, she was a warrior. I knew it and I watched the moon as she cycled us closer to the store and I was no longer frightened. The large ball morphed back into a celestial friend and I smiled back at him.

My mom docked her bike safely in the corral in front of the small supermarket and dismounted. She turned around and unbuckled me from my little harness and glided me to the ground. I took her hand and we walked through the store, picking up a few small items. I watched her as she selected spices and oranges and delicately rummaged for the prized onion. She turned around and saw a familiar face. I did not know the woman. I don't remember what my mom called her. They embraced and talked about things that I didn't care about. Then the woman leaned in and her tone changed.

"Did you hear about Barbara's son?" the woman asked.

"I did. Her husband called me," Mom responded with no indication as to what happened.

"I knew that y'all were close. I just can't imagine." The woman looked down at me and then continued in coded language. "Poor little thing. And I heard the babysitter didn't make it either. I just don't understand letting kids ride with other people like that. Babies are getting kidnapped and all kinds of things. We are going to have to just hold them a little tighter, aren't we?"

"Indeed," was my mom's only response.

It became clear to the woman that she wasn't going to get much out of my mother that night. She was as steeled as Fort Knox. Not a word or indication as to what was happening. To this day, I don't know if it was my mom protecting me or her friendship to Barbara. I've sometimes wondered if she knew this woman was just a gossip and wanted to syphon her for information. Either way, I recognized the name. As the woman walked away with her cart, I tugged at my mommy's arm.

"Is Mrs. Barbara okay, Mommy?"

My mom took a long pause. The truth is she wasn't okay, not even a little bit, and my mom took a moment to wait and not lie but trying not to tell the truth.

"No, she isn't okay right now. She is hurting very badly."

"Did someone hurt her?"

"Yes, someone hurt her in a way that can't ever really go away," she said and then hoped this would be enough; she began rustling through a selection of large tomatoes.

"Is Tommy okay, Mommy?"

Tommy was my best friend, as best a friend that you can have at three years old. Mrs. Barbara was my mom's best friend. They had been pregnant together and so I did everything with Tommy. We went to the playground together and took baths together and he was everywhere. My mom got down on one knee in the grocery store and I remember a tomato falling down to the ground and exploding in a thud. My mom kicked it under the bins with her foot and looked me right in the eyes. She was crying.

"Are you sad?" I asked, hugging my mom. She held me for a moment and then pulled me back into her line of vision.

"Yes, baby, I am sad. Something very sad happened. Tommy went to be with the angels. He is gone and it was a very, very sad accident. So Mrs. Barbara is very sad and I am very sad."

"Is Tommy coming back from the angels?" I asked.

"No, Leo." My mom's makeup was running down her cheeks. "He isn't. He is gone forever."

"I guess his mommy isn't like you!" I said excitedly. "You won't let anything hurt me."

***

We had one more story to publish. One more story to tell and then everything was going to change. That was nearly a month ago. No, we were stuck in a stasis of uncertainty. The bulk of the article was written and Clementine had a copy of it. However, the stash of evidence was with Shane and Shane wasn't there. This was not his longest adventure. One time, he disappeared with complete radio silence for an entire summer. There was no telling how long we would have to wait. We continued forward publishing what we could about other stories, but our readership, which had now substantially grown, began to inquire. They wanted to know where we were going with all of this. But we were stuck.

Life was moving forward as it does. Even though this project had become so much to us, it was beginning to feel like just another piece of the puzzle in our lives.

Clementine would send out a piece for review. Nicholas would independently publish another opinion spot. But we weren't meeting like we used to.

Probably the biggest change that had happened was that Joy and I were finally official. Well, as official as she was willing to be. Like the waves crashing against the sand in the gulf, they are certain and they are there but at their pleasure. The sand can no more hold them down than the waves can permanently hug the sand. In the same way that you can't think of the beach without the waves or the sand, we were that well associated in the minds of those who knew us. I knew that we were just as fragile. Some of the water remains in the sand and some of the sand is dragged out to the depths with the waves. I was learning to enjoy that level of intimacy and fragility.

Nicholas took it pretty well. When Joy told him he said, "Okay. Makes sense." And that was the beginning and end of the conversation.

Descent doesn't normally come in the forms you expect it. I was absolutely certain that Nick was going to give me one of those, "if you hurt my sister" lectures or something. He didn't. Instead, he just accepted this all as the new normal and moved on. I think he had long ago learned that any attempts to try to control Joy were futile. No, the hitch in the plan came from an entirely different corner: Clementine.

I guess in the back of my mind I always knew that she cared for Joy too. Of course she did. I would have been stupid to think otherwise. I suppose I just didn't care, which is a pretty cruel thing to say out loud. But that lack of caring became apparent in how callused I was in the clear sadness that fell over her face. As much as my life was being instantly fulfilled in our newfound love, Clementine was dealing with heartbreak. I was imagining a life together and the one she had imagined was crumbling around her.

She chose to pour herself into her work, not just with the paper but also other projects and sites she was supposed to be working on. She maintained full dedication to everything, but she was also what held us together on a schedule, regular meetings, and things like that. Without her leadership, we were just floating away, which, for me, wasn't that big of a deal at the time. It gave me more time to see Joy and for us to pour our energy into what we were building together.

The quiet after the storm of these last few months was delightful, frankly. We went to the All Saints to play pool and have a few drinks and talk with our other friends and acquaintances. It wasn't all business and chaos. But the calm can only last so long and so one night Joy said we needed to invite Clementine out to join us. I didn't vocally protest, but I guess I wasn't as enthusiastic as I should have been either.

"She's our friend!" Joy said, jabbing me in the side. "Since Shane decided to bounce, a lot has fallen onto her. She needs us."

When Clementine arrived at the All Saints, we did what we always do when our little threesome met sans the others. We played darts until our fingers fell off. I guess I had just been a jackass because it was actually kind of perfect. I think in our newfound couple isolationism, I had lost track of the importance and profound love I felt from our friend group. I was also suddenly missing Shane, which isn't something I did often. Not because I didn't love him and not because he isn't a missable kind of guy! It's just I have been so pavlov'd into becoming accustomed to his little jaunts.

I missed this. I missed us all together. The beauty of what we were all building together. I was letting my anxieties and fears get the best of me. And then, maybe I was speaking too soon. Out of the corner of my eye, I saw Clementine giving me a look that felt a lot like a glare. I considered ignoring it and then my lesser demons got a hold of me. Joy was back up at the bar, supposedly getting us another round, but she was flirting with Billy, as she is wont to do. The two of them were a funny pair when they got to flirting. They could have taken it on the road.

"Listen," I said, looking directly at Clementine, "I know you aren't thrilled about this whole Joy and me thing and I think I know why."

"Do you?" Clementine crossed her arms at me. This was never a good sign.

"Yeah, I think it's pretty obvious you are in love with her too."

"You are an idiot," she scoffed.

"So you are denying it?"

"No, it's just that life is so much more complicated than this box you are trying to put it into. And I think it's really dumb and I also think it means you don't get Joy at all. Have you read her work? Do you listen?"

I had read her work and I had listened. But I guess I just always thought of her philosophies as avant-garde more than praxis. However, Clementine was coming at me like an acolyte of the true teachings. She was going off and hard. I was feeling pretty stupid, so maybe she was right. The way she was speaking is how one might imagine the Apostles ranting about their certainty about Christ.

"Don't you get it?"

"No, I guess I don't."

Clementine rolled her eyes. "I'm in love with you."

That came crashing on my head like an entire stack of bricks. I had stepped right into this and didn't really know how to step back out of it. Had I missed something here? I mean I had spent most of high school essentially single and I was suddenly missing the fact that my two best friends were in love with me? Was I really this dumb?

I am absolutely certain my face must have looked pretty dumb. My brain was not rushing with information and then responding within a matter of seconds. It was trudging along and I think I was stuck there just blinking like a Hugh Grant movie stuck on a loop.

I could have really used that second round.

"I'm in love with her too." She decided to drop that on in there since I was clearly in a state of shock and I suppose she felt it best to just dump it all on me. My face remained the same, just sort of a blinking, sluggish shock, but with this new information my head sort of tilted a little to the right as if the information entering my brain was a bit more weight than it could handle.

"Let me try this again." She resolutely jumped forward. "I am in love with y'all. Both of you. Together. All of it. I am head over heels in love with all of you, both of you, and I wish that it was us, all of us."

I'm not certain my head could tilt any further to the right and so it sort of just bounced back up erect and then flopped over to the left. And then it just sort of kind of began to shake back and forth like a no but not exactly a no. And then I got center vision again and looked at Clementine.

"No shit?" was the most eloquent thing that escaped my mouth.

Clementine stood up with a giggle and ruffled my hair in motion with my head shaking. She said she had to use the restroom and walked off. I suppose it was best for me to be left alone there in my thoughts. I mean I knew the things that Joy believed, but I guess I never thought of them as beliefs. They were ideas, ways to push the boundaries, but what did this look like in reality? Mormonism minus the weird religion part? We were just beginning to broach the idea of what it would look like for gay couples to get married and these two were living in 2075 and trying to just shatter all social, gender, and sexuality norms with a hammer.

I started to wonder if they had discussed this. Or did Clementine just drop this on me as an experiment to see how things were going? Maybe this was a prank. They were fucking with me because I had been such a reclusive dick. That made the most sense. I was going to work all this out before Joy returned with the drinks.

Then the world started to move in slow motion.

Clementine pushed the bathroom door open holding her phone in her hand. The brightness of the screen cut through the red smoking fog that always hovered through the bar. She ran toward me and as she passed Joy, she made a failed attempt at reaching for her. Joy ran behind her and I watched as Clementine's knee hit the ground before she could fully reach me. I thought of my mother that day, the way she knelt down so gingerly to meet me face-to-face. Joy, now standing next to me, leaned down toward her with a similarly maternal action.

Clementine was sobbing and couldn't find words. She just held up her new smartphone toward both of our faces as our eyes desperately attempted to focus on the screen. Joy hit the floor as well and there they both lay, holding each other as they sobbed. Clementine just held the screen up as if her arm was frozen in time, as if she didn't want to look at it, as if she wanted it as far away from her as possible. I couldn't stop staring at the screen, reading the words again and again waiting for them to change. To morph. To disappear. But they wouldn't move. Gone were the days when the AV nerds would rush down the hallway with bulky TV sets on wheels to bring us the news. No, the audio visual nerds were now following us everywhere we went. Every bit of news, every tweet, every status abruptly interrupting each action. So here her arm stayed with paralysis, lingering with this glowing screen and those words piercing into our world and shattering the sanctity of our shelter from all storms.

BREAKING: Body of former reporter found, murdered.

Chapter Twelve

Until We Part

It was my first year of college and I was still living with my parents. They lived in a two-story ranch-style brick house that hadn't been updated since they purchased it in the '80s. It was a time capsule. I had a small bedroom that had its own entrance and bathroom downstairs near the laundry room. My father started to complain that I still lived there because he planned to rent it out as soon as I was gone. But every time I suggested leaving he protested in his way. "You'll never make it out there." He always said things like that as if there was zero weight of responsibility. I noticed that amongst a lot of my friends and their relationships with their parents. The grown-ups acted like they were baffled how we turned out this way. It certainly wasn't like they took a hands-off approach to us.

My parents dictated every part of my life. After my friend Tommy was killed in the car accident with his babysitter, it sent a wave through our town. It was the only thing that dominated the news for weeks. They blamed everyone. They went after the babysitter, who also died, and claimed maybe she was on drugs or drinking. When her autopsy came back, she was negative for everything. So then they went after the grandma who dropped the baby off. Finally, the parents were responsible.

Being a parent in the '80s and '90s must have been quite the anomaly. You were supposed to be Schrodinger's Parent, both hard working and never home, but also the personification of a helicopter parent. We were the last of the latch-key kids. We were dropped off at home while our parents still worked but were also filled with horror stories about what might happen if we opened the door. Some clown kid-eater might show up dressed like a mailman and then sell our bodies for parts. We still played outside but never alone. We were the phasing out of the free-range kid style of parenting and phasing in being raised by technology.

I was fifteen years old before we had a computer, but I was also instantly proficient. We had front row seats to the world changing. Society hadn't taken a quantum leap like this since the harnessing of electricity as far as technology was concerned. There was a 450-year time span between the invention of the printing press and the telephone. Then almost 120 years from the phone to in-home dialup internet. Our generation went from AOL CDs and paying for surfing the net by the minute to having combined cellular phone/pocket computers with more technology in them than our parents' at-home computers in about a decade.

We went from knowing what it was like to sit under the stars with our friends and look at old *Playboy* magazines we found in our parents' closets to suddenly never being alone and never being able to escape. Living in this middle between the way things were and the evolution of technology was a strange transition. We grew up being told to be quiet, listen, and that we weren't allowed to be adults until well into our 20s. We were inconsequential and yet necessary to teach those who made six times as much as us how to open PDF files or respond to emails. We made the world turn and didn't matter at all.

When I heard a soft knock at my door behind my parents' house at 3:00 AM, I was disoriented but not shocked. I had long ago stopped being afraid of the bogeyman or the kid-eating clown but wasn't so yet so desensitized to people showing up unannounced that I would call the cops.

It was Shane.

He was standing there, soaking wet from head to toe. It had been raining for days as it does when summer turns to winter. Autumn doesn't exist here. It wasn't a weekend or a holiday and so I was sort of shocked to see him at all. Even though his face was covered in rain, I could distinctly tell he was crying.

"I guess I should have called." He sniffed.

"Don't be stupid, get inside." After my invitation he started to knock his shoes off on the door frame and I hushed him. "Don't wake my parents up."

I gave him a pair of pajamas and he quietly went into the bathroom to change. When he emerged back into my room, we opened a window and lit a joint. We just sat in the silence for a while. Shane was normally a walking ball of words. When he wasn't rambling on about some girl or adventure or both, he was writing. This was one of the few times I saw him in a complete state of contemplation. In between drags he just stared at his feet.

"I fucked up."

The abrupt break in the silence shocked me. My head was a bit fuzzy and I was tired as hell. I was starting to float off gently into the marijuana-induced slumber and he jolted me right back into reality.

"What happened, buddy?"

He went on about how he had gotten really involved with a lot of extracurriculars at school: theatre, the school paper, he was working a job, he had a roommate, was running off to go get high and ride Splash Mountain, and then dating. He was doing a lot of dating. With this much going on, he was doing a lot less school than he was supposed to be doing while being in school. He was flunking out. He was going to lose everything. He only had a partial scholarship and so everything else, including his housing, was all being financed by student loans.

"I'm going to end up broke, uneducated, and in debt." He was distraught. "I'm messing it all up. And what's worse, I'm having the time of my life. I don't even regret it because, I mean, it's been great down there. It's fucking wonderful. But it's about to all go to hell. I don't know what to do, Leo. I don't know what to do."

It is a strange feeling when the person you think of as the strongest and most resilient is sitting before you totally broken. I grabbed him by the back of the neck and pulled him in close. I hugged him and told him everything was going to be alright.

That night, he slept on my bed and I slept on the love seat in my room. My parents hated having company over but I promised them it would only be until Sunday. I resolved in that moment that it was time to get out of there, whatever it took. The rest of that week I helped Shane email all his professors and we worked out a plan. I helped him make a schedule, something he hated but he also knew was necessary. We worked out a way that he could complete his classes and still have time to do the things he loved. It wasn't perfect, it wasn't freedom, but it wasn't quite prison.

Saturday night we went out to enjoy the town, shoot some pool, and ended it by going out to the beach to howl at the moon. I made him promise that we would be done by midnight so he would have enough time to get a good rest before having to drive back to central Florida the next morning. We lay out on the sand and watched the shooting stars.

"You are the best boyfriend a man could ask for." He tapped my hand and I knew he was smiling. "I love you. I really do. I don't know what I would do without you. You are a forever person for me, you know that, right? We are going to grow old and grey together. Next door neighbors at the nursing home kind of forever."

***

They cremated him. Everyone said it's what he would have wanted, but the truth was they had no choice. All I could think about is how I would never get to see him again, not even in death. He was just gone. He was just ashes in a shitty vase. I was numb and in the most pain I had ever felt in my entire life. All the hurt was stuck somewhere deep inside me, hidden behind a frozen wall of tears that weren't ready to fall just yet. I was being strong for Joy, for Clementine, for Nick. He was taking it hard in a way that didn't surprise any of us. I guess we all thought we had more time. I guess he thought he would one day get to make it right, say those apologies.

Shane never wanted a church funeral, but how was I supposed to have that argument with his parents? So we all filed into the church to say goodbye. Nick sat with us all the way up until he absolutely had to leave. Shane's parents asked him if he would do the funeral. He told them he didn't know how to. The old priest who both Nick and Shane were altar servers for led the service and Nick served next to him. You could see on his face he was disassociating. He was somewhere else, not thinking about his friend in the urn. Not facing reality. His mom asked me if I would speak. I didn't know what to say, but I couldn't say no, not now that Nick had.

When it came time, Father Jack called me up. Joy and Clementine were holding my hands and I hated to leave, but I needed to go. I stood there and looked out at the crowd. There were people from high school and friends of his from college. The realtors that he smoked cigars with and the kids from the comic shop. Reporters and people from City Hall. Honestly, I imagined the whole town empty because it felt like they were all here. I wondered who was in the stores or at the gas stations.

Even both Billy and Ethel were there too. The All Saints had only been closed three times in its history: the day after Ethel had been robbed at gunpoint and knocked the guy out with a frying pan, when the old plumbing busted and the whole place flooded, and today. Ethel had made fried chicken and collard greens and it was all back at the All Saints waiting for us. A whole world away from this church was our real altar, our sanctuary, the place we needed to actually lay him to rest. Some pretzels and Jim Beam, this is Shane's body; this is Shane's blood. This is all that remains; do this in memory of him.

My hands dug deep into the wooden lectern. Outside of the corner of my eyes, I could see Shane's smiling face in a large portrait that was hanging on an easel. I took a deep breath, looked right at the only way I would ever be able to see him again and did my fucking best.

"I'm not particularly religious." *What a stellar opening,* I thought to myself. "But my grandma's favorite Bible verse was, 'Jesus wept.' She said she liked it a lot because it was also the shortest. She used to tell me it mattered because it showed that Jesus was just like us. I hope that you will all forgive me my own tears because Jesus isn't just like us. He wept but then he could raise his friend from the dead. So forgive my tears as I weep, completely incapable of doing the same thing for my own friend."

I couldn't give Shane what he wanted. He had to be buried in a church and I couldn't argue. But I suddenly felt possessed by him. I was never one to buck orders or go against the grain. I was concerned with rules and order. In that moment, the only way I knew how to honor his memory was to be completely and totally irreverent. I told about the time we all went streaking through the mall on a dare and didn't get caught. I talked about the time we smoked weed behind the church while he was waiting to altar-serve a wedding. I was on a roll. Everyone was laughing, even the priest. I wish Shane had known how much he was seen and loved for being the little weirdo he was.

And just like that it was over. His parents took away the fragmented particles that remained of him and placed it in their car. The rest of him, be it spirit or the water, now floated away free. As I pulled away from the church that day, I wondered if he was now a wave or the rain or if he would become some echo as he rushed through a canyon. I pulled over on the side of the road as I cried, thinking about how he was gone but also here. That his life was cut so unfairly short but that it was also given a freedom he could never have imagined.

When I got to the All Saints, it felt strange to see all these figures inside. The place was packed with bodies that seemed out of place. Shane's parents were there. All I could think about was that his remains were in their car. I wondered if they buckled him in. Part of me wanted to break in and steal him. I imagined throwing his ashes all over and letting him become one with this place. Thinking about him being the dust in between the gravel parking lot and the chalk in the pool room or the cocaine in the bathroom. Little dust particles of Shane floating everywhere and in everything.

I was starving and wanted to throw up all at the same time. Ethel had really outdone herself with this spread. It was absolutely perfect. I imagine she had seen a lot of loss in her time. Shane was the only one of us who really knew her well. He was the only one who came up here during the daytime. He was a collector of stories and there was no better place to collect stories than amongst the day timers. He would just sit up here and talk with them about their first wives and second lives. These stories would all be penned in journals and sit on flash drives that scattered his home along with collections of old books he never read and paintings he never sold.

When he was killed, they took everything. His entire house was cleared of everything. All of the paintings he had done. Every story he had written. The evidence we had against the mayor, bishop, and sheriff. It had been sitting on his desk in a manila folder. Shane was supposed to digitize them a million times and hadn't gotten around to it. Like the jackass he was, he had written, "EVIDENCE," across the front of it in big red lettering.

It was hard not to become a bit of a conspiracy theorist and wonder if there was more to it than that these two brothers had just been greedy. That they had killed their friend for stuff. I almost wanted it to be bigger than that for Shane's sake.

Nick was still at the church, but I saw Joy and Clementine sitting at our big table. Strangers were there with them. They were surrounded having two-sentence conversations like, "How did you know Shane?" or, "When was the last time you two talked?" They both lit up when they saw me making my way through the crowd. I guess I had planned to get some food before but they looked in desperate need of a good rescuing. We hugged and someone inconsequential exited the table so I took my place next to them. A few minutes later, Nick arrived and it took him about fifteen minutes to make his way to us as he faced his own series of two-sentence conversations. "You were so brave today," or, "I don't know how you did it!"

He sat down with us and we four felt so alone in the room full of people. People coming and people going. We all just stared at our full glasses and couldn't find a way to stomach anything including alcohol. Someone across the room yelled, "To Shane!" As he held his glass high in the air, the rest of the room let out a boisterous response, "To Shane," and we all took a shot. Then a silence fell over the crowd as the door opened and three figures made their way into the bar.

The mayor, the bishop, and the sheriff.

They walked around and shook hands and offered condolences and gave out business cards. The four of us watched in complete shock as these men danced around the room. The audacity of it all. There was absolutely zero doubt that they had known about Shane's involvement in the paper. It's why he lost his job and so they knew. This was a power move. Nick looked like he was going to shit himself.

As they made their way around the room, their eyes kept shifting toward our table. They would lean in and whisper to someone looking in our direction. Finally, they were at our table. My heart was beating up into my throat.

"I'm so sorry I couldn't be there today, Father Nicholas," the bishop said, reaching his hand out to Nick. He took the bishop's hand and kissed his ring.

"I heard you had some wonderful things to say today, young man," the mayor said, looking directly at me.

"I just want to assure you that we will not rest until every rock has been overturned to catch these criminals," the sheriff said, to no one in particular.

We made our best attempts at responses but mostly looked like children who had gotten caught sneaking out of the window. Part of me wondered if I could reach the sheriff's gun before he would notice. I had nothing left to live for. Just in the nick of time, Joy placed her hand in mine. The three of them made gracious nods at us.

The bishop remarked as they left, "If you should need anything at all, here is my card."

Nick got up and left to walk the bishop out to his car. It left the three of us now alone with our racing thoughts. It suddenly became easier to drink. We drank to memories and to good health and to sex and to drugs and to the future. We drank to remember and then we drank to forget. We drank as people left and as new people arrived. We drank to the hours and to the minutes and to the years spent together. We drank to the years spent apart. We drank to Shane and we drank to justice.

When the last call rang and the lights came on, no one rushed us out. We just sat there alone in the silence of the place. Eventually, Ethel came and put her hands on our shoulders and kisses on our cheeks. She told us she was calling us a cab. We rode to Joy's house and we drank some more. Nick had long abandoned us to early morning meetings and responsibility. It was down to us to drink and to cry and to watch videos of him on our phones. I played the last voicemail he left me.

"I'm running late, buddy. I'm on my way and boy do I have a fucking story to tell you. I hope you are ready. I don't think you are ready. Don't go! I'm on my way. I love you!"

We cried and we held each other. And we kissed. The three of us lay together on Joy's bed in our tears and memories and we each held the others close like we never wanted to let go. We were as close as any three people could be. Clementine passed out first, and then Joy. I lay there, in awe of the absurdity of life and missing Shane. The world was spinning around me and I felt like I was spinning and sinking into the bed. I felt a sudden escape happening and I ran for the restroom. The entirety of innards exited my body until I dry heaved. I began to cry, laying my head against the toilet rim. I stayed there until I too passed out. Some hours later, Clementine found me and carried me back to bed.

The three of us slept there all night, holding one another and knowing we could never let go again. How could we fathom this parting? How could we truly say goodbye?

I had no answers.

DECISIONS

My first date with my first girlfriend was a trip to the skating rink. We glided across the floor to such notable classics as "Rhythm is a Dancer" and the "Tootsee Roll". The lights, the roller blades, the smell of stale popcorn and hot dog water. There was really nothing much like the skating rink. There was an old couple that still wore their '70s style disco clothing and could do some wild moves. But we all knew what the night was about, what everyone was waiting for, the whole reason that you would go to the skating rink to begin with: the couple's skate.

For those of us who weren't smooth or cool, this was a guaranteed way to secure that you and your date would absolutely be holding hands before the night was through. It was required. The couple's song hadn't been played yet and my heart was beating so fast I thought it was going to explode out of my chest like that baby alien.

Then, magically, it came. The DJ announced over the speakers, "Alright ladies and gentlemen, it's time for that special time of the night: couple's skate. If you have a special person in your life, it's time to hit the floor."

Ashley and I hit the floor at the exact moment that "Truly Madly Deeply" began to play. She reached out and grabbed my hand. I begged to any deity that was listening that my palms wouldn't get sweaty. We slowly glided across the sea of well-waxed wood. Life was perfect. I knew I was going to marry her and we would live together on a hill by a lake and have a puppy and babies.

Four minutes and twenty-two seconds of absolute bliss and then it came to a jarring end as they began "The Macarena." We quickly exited and sat down at the little tables on the side of the rink. Ashley looked at me and I thought I was going to explode with love. She gave me a big brace-y smile and said tenderly, "Will you watch my purse?"

I held on to it as tightly as I could. This was my solemn duty. I was now a man. Nay! A knight in shining armor and my quest was to keep her valuables as safe as possible. I watched as she made her way to the restroom and then she turned back around to me.

"Hey, Leo."

I looked back at her with enamored eyes. "Yes!"

"Don't look inside it, okay?"

Somehow, out of nowhere, Shane appeared. I hadn't seen him all night and so he must have been hidden in the arcade or maybe in the broom closet with someone. But here he was, morphed into existence, to play the devil on my shoulder.

"What's in the purse, Leo?" he said with a shit-eating grin.

"I have no idea." I swatted his hand away. "And we aren't looking! Jesus, it's my one responsibility."

"Don't be such a goony. We have to look." And with that he snatched the purse out of my hand.

I would be lying if the curiosity wasn't killing me as well, but I had a noble responsibility to make sure that I kept her purse safe. Her requirements for safety also included not looking in the purse. As I was struggling with all these very complex feelings, Shane opened the purse. I looked inside and we both stared.

Maxi pads.

This was a whole lot for us to process. At first, we weren't really sure what we were looking at and then it became clear. Shane clarified for me, just in case I was stupid. Not that we fully understood what this meant. I mean it certified that she had a vagina. Not that either one of us actually understood any of it. We both still thought girls peed out of their butts. We just stood there, marveling in the bastion of maturity in pubescent stupidity.

"Leo!" I could feel a chill go up my spine. "You are the rottenest boy. I hate you. I hate you. I hate you!"

With that, Ashley grabbed her purse and I chased after her. There was no use. She was gone forever. She left my life as quickly as she came into it. We never spoke again. My house on the hill by the lake, the puppies, the beautiful children were all suddenly dreams dashed away. Stupid Shane had ruined everything. He would have been my best man too! I was fortune's fool. I cried in the men's room. I called my mom from the pay phone and waited for her to arrive outside. Shane waited outside with me. He was smoking half a cigarette he had stolen out of the ash tray. He handed it to me and I took my first ever drag.

"I'm sorry," he said.

I shrugged it off. I would never understand girls.

***

In the aftermath of Shane's murder, it was difficult to make sense of anything. Weeks were passing and it felt like it all happened yesterday. Some mornings, I would feel a decade older and that this was all part of some dark distant past. It was an ugly, murky crude oil kind of feeling. I couldn't move properly. I was gliding through things at work, but nothing was making sense. I stayed at Joy's house the whole time, so did Clementine. Honestly, the three of us were basically inseparable after the funeral. I don't think any of us wanted to let the others out of eyesight. Nick came and checked on us all a couple of times. He didn't say much. I think in his own way he needed to make sure we were all still breathing for the same reason.

Growing up in the South, there is not much distinction between our religious upbringing and our superstitions. The same folks going to Mass every Sunday are the ones visiting the fortune tellers along Jackson Square in the French Quarter every weekend. We hang both crucifixes and chicken feet without any level of irony. We are seeped deeply in a mesh of cultures that to the outside observer might seem counterintuitive, but to those of us living along the swampy waters of the Gulf Coast, if God will not answer, maybe the tarot deck will. So when Death decides to ride in to collect one of our kith or kin, we know all too well that Death comes in threes and the great watch begins to hold tight to those you love, lest she visit them next.

In spite of how wonderful it was to have everyone around, I was becoming jealous. I missed the time with Joy before ... before it was like this. We hadn't even had the chance to process all these feelings and the loss as individuals or as a couple. I'm not really sure I had processed my own feelings because we were all there.

When I got home, or rather to Joy's home, early from work one night there was a note on the door. It was a notice.

NOTICE

PER YOUR LEASE AGREEMENT, NO MORE THAN ONE VISITOR CAN RESIDE AT THIS PROPERTY FOR MORE THAN FIVE CONSECUTIVE DAYS IN A ROW.

PLEASE REMOVE YOUR ADDITIONAL ROOMMATES, HAVE THEM SIGN A LEASE (WITH A RENT INCREASE), OR VACATE.

"Fuck," I said aloud.

I suppose because our cars were always parked there we drew attention. Normally, it was just me, but I guess with now having Clementine's vehicle it was really clogging the small driveway. I wasn't particularly looking forward to having this conversation with Joy and, honestly, I was getting a little annoyed as it was with Clementine there every second. I'm sure that Joy probably wanted her alone time from me too. Maybe this was a good thing, the notice. It was going to force a couple of conversations we all needed to have. First being that it was probably time for Clementine to go home. Second, it was probably best that Joy and I had a conversation about maybe moving in with each other. We were always around and at this point me keeping my apartment was making less and less sense.

I walked into what I assumed was an empty apartment and there was Clementine. She recognized the look of shock on my face and immediately responded, "My car is in the shop."

"Oh," was all I mustered.

"What's that?" She was pointing to the notice from Joy's landlord.

"Uh, yeah, it's a notice. Apparently, we've overstayed our welcome." I handed it to her.

She looked concerned as she read it for a while and said something about how she could have an attorney look at it. Apparently, she had an attorney on retainer because of all her work with the websites and stuff. I told her we would have to ask Joy about that.

"Maybe I could move in!" Clementine said excitedly.

"I don't know."

"You don't know what?" She frowned.

"I don't know." I was stuttering. "I just think maybe we need some space, you know? It's been a long couple of weeks and it's been a lot."

"Are you saying I am a lot?"

"No, I'm not saying you specifically or anything. I'm just saying everything has been. I was thinking about asking Joy about us moving in together anyways. It just makes sense."

"What about us?" Clementine looked confused.

"What us? Is that what you think this has been? What do you think? I don't know what you think. I don't know what I think."

Clementine sat down at the two-seater table in the kitchen. She looked at the notice and then back at me. She was clearly upset and confused. This is the part of humaning I am the worst at. I had a million things I wanted to say that were flowing through my brain. I wasn't meaning to be rude. It wasn't that I didn't care about her. I just… I don't really know what I was going for here.

"I love you," she said gently, holding back a tear.

"I love Joy," I said in response. "I love you too. You are my best friend! But I am in love with Joy. There isn't an 'us', right? How does that even work to you? How does this make sense? I can't make it make sense, Clementine; I don't know how to make it make sense."

"Fuck, Leo. Not everything has to make sense. Some things just are, you know. It doesn't all have to fit in a pretty little box or on a calendar. I mean I didn't ask to be like this. I didn't ask for this to be what happened. I didn't mean to love you both. I didn't want to be complicated, you know! I mean, fuck, why would I want to be complicated? I just know that I love you and I love her and I love us together. I don't know how else to explain that."

"I don't know."

"Listen, I've embarrassed myself enough for tonight. It's my birthday this weekend. I'm just… I'm going to go back home. I'm going to just go back home for a couple of days and sort this out."

I tried to stop her. I told her not to leave upset and that I was sorry. I think I said I was sorry. But she left. I spent the rest of the night trying to eat something and watching a Tarantino film. A few hours later, Joy showed up. She asked where Clementine was. I told her about the note and about the conversation. She told me I was brutish and stupid. That she didn't know what she wanted either but that it wasn't for me to decide those types of things. I was invited to go home too. For the first night in weeks, I slept alone. Not with two people but with my own thoughts, my least favorite person to try to sleep with.

I cried. Not a little exhausted cry like I did that day after the funeral. But a good solid cry. The kind that comes up from your gut and takes the wind away from you. The type that has been hiding somewhere deep in the recesses and dark spaces and finally needed to get out. I blew my nose on the old shirt I had thrown on the floor and a familiar scent came inside me as I finally took a breath in.

It was Clementine's shampoo. In that moment my heart split in two and I realized I was an idiot.

I spent the whole next morning picking out a birthday present for her. We would do something special for her when she got back from her cousin's. I was always a bit of a late bloomer. It just sometimes takes me a minute to see things clearly. See, I was still imagining that lake and the house on a hill with the puppies and the babies. I suppose that's what we are all supposed to want, right? The perfect wedding and Julia Roberts in a pretty white dress. Boy meets girl and it just all makes sense. It's what my programming had set me up for. This didn't fit. Clementine was right. She wasn't the one making it complicated. I was complicated. I wanted the rules and the structures. I wasn't willing to bend. I was afraid I would break.

I guess I was right; I wouldn't ever understand girls. But I was going to give it my best shot. If Shane had taught me anything, if I was going to learn any lessons from him, it's that life is short and that you always have to tell the people you love that you love them, regardless of whether it makes sense to you or anyone else.

And that was exactly what I was going to do.

CHAPTER FOURTEEN

THE END

I don't know how to tell this part other than plainly.

While Clementine was off celebrating her birthday she received a call from her mother. Someone had acquired some of the nude photos she had taken for some of her clients and had sent them to her father's work. The email went out to all 537 employees. Her dad was mortified and called her, "a personal embarrassment and a disgrace to her family." She was staying with her cousin and her aunt. Because her father was who he was, and his company employed a lot of family members, her aunt let her know that she wouldn't be able to stay after that night. She needed to pack up and leave first thing in the morning.

When I got back over to Joy's apartment, the day after Clementine's birthday, I found Joy slumped over in her chair. She was sitting in front of her laptop. I walked into the kitchen and set down some food I had brought with me. I had a small cake that I was about to put in the refrigerator for when Clementine got back. I was setting everything in its place and Joy still hadn't looked up. I assumed she was enthralled with some project.

"What's up, beautiful?" I was fondling a head of lettuce. "You doing alright?"

"She's dead."

I dropped the lettuce.

"Who? Who is dead?"

"Clementine. She's dead."

With that, Joy jumped up from the computer and into my arms. I stood there, holding her as she wept into my arm, and I was in complete shock. I didn't know anything. I couldn't ask anything. I just waited and waited for answers.

Clementine and her cousin had decided to continue on with their plans to celebrate her birthday. They were out all night and Clementine was extremely drunk. She spoke the entire cab ride home about how she was a disappointment; that she was a failure and that no one would love her ever again. When she got back to her aunt's house, her cousin put her to bed. At some point during the night, Clementine got up, likely still intoxicated, and she downed the entire bottle of her heart medication and then moved on to a bottle of someone else's pain medication. She took as much of it as she could stomach. Her cousin found her the next morning on the bathroom floor.

My grandma's voice came to me. "Be careful, boy, death comes in threes."

It seems everyone has a different breaking point and some people are more fragile than others. Some are fragile like a bomb and some like a flower. Clementine at times seemed both. She was fiery and explosive toward injustice when that injustice was coming for others, but when it came for her she took each stroke like a hurricane wind shattering its waves against her foundation. It seems that the loss of Shane, the fear of losing what she hoped for us, and then finally the exposure of her modeling work was a trifecta too big for her in that moment. Her petals began to fall and the only release seemed escape.

The numbness I felt overtaking my body this time was wholly different than when Shane died. This was a sinking, crippling guilt that was being held at bay only by this numbness. Deep in my mind I knew that the reprieve of this pain was only temporary. That eventually the buttress of my numbness would give way and that it would all come flowing in. That I would have to face this guilt for the things I said, my own inability to let love take me in whatever direction it would, and for pushing her away for the sake of one of the most egregious of sins: jealousy.

Less than a month after burying Shane, we would gather again. Now just Nick, Joy, and I remained to say farewell to one of the most beautiful, tender, and sweet spirits we knew. This all seemed too cruel a life to live. How much more could any person endure? I wasn't certain.

As our friends and acquaintances filed in for yet another funeral, another goodbye, another chapter closing too soon, I was still fumbling with this numbness. But I could feel it breaking down and I knew that this nagging guilt was waiting to strangle me as soon as it was released from its cage. It was something I would soon become very well known to. This guilt would grow and become ferocious. It would gnaw slowly away at my insides until I would become so swollen with its festering pain that it would render me immovable. I was becoming a shadow of myself and I could see I was aging right before my eyes. This was a monstrous burden.

Joy, who was normally so famous for her ability to reframe, was also stuck somewhere in a broken space. We moved around each other. We slept in the same bed, ate the same meals, but we couldn't see each other. We also didn't want to let the other out of sight. There was, somewhere floating in both our minds, the fear of who would be the third. When would Death come knocking at the next door? Would it be a relative, a friend, a far-off acquaintance, her cat? There was no way to know and no particular science to decode a when, where, or how.

I could hardly believe that here we were at the end of this year. What a cruel send-off. It seemed that Halloween never happened because Shane was taken from us and then Thanksgiving and Christmas weren't real. We were holed up, hiding from reality and festivities. It seemed out of place to be joyous in the midst of the worst pain imaginable. And now, this last stunning light was snuffed out. What could possibly ring in a New Year that mattered? What could matter now? It seemed like there would be nothing at all that could soothe this aching, itching pain. I wasn't even sure if I would ever be able to celebrate it, or nearly anything, ever again.

We began that year with hope and with change. It emboldened us to take big risks and reach for the stars, no matter how far away they may have seemed. No one warned us that hope and change would come with a body count. The whole world was shifting around us. The framework was being set for such immense destruction that there was no way to even fathom it. But in these last few moments of a year that was sparked with promise and ended with a crater that seemed impassable, it didn't even seem possible that this was the same timeline. Something got off track and it just needed to readjust. I wanted back onto the plane of existence where the *Berenstein Bears* existed, where I was home watching the *Looney Toons* while eating a bowl of Fruit Loops, waiting for Shane and Clementine to come visit. Not the dark universe we had been thrust into where nothing made sense and everyone was dead.

In spite of the pain, the uncertainty, and the guilt, I was becoming increasingly convinced that this wasn't an accident. These were not moments designed by some distant god who was bored. These were the acts of men, cruel men, who had their egos busted by a couple of millennials who thought they were ready for the fight but didn't realize how hard these fuckers were willing to hit back. I didn't know how to connect the pieces, but it didn't make sense any other way. The two people who had the keys to unlocking all this drama and scandal now lay dead. One by no accident and the other by their own hand, but that hand was pushed. I just didn't know how to find the truth.

But I would find it.

***

One of the many horrific things about being poor is the inability to take the time you need to heal. Whether it's physically, mentally, or emotionally, you still have to be at work. If you don't show, there is always someone else just as poor as you ready to fill the void you are leaving behind. We are trained to look at them as an enemy, someone who is stealing your job. The truth is they are just someone who is struggling just like you, and this deflection keeps the poor mad at each other instead of collectively angry at the real enemy. So we battle each other or ourselves.

I had no time left to take for myself. Shane's funeral had to be planned around my work schedule. Thankfully, his parents understood my situation and were gracious to me. I had to call in sick just to be at Clementine's celebration of life.

When I got to work that day, I arrived with a little less pep in my step, but I was fucking present. I did a good job. The kitchen manager walked in and out for the better part of an hour. One of my co-workers leaned toward me.

"Someone's getting fired today," he said.

"How do you know?" I nervously inquired.

"That's what he does, man. Haven't you noticed? When he's ready to sack someone he gets all nervous about it. He walks in and out like that, sometimes all day. He then calls them back and tells them it's time to talk to the general manager and that's when the axe gets dropped. It doesn't happen often I guess, so most miss the pattern, but I am telling you, someone is getting dumped today. Wait and see."

I was on pins and needles all through the dinner prep. Then another cook showed up. This was more than we would normally have on a Thursday night. He walked in and grabbed an apron off a hook and came and stood next to me.

"Why are you here?" I asked.

"Uh… I'm wondering the same thing. I got called in about half an hour ago. They said they were shorthanded."

Just then the kitchen manager emerged through the doors again. He looked around as if he wasn't certain what he was doing and then said, "Ah!" and walked over toward us. "Yeah, hey, Leo… Can we talk for a couple of minutes?"

"Sure," I said and I took my apron off and handed it to the co-worker who had given me the heads-up. He shrugged sympathetically.

We walked through the stainless steel doors and down a hallway to a small office where the general manager sat with his computer and screens full of security camera footage. He turned around in his swivel chair and looked at me. He was holding some papers.

"Listen, Leo," the general manager said, "you've been with us a while and I like you. This isn't anything personal, but we have to let you go. You've violated one of the employee standards and it's out of my hands."

"What did I do, sir?" I asked forcefully.

"Well, it's been brought to our attention that you are one of the editors of a website that disparages a number of our patrons." He sighed. "And, well, that goes against our company policies. I'm afraid this is a cut and dry thing. I'm sure you understand."

"I need to pee. Am I still allowed to pee?" was all I could come up with.

"We will send you a check to your address on file." He responded, "And yes, you can pee."

"Thank you, sir," was all I said as I turned around and walked out the door toward the bathrooms.

Of course I got fucking fired. This was a full-on onslaught. They were taking us down piece by piece. The halls of The Pub were a blur of paintings and dollars and abstract humans enjoying their lives. I rushed down the halls trying to make my way to the restroom before I threw up. I was so angry and my whole body was aching with rage. I wanted to punch anything or anyone. I could feel my blood boiling. I made a final turn and crashed into someone so hard I could hear our chests thud.

It was Nick. He quickly reached down and picked up a manila folder with familiar handwriting that read in all red lettering, "EVIDENCE."

He pushed me aside by my shoulder and quickly said, "It's good to see you, Leo." Then he walked on passed me. I rushed toward the corner that led to the bathroom and then turned around as he made a few taps on a wall and a door opened. He disappeared inside The Statesmen Lounge.

I don't remember driving to Joy's house. I don't know if anything was on the radio. I don't know if I put on my seatbelt. It just seemed like the thought entered my head that I needed to tell her and then I was parked outside of her house. Then I was at the door. Then I was inside and I was telling her everything about my suspicions that this wasn't all an accident. That I was just suddenly fired for no reason other than my involvement with the paper. I paused before telling her about seeing Nick heading into the club and the folder that I was absolutely certain said evidence on it in Shane's writing.

"How certain?" she asked.

"Really certain, I think." It's funny how when someone questions you, you start to question yourself, your own eyes and senses. I knew what I saw, but now that I was making the actual accusation it felt suddenly less certain.

"People die, Leo. Life is complicated. But you are talking about a conspiracy here."

"How is this so fucking odd? I mean this whole thing started with a murder."

"But Clementine wasn't murdered."

"She was as good as! I mean she's written a ton about her struggles. They knew all it would take was the right push. They made a gamble and it paid off."

"And so what? My brother killed Shane, is that really what you are saying?"

"No." I paused. "I don't know."

"You don't know if you are accusing my brother of murdering our friend?"

"I don't know, Joy."

"Well, you better get really fucking certain, Leo, and quick."

I did not choose my words wisely. "I mean Shane, Clementine, me, we've all faced consequences for what we did. What about you? What about Nick? Are you being threatened?"

"Fuck you."

"Are you?"

"You are insane. You know that? This is insane."

"What's insane is looking at this and not seeing that something doesn't fit!"

"So then say it, say you think my brother did it!"

"Fine, if that's what you need to hear. Yeah, I guess your brother is involved. And I think he is protecting you."

She shoved me hard in the chest. She did it again. She started to cry and then fell against me. I held her for a few moments and then she screamed. She pulled away from me and told me to get out. I think I protested and then she made it very clear it was time for me to leave. I made a long and slow walk to my car. With every step I kept hoping she would run after me. That she would say she was just angry or scared or both. With each step it felt less and less like a movie and more like reality.

When I finally reached my car, I realized that my grandmother was right and this was it. This was the third death in our story. The death of the friend group. It was now dissolved and I was alone. Joy and Nick would be brother and sister forever, but this group, this little company, it was gone forever. This death hurt instantly. My hurt had no more ability to suppress. I stayed there and cried and then finally drove away.

I got home and sat on my couch for hours in the silence.

I reached for my computer. I wanted to salvage everything that existed, every email, every MySpace post and message, all the pictures. I needed to document it all away before everything decayed and was lost. It was all I would have left. I would archive her and Shane forever in the only tangible way I could. When I opened my email, I had one that stood out from the rest. At first, I thought it was spam but then decided to open it.

Dear Sir,

We at Web Hosting Services would like to send our sincerest condolences for the loss of your family/friend. We understand that this must be a difficult time for you.

It is our responsibility to inform you that you were chosen by the domain holder to be their successor in the event of death. You have three options: you can delete the site, archive the site, or you may assume responsibility of the site.

You will not be charged for the next three months as you take time to deliberate.

Please click here when you are ready.

Sincerely,

Management.

This didn't die with them. I had everything. And I was the only one who knew. I was given one of those choices, go right or go left. Should I let this chapter die with them or should I press on?

I looked at the clock. Tomorrow was New Year's Eve. *Happy fucking New Year,* I thought. In that moment, I knew exactly what I was going to do. What a bunch of idiots. The one thing that rich people always underestimate is this: the audacity of poor people when they have nothing left to lose, especially if you are the one who took it from them.

This was going to be a wild decade, fuckers.

ACT II
TWO THOUSAND NINETEEN

CHAPTER ONE

GHOSTS

Everything this side of thirty hurt just a little differently. I had rung in the New Year like I was a kid, but today I was paying for the borrowed time, especially since today I had to celebrate a very special birthday. Somehow, with the help of electrolytes, ibuprofen, and a healthy diet of Waffle House, I had survived the day and now it was time for a bit of the hair of the dog that bit me. I walked down the familiar corridor. The wall was now illuminated by a faux retro neon sign with those comforting words: All Saints Hotel and Cocktail Lounge. This was one of many additions that had been collected over the last decade as the bar shuffled hands between a couple of new owners. No changes were so big that they took away from the atmosphere of this place. It stood as a last vestige to a time when dive bars were filled with smoke and one-night stands. With all the many changes that had been made, waiting for me at the end of the corridor was that ancient church door. She looked older and as if she was sagging a bit at the hinges.

"I'm sorry, boy," said the Bar, "I don't have much left to give you. Your friends are all gone."

"I have a lot of work to do; I don't have much time for friends anymore," I said.

"The old round table is occupied by someone else, now," said the Bar.

"That's alright, I don't need much now," I said. "Just somewhere to sit and rest. I am very tired."

"Well," said the Bar, straightening herself up as much as she could on her hinges, "well, an old bar stool is good for sitting and resting! Come, sit and rest."

At the urging of my old friend the Bar, I rounded the corner and made my way into the main bar. It was full of faces all well acquainted with me. This room was still full of happy haunts and memories of times that seemed so far way and yet here in this space wrapped around me. There, in the center of the room, I could see the ghost of Shane laughing at a story as he sat at our round table. This table was now occupied by a new crew of young and ambitious folks ready to embark on their grand adventure. Behind them, I could still see the shadows of Clementine throwing a dart and hitting a bull's-eye and then jumping with Joy in excitement.

The harder specters to live with were those bodies that were still warm but doing so in other places than here. The walls were now filled with many faces and many more news stories. People who had come and those who had gone. For some, this lovely space was a special graveyard to come and commune with all who had gone and yet for others it was a garden where ideas of the future were just beginning to bloom. They had yet to see loss or failure or disappointment. The younger batch of millennials were all too accustomed to their phone firmly planted in front of their faces and under the sound of the jukebox you could hear the fluttering of tweets and snaps and statuses flowing from their fingers.

Like all of human history, the new was being built directly on top of the ancient ruins. The same was true for my life. There was a time when I felt that I couldn't ever step foot back into these hallowed halls. The pain was too great. But with age comes the understanding that pain is where we learn and grow, if we allow it. It became eventually alright to sit here with these ghosts and enjoy their company.

There is the chair where I fumbled with a ring in my pocket that I never got to use. That was the wall that the beer bottle shattered against the night Joy and I finally said our goodbyes. That was the barstool where I got the text that turned into a call that would forever change the trajectory of my entire life. That was the television where I saw the news that the Pope had selected a new bishop for the diocese and a familiar name was declared the youngest primate in the United States. It was here that I held the interview for the first new staff writer at the *Panhandle Free Press* after landing our first big ad contract.

Life is full of memories, good, bad, ugly, and beautiful. It's up to each of us how to choose to digest them and what to do with them once they are inside us. There was many a night I drank to the pain or to our good health.

Tonight, I would take up residence at my now familiar seat at the bar, having long abandoned that table to those who still had dreams to dream and hopes dripping from their bleeding hearts. My drink was sitting there waiting for me. The bartender leaned down low.

"Shall I start you a tab, sir?" He smiled.

"I think it'll just be one for me tonight, Mikey."

"You got it," he said as he handed me my change. I lifted my glass, as I always did, to the picture of Billy that hung behind the register.

"How did Clementyne's birthday go today?"

"It was great. The perfect party. It was *Frozen* themed, but I guess everything is now."

"What was the big number?"

"Eight, hard to believe it."

A girl tapped me on the shoulder and her boyfriend stood behind her. "One round of darts, Leo?" she asked and I smiled back at Mikey asking if he would open that tab after all. It's a strange feeling being the one who survives. The one who is still here. The one who is seen as the elder. Tomorrow, I would have work and responsibilities and then it would be my weekend to take the most important little girl in my life. But for tonight, I wasn't ready just yet to join the cast of characters that left before 10:00 PM. I wasn't rushing to become a day timer. Another round then. To Shane. To Clementine. To impeachment. To a wild ride. To maybe this year finally being seen as an adult. To student debt. To that feeling that, for whatever reason, won't die along with everything else: hope and change.

***

I never really thought I would have friends again. I suppose it is the same feeling one feels after a divorce. "I'll never love again!" But then, somehow, in an unexplained way, your heart opens back up. You slowly discover that there is still room in your heart for someone else. It will always be a little different. With age comes a whole different understanding of love and passion and responsibility. Yet, somewhere deep down, you are still that same person. The mirror might be telling a different story but you are still young at heart or some shit. So here I would stand shooting darts and waiting for the next evolution of forever people to arrive.

Alexandria walked in and waved me down, causing me to miss a shot I was certain would have been a bull's-eye. She was the first person I dated after I finally decided I could do that again. She was a very special person to me. We realized pretty early on that we made far better friends than lovers. It was strange to now live in a mature enough space to be able to let relationships evolve instead of die. But there was no better teacher for that lesson than someone who had evolved more than anyone else I knew.

She used to always say, "If I could grow from Alex into Alexandria and struggle through all of that self-actualization and reach this place of being comfortable in who I am, love myself in this skin, well, then I don't think most people have an excuse for not constantly growing into who they are really meant to be."

Those words impacted me and I am in a constant debt to her grace and beauty in how she chooses to see this world.

"How did today go, Daddy?" Alexandria asked as she wiped a piece of blue glitter from my cheek.

"It was hard to let it go," I quipped.

"You know these dad jokes are getting worse and worse the older you get."

"Yeah, I can't help it. They are overtaking me." I looked past Alexandria to a dark figure now engulfing the bar well. "Would you look at that? Someone's bar ban must have been lifted."

There stood Blake, holding his rum and Coke in one hand and another glass full of just Coke in the other. This was always a sign that he was going to try to take it just a little bit slower that night. He took a glance around the bar to see who else was here, scoping the place out for some familiar faces and also hoping to maybe see someone who might not yet have heard all of his well-tried pickup lines. Finding no one yet, he shuffled his way over toward us and took up a barstool at the edge of the bar.

"Who's got next game?" he asked nodding at the dart board.

"I suppose we do. Where's Parker?" I looked at Alexandria.

"I'm not sure he is coming tonight," she said as if there was more to the story.

"Oh?" I said suspiciously.

"Did I miss that much in two weeks?" Blake inquired with a smirk.

Alexandria took a deep sigh and said, "Well, remember how last week he said that he and Jenny had an open relationship and we shouldn't judge when he left with that brunette? It seems it was a little less open than we were led to believe and well…"

I shot Alexandria a look and she responded with disdain. "I know, I know! 'We don't write about that sort of thing. People's personal lives are their personal lives blah, blah, blah!' But I'm not writing it, I'm just gossiping it!"

"He's our friend."

"Fine!" Alexandria grunted, rolling her eyes.

"Is the brunette here now?" Blake asked. "She must be absolutely heartbroken."

"You deserve to be banned for life," I said, pushing him aside with a laugh and then pointing to the dart board. "It's our turn, y'all."

The young couple that had been playing handed us the chipped jar of darts and suddenly I was transported to another place and another time. For a moment everyone was well and I could imagine in my mind's eye what the world would look like if life had gone just a little differently. I watched as Clementine handed the darts to Alexandria and they giggled off to select the game. Nicholas was standing there explaining to Blake how important it was to respect his body and that maybe he should slow down just a bit. Shane was over here convincing Mikey that it was really alright to put just one drink on my tab and the new bartender was too new to know the ropes just yet.

There was Joy. That ring that fumbled around in my pocket on her finger. We'd been through a lot, but we'd weathered it. My parents were babysitting our little ones and it was a wonderfully rare night out with friends. Or maybe we would be standing here with Clementine.

Maybe it was all different. What if I had made every right choice?

Bull's-eye.

Parker had arrived. There was absolutely no point in playing now. We were all done for. This was my new life and it was beautiful. It was a different kind of beautiful and it certainly was filled with its own downfalls. I was not immune to pain or disappointment or loss. Tomorrow, I would go pick up my daughter and would get the wonderful experience of seeing Joy and her boyfriend, a constant reminder to me of all my failures and missteps. I was sleeping in the bed that I had made by living in my hurt instead of learning sooner that life isn't perfect but that it is perfectly flawed.

I guess the weirdest part about life is that just as soon as you think you've come to terms with those realities something will happen. You will smell someone's old shampoo wafting through the wind. You will be forced to face down the things you've abandoned. Demons will come back to haunt you that you thought were long ago buried. Sometimes you will get answers to questions you thought would never come.

I picked up my darts from the table in between drags on a cigarette. I looked up and everyone was in a stunned stance with their necks compelled upward like they had seen the face of God. I began to turn around and Alexandria grabbed me and held me tight. She gave me a pained look, the kind that is full of empathy and compassion. She knew that whatever was behind me was a monster I had long buried and she wanted to look at my face one more time like this before all that pain came crushing back down on my chest and before my countenance dropped. One last look at me before that monster grabbed me by the neck and attempted to drag me back into the dark cave of despair where it would gnaw at my bones as I wailed for lives lost and words unspoken.

"Leo," was all she said with such love and concern.

As I turned, I saw Shane's face smiling and laughing in the photo they always used for every news article. And then suddenly the two faces I hated the most in the world flashed across the screen and I was now breathing heavily. It had been years since a story had run on what happened and there they were, those two horrific men, but they looked older and worn. These were not the same recycled images. These were new mug shots.

"Turn that up!" I yelled to Mikey. He fumbled for the remote and clicked it off mute.

"The two brothers had been on the run and living off the grid in rural Arkansas. They were wanted for another crime when law enforcement finally apprehended them. The sheriff has announced that extradition papers have been filed and they will finally face trial for the murder of former reporter Shane…"

My mind went numb. Would this be the moment that forced us all back together? Were we finally going to have to exhume all the remains of emotions and sadness and would Shane be able to now rest in peace? I quickly pulled my phone out of my pocket and swiped up on the screen.

Alexandria looked worried. "What are you going to do?"

"I've got to warn Joy," I said calmly.

I stepped outside of the bar under the light of the neon sign. I lit a cigarette and put my ear buds in. I took one big, long, deep breath and clicked call.

Here we go again, I thought. And the Bar sighed along with me and rested into her hinges.

"Joy," I said.

And the Bar was happy.

CHAPTER TWO

GLASS HOUSES

For a brief period I was what I think an adult is supposed to be. The world came crashing down around me in a flash and then suddenly … clarity. The time after losing everything—Shane, Clementine, my job—it seemed as if depression itself had manifested into our world and was walking around amongst us. A foggy cloud of confusion and disillusionment. The doubts that floated in my mind about Nicholas still lingered, but my heart couldn't allow me to lose Joy. The loss already experienced was too great a burden to bear and so, for a time, it became easy to lay those intellectual understandings aside for a season.

Life began to flow forward and it felt like Joy and I had dodged a bullet. Somehow we were still here, still alive. The silence of our paper seemed to appease the demons that chased us. Over time it began to feel like maybe my suspicions were nothing more than fantasy and the further away I got from them the easier it became to just let time pass on by. I began to gaslight myself into just believing that this was all my mind's way of trying to reconcile the unimaginable. So I placed their emails, texts, messages, photos, stories, lives, memories, and the truth inside another manila folder and put it safely on a shelf. They could live safely there, close but far away. Slowly, life began to fill itself with moments that felt less miserable and some of them even began to feel pleasurable again.

With this newfound discovery that life could, in fact, be lived by us in spite of all the loss, we jettisoned forward into a maze of drinking our memories away. We met new people. We made fake friends and had real experiences with them. Their bodies were warm but our hearts were cold. They had been consumed by the icy crystals of sadness that loomed around our cockles until we couldn't feel anymore. Numbness masquerading as living. It sort of felt the same but nothing would ever feel the same again, I was sure of it.

As the novocaine slowly seeped through our veins we kept trying to find new ways to feel without feeling. To experience without getting too close.

The problem is that hiding pain behind synthetic blends of nothingness does not make the ache disappear;

it is hiding there, lurking behind the anesthetics just waiting for its moment to pounce again. Then, one especially unimportant night, that entire facade came crashing down around us and the only thing that can truly dispel the pain of living a false life is genuineness. We confronted that darkness together with our words and our emotions and our tears flowed out deep from within our souls. Rivers of salty exasperation walked out of us like corpses from their tombs.

We collapsed into each other and suddenly we could feel. It was like, in this moment, our bodies were finally able to release all of the indulgence we had been deprived of. The air we breathed was like inhaling flowers. The silk sheets underneath us engulfed our bodies the way that chocolate consumes and attaches itself to a fruit dipped into it. Every inch of the room felt like electricity. As we lay there in this blissful release our fingers found each other's flesh. Mine walked around the curves of her until they dipped deep down into the recess of her hips.

These motions moved organically and rhythmically. It was as if we were discovering each other again for the first time. The beauty of the broken monotony was shattered as I reached for the night stand drawer and pulled out a condom. She wrapped her fingers around me and pulled me close.

"I want to feel you, all of you," she breathed into my ear. "I need to feel. I need to feel you. I want you to forever be with me and me with you."

We lay there together, experiencing the fear of living in this moment. We jumped off the base of the cliff, no parachute, into the dangerous and uncertain waters below. And as we crashed into the warm wet sea of unknowing before us, we became enraptured in the release of that terror and we fell deeply into the depths of its refreshing disquietude.

Her screams released her from the binds of all we had been terrified to admit. Could we find love again? Was there anything in this life that could every truly erase all of this misery?

And what seemed like moments later she screamed again and here she was: a beautiful baby girl.

Nothing in life would ever be the same. With this sudden thrust into parenthood would come another stunning reality of how much this would in no way make us adults in the eyes of those who lorded over us. A generation still unwilling and unable to accept the reality that our lives lacked purpose or meaning. They drank from the chalice of eternal youth laced with cocaine and good mortgage rates. Too selfish to grow up, too afraid to grow old, they infantilized us for their own self-preservation.

Grandpa! My father would rather have taken a bullet to the chest than admit his new title. The week our Clementyne was born they took a two-week vacation to explore the wild world and show us how young they were. They had raised a child; they weren't interested in raising another. They let me know I knew what I was getting myself into. They hoped I would enjoy it.

No one was there to help them. No one at all ... other than my grandmother, a robust after-school care program, and the nanny they could afford to watch me so they could both go to work. The entire world had been given to them and then they suddenly decided to do a reverse mortgage on the economy so they could live life at the same pace of the youth they also got to live.

We couldn't afford for Joy to work but we couldn't afford for her not to. So one day, in between my second shift and my third job, I opened my laptop and looked at that portal that haunted the back recesses of my mind. There was a truth still to be told. There was a resource yet untapped. Had I missed it all along? No, I had just been living and leading with my heart and then, in a moment of clarity, I allowed my intellect to shine back through. It was time to tell the stories that needed to be told. This was the only way to keep them truly alive.

If I was going to make it right I was going to need to write the wrongs.

***

Journalism is never where I thought I would find myself. I could never have imagined myself as an entrepreneur and working for myself either. These were two gifts, each given to me by the spirits of my friends who left me all too soon. Though I could never fully tell a story in the way that Shane could, he gave me the ability to do enough in his memory that I could occasionally cause a little bit of damage. I was never quite certain why Clementine picked me as the person she left the paper to. Some part of me wondered if it was that she had started to get smart to the fact that Nick was a snake in the grass and was afraid what Joy might do if it was left to her. No matter the reason, she left it to me and I did the best I could with it.

I never finished the story of what happened with the mayor, the bishop, and the sheriff. The sheriff eventually met his own fate when he pushed too far and even the big paper turned on him. He lost his re-election campaign to a young and ambitious man who was focused on community policing and dismantling the good ol' boy power structures. He installed body cameras and accountability squads that looked into any shadow of wrongdoing. The mayor eventually retired and was replaced by another version of himself with a brighter smile. But with the structure broken with the new sheriff in town, it wasn't the same City Hall.

Then the bishop died.

The scriptures say, "Be sure your sins will find you out," and I was now having to face the reality of my silence. I had sat by and watched as Nicholas ascended over the years. He worked as the bishop's secretary and then became a monsignor. He traveled to Rome over the summers and studied and became a shining star. I always wondered what Judas would have spent his silver on had he chosen to live and in Nick I got a pretty good glimpse at what it might have looked like. He would have purchased silence and a throne.

In the early years, I told myself that I was probably crazy. It was just silly to think that Nick would have betrayed us all. I took the paper in a different direction. We still pressed forward on tough issues. It did its part in our town to hold feet to the fire and create another level of community-level accountability for power brokers and government officials. In truth, before ever pushing the publish button I would always think in the back of my mind, *Will this get me killed or just make them mad?* That was the test for everything I wrote. Tell just enough to push the envelope but never enough to end up pushing daisies.

The call I made to Joy about Shane's murderers being captured was far less ceremonious than I thought it would be. Clementyne was fighting bedtime and there was a new episode of *Outlander*. Her world was moving forward and I was still chasing shadows.

My dad kept wondering when I was going to get a "real job." When would I buy a home or drive a car with a warranty? I wondered those things too. I suppose if I had the courage I should have asked my dad if he thought it was that I didn't want those things. That's how he always acted, like I was some petulant child who didn't want nice things like it was some kind of rebellion.

I would have loved nothing more in the world than to have bought a decent-sized home and built a playhouse in the backyard. To lie out under the stars in a tree house with Clementyne and watch as meteors fall across the deep black backdrop of outer space. I wasn't avoiding it; I couldn't afford it. It wasn't for a lack of hard work. I woke up every morning and poured myself into my work. Every day I wrote and took chances and sat through editorial meetings in a real office that I paid for. In the afternoons I haggled with advertisers and in the evenings I sat with my staff as we hand-selected the stories to tell for the next day, assuming nothing new broke before dawn.

Then I would make my way a few blocks across town and feel that gravel under my tires. I would spend the nights drinking with ghosts and new friends. But I guessed, someday, I would grow up. Someday I would buy a house and a big fancy car. Maybe it would all get better and I would stop breaking even. At least I wasn't standing in front of the grill anymore, I guess. I wasn't a dollar richer for it.

At least it afforded me something that was much more than just a little luxury; when it was my weekend to spend time with my little one I could actually spend time with her. So we would go to borrowed play sets and lie out on the sand of the beach and dream about building tree houses. She would put her little hand in mine and say, "Wouldn't that be an exciting adventure, Daddy?" and I would agree.

Some days I would look at her and wonder if maybe she wasn't mine. There was all of Joy and all of Clementine inside her, but I wasn't sure where I was. She was so full of hope and adventure and a deep melancholy that defied her young years. All I wanted in the whole world was to build a space where she would be safe and protected. And maybe one day I would, whenever I grew up, whenever that would be. I was still waiting in line for our parents to admit that they were adults so that I could give it a try sometime.

Chapter Three

The Luckiest

I have yelled at my father exactly one time in my entire life. There were a great deal of back payments packed into that explosion, I can assure you. Countless times over my life I had felt my chest swell with things I wanted to tell him, but fear always captivated me in those moments and silence prevailed. I am not even really sure what I was afraid of. I already felt deprived of his love and affection, did I think there was a lower than here? Could I fall off the cliff into the pit of indifference? Whatever it was, I held back and refused to defend myself against his scoffs and snide remarks.

I am lazy. I am entitled. I am liberally biased. I am nothing. I am a child. I am defiant. I am failing. I am flailing. I am not determined. I am my own worst enemy. I am not listening. I am the problem. I am just stubborn.

I am going to understand some day. I am spoiled. I am unappreciative for all his hard work. I am unwilling to try. I am nothing like him. I am not doing enough. I should go to college unless I want to flip burgers for the rest of my life. I should be happy with my job flipping burgers. I am doing too much. I am the sum total of my own choices. I am glued to my devices. I am going to regret it. I am missing the point. I am just a liberal because I am young. I am going to understand, eventually. I am too angry. I am too unwavering. I am too bitter. I am nothing. I am a millennial.

When I looked down at Clementine's still face there were a million things I wanted to whisper into her ear. I wondered if she could still hear me. Was her spirit still floating nearby or was the whole concept of a spirit something humankind created for consolation? I didn't know. She looked so beautiful and peaceful. I wasn't angry with her for deciding to leave. I understood why she felt she needed to go.

Shane once said to me, "I sometimes wonder if humans are all given the same amount of energy when they are born. Kind of like lives in a video game. We are all doled out three lives and some of us just use that energy in different ways and collect different abilities or disadvantages as we go along. Then one day, just like that, you don't have any energy anymore. It's all used up. Some of us use it all up before we are twenty and some of us reserve just enough to say goodbye at a hundred. Different things like trauma or hurts can drain us. Who knows? Maybe we just only have so much."

I know there were days I felt like the energy was being sucked out of me like I was attached to the torture device in the Pit of Despair. A year just gone, disappeared, into me making another dollar to survive and another person rich so they could truly live.

Clementine loved so deeply and purely that I bet energy flowed out of her like rushing waters from a dam. Now she lay before me quiet and gone. I wanted to hug her and thank her and I didn't want to see her disappear forever into the ground. I wanted her to know that I loved her. I wondered if she knew that now. Was she somewhere able to see it all play out like some sitcom in a heaven far away and she could now know that Joy and I had talked about her? That I was changing. Did she know I loved her? Could she still love me?

People spoke words and sang songs. Faces I didn't know. Family she rarely spoke about that now claimed her body. They took gallons of whitewash paint and cleaned up her life to appease grandparents and the preacher. No one talked about her art. No one mentioned the painting she did where the lady spread open her legs and the waters flowed out to nourish the earth. There wasn't a mention about her modeling or how she was excited for advancing the cause of deconstructing beauty norms.

She was good in school. She was sweet. She went to church. She died. Amen.

Just like that she was gone forever. I would regret not kissing her cold face or touching her folded hands. What was I afraid of? Everything I hadn't done was because of fear. I was afraid to risk and scared to dream. I looked back from the parking lot of the funeral home and across the grassy fields fertilized with formaldehyde and missed opportunities and up the little hill to the fresh patch of dirt where she lay down in a box far away from me now and I made a promise.

"Clementine, I'll love you forever. I'll be sorry forever. I promise not to let another moment pass me by, if I can help it, and I'll chase after every opportunity that life gives me. It might never give me another and I know I'll never meet another you. I'll say what I am thinking and I'll speak my feelings and I'll never miss the chance to say what needs to be said again. I promise you. I promise me too."

My parents were waiting by their car. They had offered to take both me and Joy to dinner after the service. Part of me wanted to run back and lift that dirt back like a blanket and just lie there with her until the end of the world. I took Joy by the hand and decided to stay with the living just a little while longer or maybe fifty more years. As I made it to my parents' car they were exercising Southern discretion as they spoke in loud whispered tones. My dad looked at me with a look that I mistook for compassion.

"I don't understand," he remarked, looking directly in my eyes, "you kids have been given everything in the world. We did everything. You live in the greatest country in the world, no wars, no famines, just buckets of opportunity, and you squander it."

"What?" was all I could squeeze out.

"I'm just saying, why a girl so young would just decide to kill herself is beyond me. This is what I've been warning you about with being spoiled, ungrateful, and entitled. A life wasted because someone got the wrong order at Starbucks or some other useless whiny bullshit."

Joy squeezed my hand tightly. It wasn't like she was holding me back; I don't think she even could have thought to. She was just holding me and maybe letting out a bit of her rage as well. I jerked my hand away and in a single motion shoved my dad against his silver sedan. He looked confused for a moment and then his pride rushed out and he knocked me back. Then he took the stance with both dukes up.

"What the hell is wrong with you, boy?" he screamed while using one of his knuckles to sniff his nose.

"No, what the fuck is wrong with you? You think she died because she was inconvenienced? You are a fucking fool if you think life is so goddamn perfect for us. It's like…"

"It's like what?"

"It's like you got it all and as long as you got it that was enough. You didn't give a fuck if we could afford school or insurance or get our teeth fixed. The last time I went to the doctor was when Mom took me for my check-up when I was seventeen. Not a single dentist appointment, nothing. I can't afford that shit. Clementine couldn't either. There was obviously some deep stuff going on, stuff we didn't know or didn't see. Or maybe she was just fucking done, Dad. Maybe she looked into the crystal ball and saw everything that was coming. A forever collapsing economy and working forever and with nothing to show for it."

"Bullshit."

"No, it's not bullshit. It's the fucking truth, fair and goddamn balanced. And you know what? It could have been me in that casket. You know how many fucking times I have wanted to just put a rope around my neck and just be free? Free from bills and free from fear and free from having to wonder if I filed my taxes the right way because you never took the fucking time to teach me and you voted to cut spending in schools for them to teach me too. I understand why Clementine left and I don't blame her. But I sure as fuck blame you."

"Of course you do. That's all you millennials know how to do, displace blame and take zero—"

I assume that what he was going to say was responsibility. I'll never know and I really didn't fucking care. In a moment of uncharacteristic resolve he dropped his guard for just a split second and I saw it. I took it. I knocked my dad so square in the jaw that he stumbled back. I remember my mother screaming something like, "What are you doing?" and then I stepped away. I spit on the ground toward his feet. We never talked about it. Over the years I would go to Thanksgiving and Christmas and we would debate and I would listen and we would never speak of that day again.

Nothing changed. Not with him, not with the world.

I would have done anything to have been burying him that day instead. Your parents dying is normal. Plenty of people my age have done it. But seeing Clementine go, dust to dust, and then gone forever, this wasn't natural. I didn't resent her choice, but I resented him for it. He killed her as much as anyone. A land without hope or promise or opportunity or forgiveness. That was the legacy and we were all dying to keep them on life support. They harvested our organs for just another decade in Congress or as a CEO. If there was a God and they granted me one wish, I would have dug her up and placed him in that grave and corrected the mistake of them burying us all in debt, in a dying planet, in missed opportunity, in wars for oil, in wars over drugs, stacking us in prisons while bragging about being the freest country in the world. We were buried in bullets, in grease, sinking into a plastic ocean, and all they wanted us to do was thank them for it. I would rather die.

***

I walked down the long corridor that led to my office. It was a small space. There was one open room that was full of framed articles and had three plastic folding tables that were used as desks. One unisex bathroom and another small room that was barely a broom closet that I called my office. I never really spent much time in there. As I rounded the corner I passed the other rented offices in the large building named after some family that mattered. When I reached the door and emerged inside, my singular staff person jumped up and said, "Why are you here?"

Suddenly, I realized this wasn't where I was supposed to be at all. Today was the big day. The new bishop was about to be installed at the cathedral. This was the story. I looked at a large clock on the wall. I was going to be late, very, very late. But what did it matter? I just had to be there.

When you have lived in a town this long, it is hard for every inch of it not to have memories, big and small. There was the fountain where Joy jumped in and danced in the water. It was also the same fountain that Shane and I put soap and food coloring in. The sheriff's department looked for the culprits but never found them. It made the front page of the paper. There was the alley that Clementine and Joy disappeared down the night of the Alternative Prom. And this, this was the church where my friend would soon assume the mantle of bishop. I guess that means we were all just pawns.

As I pulled into the parking lot, I quickly discovered there was nowhere to park. I had to drive around until I found a space near a playground a few blocks away. I lit up a cigarette as I made the stroll up to the brick and stone building. Inside, in the bowels of this mammoth building, he was being anointed again. Had he used all his silver yet? Or were there still higher places to ascend from here?

Before I finally made my way inside a thought came to me. "I wonder if he is still Nick."

We had watched him transfigure from Nicky to Nick to Nicholas to Father Nicholas and now the bishop. With each transubstantiation a bit of him disappeared forever. It was replaced by certainty and self-fortifying belief. I thought that it was supposed to bring you happiness and fulfillment. But with each step up the stairway to heaven, Nick stopped loving, stopped smiling, and stopped laughing. I guess he had reached the final stage of process: he was the bishop. Now he had perfected these gifts inside himself he would be able to teach others to stop loving, stop smiling, and stop laughing.

After the long and prestigious ceremony came to a grand end, we were all ushered into the reception hall where enough food had been laid out to feed an army. I couldn't help but think how dissimilar this looked to the last supper. There were no hookers or beggars or lepers in sight. I did see the mayor and the sheriff and the CEO of the hospital and lawyers.

"Daddy!" I knew that voice. Before she could reach me, her mother appeared.

"No, that isn't Daddy; that is the editor in chief. He won't be Daddy again until Saturday," Joy snarked as she kissed my cheek.

"He is the daddy in chief!" Clementyne observed.

"My girls." I smiled. "It's good to see you."

"Have you congratulated Nicholas yet?" Joy asked without irony.

"You mean the bishop? Oh, no, not yet. I'm sure he's congratulated himself enough for the both of us."

"Nothing changes." Joy almost laughed.

"And yet nothing stays the same." I mourned behind a smile.

With it she cordially walked away. It didn't matter how many years it had been, how many times I had seen it, it broke my heart every single time. She was always approaching and I was always pushing. I wondered when I would never see it again. When would be the last time she walked away? Would I ever get up the courage to run after her? Was it even fair at this point to try? Would she even care for me to anymore? I suppose I broke my promise to Clementine that day as she lay freshly in her grave. I told her I would always speak my mind and tell the truth and say, "I love you." But a hundred thousand times I watched Joy walk away and a hundred thousand times I froze. I didn't chase. I didn't yell from the rooftops. I didn't scream, "I love you." I didn't make grand pledges I could never keep. I just watched as she strolled away. I was missing it, all of it, and someday the clock was going to run out on me.

A whirlwind of curls came crashing into me. "I love you, Daddy! We have got to go." And she hugged me. She kissed me. She took her mother's hand and off they went.

A hundred thousand and one.

CHAPTER FOUR

THE ANTI-FASCISTS

My whole youth, like most kids my age, I grew up on *Indiana Jones* and *Star Wars*. They acted as some of the greatest anti-fascists propaganda films known to humanity. Shane and I would roam around the neighborhood searching for hidden treasures and swinging from trees with makeshift whips. We would run through fields and sand and chase dreams. Countless times, "Nazis, I hate these guys" passed our lips. And we meant it! This disgust for Nazis, and love for Spielberg, followed us into moving from action films and into absorbing the true horror of the Third Reich as we consumed the more reverent work of *Schindler's List*.

No amount of lightsabers slashing Imperialists could prepare us for the truth. Fantasy can never really fully convey the readiness of reality. They act as frameworks for noticing the broader picture but none of it could help us know how to fight fascism when it began to rear its beastly head right here at home. Not appearing as an ideology floating upon our shores from abroad but swelling up from right within.

Inauguration Day had long been the tradition for our friend group but now only three remained and we were as fractured as our own country as they headed to the polls on November 3rd, 2016.

Nick and I had barely spoken since the day I saw him enter The Statesmen Lounge. All of our conversations were surface-level pleasantries for the sake of congeniality. We spoke at birthday parties and family events and only in the simplest terms about the weather or when the new bridge would be complete. We didn't even feign interest in times of the past. He was as disinterested in my existence as I was in his. A million times I had thought about breaking into his apartment and rummaging to see if I could find that file with the red letters written on it. Sensibility ruled the day every single time, but the desire remained deeply implanted in me.

He now stayed as far away from politics as possible which, ironically, was a completely political move. There was no doubt he was conservative, but he sat firmly right in the center of the fence so that no one could accuse him of landing any which way. I'm sure if you asked him he would have said it was pastoral in nature; that he was attempting to be all things to all people. But I could tell the truth was he wanted to be as center as was reasonable in order to continue his ascension to the top. Even then, there was zero question about his trajectory.

I think the thing that so many missed about our concerns with the rise of fascism under Trump was that many equated the rise of Hitler with the ends exclusively and not the danger of the means. The comparisons made between the fear of fascism in the rise of Trump were not merely a fear that he would lead us in the same direct path as Hitler but that he was using the same model. But the evils of the Third Reich were not all carried out on day one. It was a slow and steady rise to power, a complete cultural shift, that brought about a totalitarian regime. It was the gifting him this power, by the people, that gave him the authority to then commit his heinous crimes against humanity. Without the power, the atrocities could never have taken place.

The concern was not that Trump would necessarily reach the same end conclusion, but that type of power, in the hands of any human, could be used for these means and that, in and of itself, is reason for fear.

There were also plenty of reasons to be concerned that a President Trump could, in fact, come to similar conclusions as his ideological predecessor. There was every reason to believe that he could reach these same conclusions about any group, be it Muslims, transpeople, women, or people of color. The fear of what he could conclude as a solution to those who disagreed with him was unprecedented, except in their comparison to fascist dictators. But warnings of this potential fall as a Democratic Republic into a Fascist Dictatorship were scoffed away as hyperbole. Our nation instead clicked their boots together and marched directly toward doomsday.

Trump embodied all of the worst parts of our parents and they flocked to him in droves. Is it any surprise that the generation who adopted the model of Helicopter Parenting elected fascists? They wanted absolute control in every aspect of our lives. They believed they could control us even into our adulthood by gaslighting that such an adulthood even existed. They would say "millennial" like it meant seventeen-year-olds when, in fact, we were starting to get cancer, arthritis, and default on student loan debt. Our parents would complain to managers and principals and get their way. They demanded we all got a trophy and then called us weak for it. Trump was them and his children were the minions that our parents had hoped, and failed, to turn us into. They were subservient lap dogs that lifted him up and never aspired to be anything other than basking in his shadow.

We had all been living under micro-fascist regimes from our inception and so how unsurprising is it that we all fled the final boss when he arrived? Trump embodied everything that had destroyed the dreams of the average millennial: he was a racist, narcissistic, billionaire landlord who made firing people an American pastime. His gluttony and cruelty were his trademarks. He was the worst parts of Reaganism concentrated into its most grotesque form.

Election night, I sat at the bar with Alexandria, who was my girlfriend at the time. The news stayed on in the background and I kept checking the election results on my phone at a manic rate. Things would look promising and then not. Slowly I began to see the writing on the wall, but somewhere deep inside me I began to panic.

"Oh, God, she's going to lose," Alexandria finally said out loud.

"It's not possible." Denying reality, I scrolled through my phone.

"You voted, right?" she asked.

"What kind of fucking question is that? Of course I voted." I was indignant. "How could I not vote?"

"I know, I just… I can't right now, Leo."

The risks were higher for her in this round, without a question. Her entire personhood was on the line. Even her using the bathroom had been politicized. We drank and were as quiet as we could be. Suddenly, the All Saints didn't feel the same. Nothing felt the same. The day timers had long overstayed their typical welcome past 10:00 PM.

No, the place was packed and the big screen that had normally only been reserved for football flipped on.

The race was called. We watched it flash across the screen and someone screamed, "Trump 2016!" In the background Alexandria flinched. I watched her whole body tense in a way I had never seen before. She reached under the table and grabbed hold of my leg. It wasn't affection, but it was intimate. She needed to be grounded in some way to anything that didn't feel dangerous in this moment.

People began to chant, "U.S.A.! U.S.A.!" And it was clear we were somehow outnumbered. I looked around the bar and saw a few of the folks come in from the pool room that I knew. We made eye contact and metaphorically shrugged in our confusion. Who were these people? Where did they come from? Was it always like this and I had somehow missed it? Had they just been hiding in the cracks of our little safe haven waiting to emerge for a moment just like this?

Emotions rushed over me and I couldn't help it, a tear rolled down my cheek and then it just began to flow. I was terrified. For our country, for anyone who looked different than the old white men bellied up to the bar in their red hats. I cried for myself, for my daughter, for the future, for the Republic, and in the most realistic and micro way for Alexandria and the fear she was feeling in this moment. I felt someone poke me in the back and

I turned around to some guy I had never seen. "You crying?" He did not look especially concerned for my well-being.

"Yeah, I am," I said defiantly.

"Fuck your feelings, faggot." He gave me another shove.

I was shocked at first. It felt strange to protest that I wasn't gay; that would somehow seem to validate his feelings that being gay was shameful. So I just stood up and looked at him. I had a good two inches on the guy and he was easily my dad's age.

"What's your deal, man?" was the best I had.

"How about you and your little boyfriend get out of here? It's Trump's American now, baby." He was not kidding around either. But this was our bar. Who the fuck was this guy? Almost instinctively I looked around for Billy and then my eyes caught his photo behind the register. Instead, I was met with an equally scared Mikey standing behind the bar, not sure what to do.

"This is my girlfriend," I said with pride.

"He's got a dick. A dress and some tits don't make a woman. We are taking this country back, you bitch."

"She's none of your business and you've got about three seconds to back the fuck off..."

"Or what?"

Suddenly, Mikey screamed, "Closing time!" and hit the lights. Everyone began to grumble and make their way to the bar. Everyone except our MAGA dude. He was ready to finish this fight. I had positioned myself in between him and Alexandria. I wanted to look back at her and make sure she was alright, but I knew better than to take my eyes off this guy. Finally, Mikey interjected again.

"Hey buddy! Porch time, now!" And the guy backed up slowly and made his way to the door.

As soon as the room cleared I hit the ground on one knee and Alexandria was crying. I held her tightly and she sobbed into my shoulder. We could hear through the walls as the chants of "U.S.A." and "Trump 2016" began to rise so loud I was sure we would hear police sirens at some point. But they never came. Mikey told us we could stay as long as we needed until the crowd cleared. The chants continued to rise up. Trump 2016. Trump 2020. Trump 2024. Trump 2028. Trump 2032. Trump 2036. Trump 2040. Trump Forever!

This is how liberty dies, with thunderous applause.

***

The problem with not being a college football fan living in the South and, instead, being someone who treats politics as your own version of sports ball is that your major events only happen every couple of years. Not that politics isn't a daily reality, but the big elections come and go and then it's back to the normal protests and writing about the daily struggles of the fight of the oppressed and the luxuries of the oppressors.

After going through our first election together, our friend group had always committed to still gather on January 20th of each year to plot and plan our futures and hopes. Even in the absence of so many of our friends, Joy had promised to keep the tradition up with me. New people became grafted into the tradition and so it came that day again, 2019.

We now lived in a very different America. The worst parts of us were rising to the top and we failed on so many fronts to suppress the rage that was building up. Being a son of the South, I feared civil unrest as much as I feared the full rise of fascism under the regime of Trump. The rhetoric was shifting toward violence and tensions were rising. I had once described it as a Cold Civil War. We all waited to see what would be our Fort Sumter moment. Would it come? Were we facing an actual insurrection or could tensions cool enough to survive these four years? We had certainly prophesied such a doomsday scenario back in 2016 as we watched Trump inexplicably defeat his Republican challengers.

After a small struggle, we were able to preserve the All Saints as a safe space. Fortunately, the current owner sided with us. He was a centrist Democrat but he still had no stomach for fascists or confederates. It did, however, result in him completely banning politics and the news being aired on the television; a small price to pay for preserving our bar. It didn't stop us from still gathering every January to celebrate democracy.

The strangest part about making new friends is that they don't truly know your experiences except by your own record. As I sat around this table and looked at all my new loves, they only knew of Shane by legend and Clementine through my oral love stories. Joy was the only other soldier still standing from a bizarre time in our history. I was so old and yet nothing more than a baby in the eyes of the world. My grey hairs were defying the lie that millennials were just spoiled children.

Alexandria probably understood the most because we had gone through all the stories in a different way when we were dating. Now that she had morphed into being one of my closest friends, she could see me from multiple angles.

"Is there a seat for me?" cut through the smoke and red hue of the lights. It was Joy.

I was shocked to see her. I sort of sat there looking like an idiot until Alexandria kicked me under the table and I jumped up and offered Joy my seat. I found another chair and brought it over to rejoin the table.

"I didn't expect you." It was supposed to be a sign of excitement but it came out much more shocked.

"It's tradition and I'm a traditional gal."

She was. She loved all things Americana. Joy was such a beautiful juxtaposition. She lived in constant contrasts. She loved tradition and bucked it in equal measure. She loved to read wedding magazines and never wanted to get married. She loved romance but never wanted to be romantic. A stunning display of the majesty of contradiction.

Once, she told me, "I would have married you though."

She would have but I was too big a fool and too determined to destroy the one thing that mattered most to her: family. My hatred for Nick ultimately destroyed us. She never once prevented me from writing about him. She supported my work completely. I never even did it. The truth was I think I took out my own rage at myself for failing to expose what had happened on her. It eventually tore us apart. I fell deep into my own darkness and I couldn't rise back up out of it. The burden eventually became too much for her to bear. She wanted adventure and romance and the ability to explore life in the truest sense of the word. She wanted to kiss a stranger under the Eiffel Tower and then spend the next day traveling to Tuscany with me. She wanted it all, everything, and she didn't want anything to hold her back. "I don't want anything extravagant, Leo, I just want the whole world." And she meant it. She wasn't jealous about things like sex or love or intimacy. She didn't hate people who saw the world differently. Her only animosity was found in that she was jealous of everyone and hated that anyone got to see the world at all, except her.

I was married to this town. I was unconcerned with the world and its problems. My only worry was making this community better in whatever way I could. I didn't need to see the Mona Lisa in person, I had Google.

The part I had missed in my own ideology is that I would have loved to have seen her seeing the Mona Lisa or kissing that stranger under the Eiffel Tower or sipping wine in Tuscany. By the time I finally realized this, that she was my joy and my happy thought, it was too late. I had to "maybe tomorrow" or "next year when things get better" my way into her having to leave.

In my absence, she didn't fly to Paris or see the paintings or kiss those strangers. She wanted to do those things with me. I just couldn't see the forest for the trees. The world was so big and yet tiny. Our entire love was consumed by my selfishness and inability to yield or give creditability to her needs and desires. We had become the one thing that she had attempted to avoid her entire life: normal. We had grown into being the coldest parts of what traditional marriage can become. So I lost her.

And yet, she was right here, sitting next to me.

We talked for hours. We told everyone stories about how Clementyne was doing in school and someone didn't know where we got the name from. Soon we were telling stories around the real stories, finding ways to make it make sense without telling the whole truth. It was a tango we danced often.

The hours melted away. I was shoved aside at one point so that Blake could take his shot at flirting with Joy and he gave it his best go at trying to take her home.

"I've known too many of you over the years." She chuckled. "Oh, if only you had only gotten here sooner, you might have won me."

"I'll build a time machine," he said and ran to the bar and got himself some toothpicks and cups and built a time machine right there on the table. He imagined with her that they had met years ago and they flirted as if they were their younger selves. My heart kind of started to race that he might succeed. There was that painful sting of jealousy, the beast I kept being unable to conquer.

Alexandria took me by the hand to play darts.

"You know," she said, "one of these days it won't be a theory. Whether it's a wedding band or death or a job offering in Bangkok, something is going to whisk that woman away and airport reunion scenes are played out as fuck."

I looked at Joy as she smiled and she laughed. With each sip of her beer her boisterous chuckle evolved into that endearing cackle. I wasn't jealous about Blake sleeping with her or taking her on some date. I was afraid he would be a better man than me and fly her across the ocean. He wouldn't actually give a fuck about her face as a tear dripped down her cheek as she looked at the snarky smile on Mona Lisa. He would probably even foolishly wipe the tear away instead of letting her deliciously enjoy it.

"But I have to fix the world before I can see it," I told Alexandria as I took a failed shot at the board.

"You are so dumb sometimes." She shook her head at me. "You can't change the world; you can only change you. The world is going to transition as she should into what she will. Yes, play a part. Yes, do your part. How very colonial of you, why do you want to change something that you haven't even seen, experienced, tasted, or explored?"

The truth was I was afraid. I was afraid of the cost. How could I do this when I needed to get my teeth looked at and my car was in desperate need of an oil change? Could I really be reckless? I guessed I wasn't getting any younger. Maybe it was time to try just not giving a fuck anymore. Not splurging on a Starbucks wasn't going to help me get a mortgage. Taking a vacation probably wasn't going to kill my credit any more than it already was. I might never own a home but at least I would have finally seen Buckingham Palace.

"You're right." I gave Alexandria the darts and began to turn around. "I'm going to tell her."

"Not tonight," she said.

I turned around just in time to watch Blake pay the tab and wave at Mikey. He slipped out the door tipping his fedora and I saw only the faintest sliver of Joy's purse exit around the corner to the door. One of these days, that would be the last time I saw her walk away. Someday I would see her walk down the aisle, down an airport terminal, or down the hallway to surgery. Someday, it would be the last time. Thankfully, knowing Blake's track record with actually sustaining a relationship of any semblance beyond a one-night stand, tonight wouldn't be it. But I needed to stop playing roulette with our lives; there was a bullet in there somewhere.

CHAPTER FIVE

YESTERDAY

You never know when something is going to be a last memory. I would have done everything so differently if I had known that I would never see Clementine again. I suppose if I had done things differently, I probably would have seen her again. At least that's what I always told myself. For the rest of my life I would walk around just a little bit sure that I was a fragment of the bullet that took her life. I was one of the pills that slipped down her throat that night. Not the only thing but part of a collection of things. Could I have been enough to save her? And is salvation what everyone wants or needs?

Maybe this one big mistake doesn't have to be the last memory. Can we reorganize our memories so that the first thing I think of when I recall her isn't the last moments of her life? Can it be anything else? Do all stories have to be told in a linear timeline or can I rewrite this one, just a bit? I close my eyes tightly enough so that, maybe, as I drift away to sleep…

"Leo, are you awake?" Clementine was way too close to my face.

"Um… I am now?" I blinked.

She jumped up and down with excitement. Joy had gone to her parents' house for something, I was too tired to remember. Clementine made breakfast. I sat at the little table in Joy's kitchen and responded to emails. At some point Clementine rustled my hair and I took my headphones off. Breakfast was ready. We ate eggs and sausage with burnt toast.

After breakfast, we curled up in bed and watched a show on Netflix all day long. I don't even remember what we watched. I fell asleep at one point and then we played a card game with the show as noise in the background. I got a text from Joy saying that she wouldn't be home that night; she was staying at her parents'. Clementine got the same text.

"Truth or dare?" Clementine asked.

"Uh … truth."

"What is your biggest fear?"

I thought for a moment. "I guess at one point I would have said dying alone. Now, after losing Shane, I think that is my new fear. Losing everyone I love."

"Isn't that the same fear, just in different packaging?" Clementine took my hand for a moment.

"Alright, your turn!"

"Fine, truth or dare?"

"Truth."

She smiled.

"I guess the same question."

"You can't just pick the same question. That's boring."

"Fine," I said again. "What do you want to be when you grow up?"

"Happy," was her simple answer.

"You aren't happy?"

"I mean I am happy … sometimes." She looked down at her hands for a moment; they were still holding the cards. "I guess … I don't know, I am happy right now. With you like, like this, this feels like family or normal. Today, there are no expectations and nothing is bearing down on me. I am happy to be here with you. This is happy, I suppose. But I want tomorrow to be happy and the next day. I wish yesterday could have been happy."

We played truth or dare for hours. We told each other many things. You think you know everything there is to know about a person if you grow up with them. But there are all these pockets of life that they live when you aren't around. In a weird way, I suppose, we are all a bit narcissistic and as we walk away, we don't think about all the things that someone else is doing in their day. People aren't secondary characters or sidekicks; everyone is a main character in their own story. As I listened to all the parts of her main storyline that I had missed, I wanted to know more and more. There were a lot of questions I didn't ask that I should have. I know that now.

She dared me to streak through the house. I changed my answer back to truth.

"You never take the risk!" She shook her head at me. "We are playing spin the bottle next."

I never picked dare because it was scary. I wanted certainty. I don't remember what show we were watching. I do remember the feeling of it all. This is love, this is happy. For just that one day we didn't have any responsibility. There were no bills to pay or our jobs demanding we exchange our life for a few measly dollar bills. The outside world was outside and no one was judging us. We just lay in bed, enjoying each other's company and learning about how we ticked and what we thought.

I am not sure how many perfect days we get in life. So much of our lives are sold to the highest bidder in order to pay for the privilege of being alive. I once had a friend who opened a taco truck. He saved up a bunch of money and purchased the truck and did most of the work himself on it. He was so proud when he passed the inspection. One of the bars downtown let him park it there for a while and eventually he found an empty parking lot on a busy street and they let him set up there.

His taco truck became super popular and the local news station even did a story on him. Then he kept getting more and more business. He had to hire someone to help because he couldn't keep up with everything.

One day, I asked him when he was going to get his car fixed now that he was successful.

"Man, I can't afford that right now!" he said.

"Dude, there is a line out the door every day at your taco truck." I laughed.

"Yeah, that doesn't mean anything. I had to give myself a pay cut to afford the employees to keep up with the demand. They doubled my rent for the spot now that I'm doing well. And the restaurant down the street got us shut down for a few weeks because they felt I was encroaching on their business." He sighed. "I kind of liked it better when it was just me. The only place to go from here is corporate. You can't get rich and powerful without hurting a few people along the way."

The more my friend succeeded the less money he was making. The system was designed to never let us break through. No matter what, they wanted to ensure we stayed poor. I could flip burgers for someone else or I could try to flip burgers for myself, did it really matter? We were all just selling our time to survive. The only question you had to answer was what flavor you wanted your survival to be.

Today, we weren't thinking about surviving. We were just alive and happy to be alive with someone we loved. I wish I had said it more. I wish I had done things differently. I suppose if I got a second chance to live that day, I would just destroy it trying to find a way to make her survive. It was a perfect day. It was a happy day. It wasn't the last day I saw her, but we said, "I love you." Those weren't the last words I said to her, but it's how I hope she remembers me.

…Just before my eyes flickered and I fell asleep, I prayed, "I would like to change my answer. I'll take the dare instead."

***

I sometimes wonder what it would be like if I could do it all again. What if I was given the opportunity to change a day, change a moment, change my life. Would I take it? What day would you change? Where is the moment that everything went off track? For the longest time I blamed that day at the All Saints when we decided to start the paper. Was that the moment it all went wrong? Probably not really. It just became an easy scapegoat to blame. That specific time in our history wasn't what made Nicholas whatever he had become. That character, or lack thereof, was imbedded into him long before we signed away our fates on a cocktail napkin. He must have been treacherous within his nature. So, I wonder;

if given the opportunity to bounce through time, would I only change the circumstances of his betrayal and not the inevitability that he would, in fact, betray us all at some point?

Some days I would ponder that idea about human nature. Are we a product of design or accident? And I don't just mean the whole idea of a god out there in the universe attempting to motivate and control the actions of their creation. I mean more micro than all that. Are we the sum total of our parents and environment or is there some spark inside us that is always there, a personality that is free from the influences of circumstance? Maybe our circumstances are what unlock our personality. Without experiencing certain traumas would we have even attempted our coup d'état? Is the struggle necessary to craft us into the people we become or would that longing for change have always been there but the potential would never have been unlocked if our hearts hadn't been broken one day?

If a potential for goodness or evil is somehow marked within our genetic coding, can we overcome it and is there something that exists outside of this binary of good or bad? Look at my life; all the indecision that marked the first quarter of it, was I not complicit in the world's atrocities and has the attempt, now, to make a better world absolved the sins of my youth? What youth! We grew up in a war zone of terrorism and guns in school.

No, we learned to hide under desks in case one of our classmates finally snapped. Our parents came after our movies, our video games, and our music. They looked everywhere for the culprit behind our angst and anger and pain, everywhere except for inward. Could it be possible, Karen, that the cause of all of this suffering was something deeper than Nirvana, *The Matrix,* and *Grand Theft Auto*? I fucking think it's possible.

We were told that the towers fell that day because we were the greatest nation in the world and everyone was jealous. So some terrorists just decided to take a box knife and bring that nation to its knees? No inward thinking, no questioning, just accepting this jealousy narrative all the way into a decades-long war. It couldn't have happened because of our constant meddling in destabilizing other nations in order to keep gas prices low or that the war machine makes literally trillions of dollars for the elite and only costs them a few Gen X'ers and Millenials. Just 7,036 American youth blown up on battlefields was a small price to pay for global domination. But sure, Dad, blame Neo for the death and destruction happening in our country. Blame everything except for the world you built. It was MTV and Madonna that caused Eric Harris and Dylan Klebold to rampage their high school; it couldn't possibly have been that they had easy access to guns, no access to healthcare, and that they grew up miles away from the literal guts of the war machine?

I guess, in a way, it's fair to say it's our own fault and not yours, since we were left to raise ourselves. Y'all were out living your best life and then whenever you were around it was to micromanage all our bad decisions. Sorry, we weren't the best parents to ourselves. If only there had been another option. But you were too busy voting against your own interest getting hard thinking that one day you too would ascend to becoming a billionaire with a bad tan.

Blame the malls; blame the schools; blame anyone but yourself. But what the fuck do we know? We are just a bunch of entitled Starbucks drinkers lounging on avocado toast, amirite?

A professor once said to our class, "Success is found in the struggle and happiness is found in the ability to be at peace." If my professor's quote is correct, can you not be successful and happy? Peace is the absence of struggle. Success, in this system, can only be achieved through struggle, conflict, and exploitation. Free from disturbance, worry, war, famine ... peace is the opposite of struggle and if peace is necessary for happiness then you cannot succeed and be happy. Maybe that was the punch line.

I think in many ways that was the struggle that our parents were collectively going through. They were all told by Bush and Reagan that if we stopped taxing the wealthy there would be more jobs, more opportunity, less struggle, and maybe you could exchange a little bit of your success for some happiness. Not for a long time but maybe just a little bit, two weeks at a time once a year. Then, somewhere out there, would be retirement. But like a big bully, they kept moving the goal post. Eventually, by the time it became our turn, we would have the opportunity to retire when we were dead.

That became the race to the end game: trickle-down economics. The finish line was to reach the top because no one wanted to be trickled on and everyone wanted to be the one taking the piss from the 94th floor. And then our whole generation watched in our classrooms as the towers fell and none of us wanted to ascend so high again. None of us wanted to be set on high towers where someday we might have to jump from the smoldering ashes of an economic fortress.

I've sometimes wondered was the Tower of Babel just a terrorist attack attempting to destroy advancements in technology that had allowed all of us to reach a level of mass communication? Had we ascended to a time like this and the world was at a place of economic and communication glory but the terrorists won and we gave glory to God for separating humanity so that one day we could knock over their towers and then they could knock over our towers until the end of time?

So what would I do if I could jump through time? Would I jump back to Babel? Should I assassinate Hitler?

Would I sit under a shady tree with Clementine and say yes to lunch? Maybe we would go to that little Cajun restaurant next to the park. We could talk for hours and hours. Would I decide to show up just in time to save Shane from being murdered or should I go back further than that? Do I show up at that the moment he is born and alter every event of his life in order to change his entire personality so that he isn't the type of person who would invite relative strangers into his home so that they wouldn't have the chance to murder him?

I suppose I could go the way of our parents and just make letting anyone, at any time, have someone else stay in their home illegal because I lost my friend that way. Of course, I would have to make a caveat in the rules that allows me to do it; I just don't want anyone else being allowed to do it. Trust me; it'll all make sense when you are older.

Maybe the best way to remember Shane isn't by trying to sterilize the world. His death can be both a horrific thing that we wouldn't wish on anyone and also a beautiful reality of his personality—or is that too grim? Is there such a thing as too safe? If I traveled through space and time in order to protect my friends from the fates that awaited us, would we have had fun or would we have just survived life? Would we have ever shared a meal, driven to the beach, swam in the moonlight in the warm waters of the Gulf, jumped from that bridge, outrun the cops, would we have lived? Is it possible that living is just risking not living?

The problem became that in every single scenario in my entire life there was one constant: me. I was always there, always in the way, always causing problems.

I guess growing up I always thought of time travel as being about going backwards. The premise was always about going back in time and trying to correct a small moment in time and then the world would be a better place if we could just make one minor tweak. Get in the car, Marty, we've got to save your parents, no wait, now it's your kids! Whatever you do, don't worry about saving yourself. Some nights I couldn't sleep as I lay there in my mind going through each memory one by one hoping to isolate the exact moment when I could have fixed it all and made everything better. Save Shane. Save Clementine. Love Joy the right way. Punch Nick. Forgive Nick. Hug Nick. Tell Nick I love him. Save Nick. Let Nick be himself. What would you change? Maybe everything got off track that day Shane gave me the cigarette at the skating rink. Was it those six steps to the ashtray that created a ripple effect and now he's dead?

I am a time traveler. I am traveling through time. I am not going backwards, we are all moving forwards. Everything we do is making a difference. We are killing people we love right now. Everything is being set into motion and it's up to us to grow and change and make it better. But I can't change the CEO or the president or my father. I can change me. Is this the beginning and end of responsibility, to work on ourselves? I don't know.

"Earth to Leo," Alexandria said.

"What? Yeah, sorry." I took the darts that Blake had extended to me.

"Where were you?" she asked with an inquisitive smile.

As I took my shot, I thought that if I kept jumping to the past, I was going to miss the future. We look back on our parents and resent them for doing too much to reshape the world in their image, will the next generation look back on us for not doing enough? Fuck. The next generation is already here and they are nipping at our heels before we've even got a chance at a shot. No time for peace just the struggle. No playing with your friends, no going to the movies; no you can't go to that concert, just do your chores.

I guess our parents meant it when they said they would ground us for life.

CHAPTER SIX

BIRDIE GOES TWEET

My grandmother died just before the 2016 presidential election. All my memories with her were the happy kind of moments. She was my reprieve from the chaos at home and in real life. Going to stay with her at that little cottage farm was like disappearing into another time. She lived in a different kind of way. She had survived the Great Depression and the Second World War. Time and generations are strange in that way. My great-grandmother had a father who fought on the wrong side of the Civil War. This was all history, but I held great-grandma's cold and thin hands as she would tell me stories of our kin. She would talk about her daddy and there I was, touching back to a moment in time. My connection to this horrific moment in history was no further away from me than her breath.

At this moment, as I stood before the corpse of my grandmother, there was, somewhere in the world, still a surviving Civil War widow living in this same space with us in 2016. That is the strange part about time. It moves and it flows. Its cold touch can reach out and grab us at any moment or its warmth can glow around us. It all depends on the memories attached and the energy it possesses.

I think my grandmother and I were always kindreds because I had more in common with her as a millennial than I did with my own parents. Grandma and I had both gone through an economic depression in our youth, we understood sacrifice. We knew the fear of watching our friends pack up and go off to war.

"The problem with your generation is that they don't respect their elders," my dad would say to me. "All of your problems boil down into that issue. You refuse to respect authority."

Ok, boomer.

I always had such a hard time with this concept that respect was supposed to just be gifted to him by virtue of his eldership and yet my dad's other favorite catchphrase was that respect is earned. What he actually meant, I guess, is that everyone else had to earn respect but that he was entitled to respect because he had passed a particular benchmark. He never wanted to be old but also demanded to be respected on the sole basis of being old. It was in this space of dichotomy that my dad and many others in his generation loved to bask.

The truth was I loved people who were older than me. It wasn't just my grandma either. There were people in my life, in big and small ways, that I admired and were examples to me of what could be. I don't know how you could call a generation obsessed with Mister Rogers and Bernie Sanders ageist. We didn't grow to hate boomers because of their age. That wasn't it at all. I couldn't quite put my finger on what it was, but I think it might have been the economic crash, wealth hoarding, crumbling infrastructure, infantilizing, lack of healthcare, fighting against a living wage, and setting the planet on fire that sent us over the edge. It had absolutely nothing to do with age; it was about a misbalance of power. My generation was quickly approaching our forties and we were still being expected to sit at the kids' table.

You are talking about a generation where those that survived did so by dodging the draft and then turning around to watch all of their friends die of opioids and AIDS just to shrug their shoulders and say, "Well, if they aren't going to eat it that just leaves more for me."

As the AIDS epidemic ripped through their generation and drugs were pumped into the cities, silence equaled death. The religious right began their ascension and Reagan promised a McDonald's franchise to everyone who remained quiet. Don't fight for the dying hoards in your streets. They don't need a vaccine, they don't need healthcare, just let nature take its course. Slowly the growing multilevel crises of Vietnam War vets, people dying of an unnamed virus, and the war on drugs raging forward created a perfect storm. The dead can't vote and neither can the incarcerated. If you just remain good little boys and girls, you too can have three ex-wives and your name plastered on the side of a hotel.

Eventually, the scale shifted red and they built the world (and God) in their own image. In reality, they were fascists the whole time and they just lacked a leader to take them the rest of the way. What Trump was too stupid to see, that any of us could have warned him, is that when you've got a generation of people who were raised being told the world belonged to them, you were just a means to an end. Millennials knew all too well that our parents used us as little remote controls and to fill the gas because they were too afraid to get their hands dirty. They didn't just want Trump because he spoke like them and gave them permission to be their most vile selves in public; they wanted someone to do their dirty work for them.

Is it any surprise then that when our generation saw that familiar red flag of totalitarianism rising up above the horizon we didn't look within our own ranks but ran to an adult? Just like we did with our teachers, youth pastors, and the nice man who pushed the carts at the grocery store.

We knew cognitively that not all Baby Boomers were the same. Yes, they are not a monolith. But we also couldn't ignore how many bodies lay in the wake of their generation. They kicked everyone with mental health issues out onto the streets, watched as cocaine was flooded into Black neighborhoods so they could arrest all the Black fathers, they looked on as their friends died from heroin overdoses and the AIDS epidemic. They titled their heads and said, "Arrest them all." Criminalize homelessness, make healthcare a luxury, stigmatize being gay, and call everyone who disagrees with you lazy and crazy.

I was eleven years old when my dad said in front of me, "If these queens don't want to die, they shouldn't stick it where it doesn't belong," as he walked out the door to go fuck his secretary without a condom and act like he was somehow the moral majority. Hate everything that is different than you.

So as my generation faced down the trial by fire of whether our country was going to try on fascism to see if it fit, we chose to chase after a man who embodied what we actually respected: consistency.

Our parents seemed to have two different sets of standards, "Do as I say, not as I do," my dad would always say. That wasn't just a mantra but his singular theology and political ideology. He wanted to dictate others' ethics and morals but wanted absolute freedom for himself.

He wanted to watch Black men fry in the electric chair and see children scorched for the sins of their fathers in Iraq. However, he wanted a god who absolved him of anything he did. That same god would hold everyone else accountable. The rules applied outward. He had freedom, liberty, and forgiveness.

He would smoke a joint while watching Fox News and cheer on the capture of immigrants jumping over the border.

"They are just smuggling drugs into the country! They say they are just scared parents coming here; if that was true, they would do it the legal way." He would take a hit.

An image would flash over the screen of a young Black kid who got arrested for dealing drugs. My dad would give nodding approval.

"He had a gun too. If they care so much about Black lives, maybe they should stop killing each other. Drugs and violence are destroying the Black community, not the police." Just one more drag before bed.

Sure, it was illegal, but if he voted to make pot legal for everyone, where would his justifications for hating and fearing his neighbor go? The laws were needed because they would never apply to him but he could easily apply them to anyone he disagreed with. It was a perfect hypocrisy.

If you wanted to survive in this dizzying game of gaslighting you just had to learn to do as they say, not as they do. Never question the hypocrisy, never mention that the emperor had no clothing, just comply or die. So our generation ran to the man who looked like the college professor that believed in us and not like the reality star who wanted to fire us (or fire on us). It's not that we didn't trust people who were older than us. We didn't fear someone's age, we feared a generation that followed a leader who said, "I could stand in the middle of Fifth Avenue and shoot somebody and I wouldn't lose any voters." We were afraid we might be the person shot. More than anything, we feared that our parents might be the ones eventually doing the shooting.

"I'll live forever," my father would say. "Just wait and see; soon we will have the technology."

I believed him, just so long as they had a leader who was willing to shoot us on Fifth Avenue to harvest our organs so they could eat their own young to survive just another decade. Just another dollar earned, another hour worked; he was willing to offer them the world. This was the salvation they had all been waiting for. Jesus was so last year; they had found their knew Messiah.

***

On February 19th of 2019, Bernie Sanders announced his second presidential run against Donald Trump. A few millennials and boomers gathered at a local Mexican restaurant in town. I looked around the room and saw faces, both young and less young, looking toward more than just a future but what felt like a final hope to save the Republic. We knew that Luke and Leia would never have gotten where they needed to be if it weren't for Obi-Wan. If we were going to fight the fascism rising around us, it was going to take more than just youthful ambition but also aged wisdom. But there was a notable defeatism this time around. Cynicism had imbedded itself deeply into our culture over the last three years.

"I think we lost our moment," an older woman said as we stood near the bowl of guacamole. "I want him to win more than anything. Ultimately, I think we will go for the safest win because we will do anything to defeat the bigger scary."

"So what do we do next?" I asked in earnest.

"Baby, you do the same thing we've always done. We go to the next picket line, we minister to the sick, we give a blanket to those sleeping on the street, and we teach." She slopped some guac on her plate.

"Teach?"

"Yes, baby, I am a school teacher. Probably most of your school teachers were just like me. We are the boomers who missed Woodstock and were a little too scared to party. Yeah, we got outnumbered, but we are still fighting, in our way. We are teaching; we were just getting you ready for this moment. Don't miss your chance; we've been rooting for you."

She smiled and joined a table with a group of folks who did, in fact, look a lot like all of my teachers in school. They were wearing shawls and big earrings. There they were! The grown-ups! They were the ones we ran to. They were the ones we could talk to when our parents wouldn't listen. Yes, they were outnumbered because their peers had left all their friends for dead on the battlefield of the War on Drugs and the War on Information. They are the nurses that administered to those that no one else would touch during the AIDS epidemic. They watched as their conservative counterparts allowed the artists and the thinkers and the writers and the dreamers to die, cut off from needed healthcare and innovative measures by their government.

So they retreated to the universities and kindergartens and taught us to paint and to write and to dream and to think. They told us that we could be anything we wanted to be and that we were special. They told us to think big and to shoot for the stars. They read us stories where women were presidents and taught us about leaders that changed the world. They couldn't outnumber their conservative peers but they could train up the next generation and prepare us for a fight we didn't even know was coming. Suddenly, those college loans were feeling worth every penny. I had been training under General Ortega the whole time and I didn't even know it. They were getting us ready for battle. They gave us *1984* and the *Handmaid's Tale* and *Animal Farm* and *Fahrenheit 451.* They made us watch *Schindler's List* in class. They fought for sex education and gave us condoms and told us to protect ourselves. They gave us all the information that our parents had been hiding from us. They were the ones who had the AV kids run the televisions into the rooms as the towers fell so that we could see, so we could learn, so we could be ready for this moment and the battle in front of us.

They were the okay boomers.

Across the room my ears zeroed in on a familiar cackle. I looked up and saw there was Joy standing by the entrance to the large room we were all filing into. She was signing some piece of paper giving emails, making donation commitments, and she was so lovely. Our lives were weaving together again in this constant back and forth dance of maybe somedays and tomorrows. I made my way across the room to her.

"Hey." *Classic move, idiot,* I thought.

"Fancy seeing you here. We have to quit meeting like this, people are going to talk."

"Yeah, well. I have to come and make my twenty-seven dollar average donation. Just doing my part." I was a bumbling fool. It was funny how, after all these years, I was still just that nervous kid who thought she was the most perfect person in the whole world. Nothing had changed that. We weren't together because of anything other than my own fear. Fear to commit, fear to let go, fear of adventures.

I used to tell myself that we never drifted apart because of a lack of love. That's what I would always tell people when they asked, "It wasn't for a lack of love." But that's a goddamn lie. If I had loved her more and more completely, I would have done things differently. I could have done more, even though I had less.

Maybe it was the fear of fascism rising, maybe it was finally getting older, but I was ready to make a change. To take a chance. Who knew what tomorrow was going to bring? These fuckers wanted to tear our republic down brick by brick and if given the chance, just at the saying of a word, they would do it. When was I going to ever get to live if not today?

"I did something kind of wild," I said with pride.

"Oh? I'm all ears." Joy leaned in.

"I got my passport."

"Shut up! I am in shock."

"Yeah, so I was curious. Would you like to get some Mexican food?"

"I don't mean to alarm you, Leo, but we are currently at a Mexican food restaurant and it looks like you are, in fact, already eating Mexican food." She tapped me on the back like I was in need of being ushered out by the medic.

"Yeah, I know, but I was thinking somewhere a bit more authentic. Just about thirteen hours to the border. If we leave now, we could be eating lunch in Mexico."

She gave me that, "who are you and what have you done with Leo?" kind of look. She grabbed a plate at the buffet and we drank margaritas and laughed with our new teacher friends. We closed the place down and an Uber came to pick us up and we drifted over to familiar ground. We sat at the All Saints and talked about the state of the world and our hopes for our daughter. We were lost in time and lost in this moment. The lights clicked on.

Closing time.

"Listen, Leo, were you serious about going to Mexico?"

I was tired and drunk and terrified she was going to ask me to drive to the border right that very minute. "Yes, I was. I mean I am. I am. I am ready to do it."

"I am glad you are growing. You are going to make someone very happy someday." She kissed me on the cheek.

I wondered if this was it. Was this the moment I was dreading when I was going to have to realize I had used up all the chances and I had finally crossed over that invisible line called the last chance at some point and didn't see it, didn't know it, but she had finally, truly moved on? It would be only fair. It wasn't her responsibility to wait around for me to finally get it together. But I wasn't ready yet to let this all go. I wanted so desperately for there to be some other chapter in this story. She was out there writing a whole new book and here I was stuck on chapter thirty-eight of high school. There she was, walking away again.

She turned around. "Hey Leo."

"Yeah!" I stood up.

"Don't lose that passport or let it expire… I'm going to cash in on that adventurous spirit you've found someday." With that she winked and vanished.

And as she walked away this time all I could hear in my head was Jim Carrey screaming, "So you're telling me there's a chance!" My life was a meme.

Chapter Seven

Summer Anthem

From spring break to the end of August the Gulf Coast becomes one massive party. Even as a local it is hard not to get caught up in the chaos and the wonder of the lights and the nostalgic MTV atmosphere that the community suddenly transforms into. Like most things in life, you never know what will be your first or your last. Wild nights full of tequila and sweat would morph into long weeks of hedonism. You would spend most days working hungover, serving up meals and drinks to eager tourists looking for fuel to compel them into the next bender of days dancing to live music along the boardwalk that would melt into rhythmic nights with raging DJs mixing hot tunes and indiscretion.

Southern summers are a wholly unique experience and it's no wonder that people travel all over the world to party with the wildest locals that the United States of America has to offer. Would you like to get a henna tattoo from an alligator doing shots of 151? We can make that happen. Come get your fortunes read while you step into abject uncertainty. "Here we are now, entertain us," the hordes would scream and we would be all too happy to provide them with their Southern fried fantasies for a gratuity. From the blizzard of beads flying across flashing flesh in New Orleans all the way down to the Cuban nights of Miami, the emerald beaches of the Gulf Coast provided a central resting zone to a myriad of beachside cultures inspired by Spanish, French, and Caribbean settlers and immigrants. Sun-kissed bodies of every shape and size lined the beaches as the waves crashed orgasmically against the crystal white sands.

Of all the sins and sweet summer nights, nothing is more decedent and hedonistic than the suicidal dance with death known as the hurricane party. This is a party planned by the gods themselves and comes with limited warning. As soon as the fates decide that the waters are warm enough and the winds begin to sing their howling song, it's time to choose the location of your death. The nightclubs and bars begin their process of boarding up and hiding their valuables. The sudden run on the liquor stores begins and you'll be lucky to find a red solo cup anywhere along the coast.

For whatever reason, the year we decided to try to fuck around and find out with nature was September 2004.

There was an eccentric business man who had built a house on the beach that he promised would be hurricane-proof. The place looked like someone had taken a massive golf ball and dropped it into the sand and then attached dueling staircases in an attempt to class the joint up. It was a bizarre dome, the interior of which was quintessentially beachside, full of bleached-white couches, turquoise dentists' office paintings, and surf boards that would never feel a wave hanging above the doors. Shane knew the owner, of course, and gave him a call asking if he could borrow the house for the hurricane to have a party. He told the guy that he would write up a story about how well the dome home stood up to the storm. "You know, if we survive." The owner inexplicably handed over the keys to us and we invited a few people to join us.

The thing about living in a small Southern town like this is that there really ain't much going on and all it takes is the smallest nudge to turn a Walmart parking lot into a full-on rager. You throw in the promise of prescription pills, a crawfish bowl, or the chance to yell, "Hey y'all, watch this!" and you've got yourself a bonafide historical event to be added to the pantheon of local legend. Many a hapless college student has been eulogized for thinking they could keep up with the spirits of the Redneck Riviera.

"Here lies Ashley, she was just trying to see if this party was cool."

Nick was the last one to arrive. He opened the door and popped only his head inside. He had a look of genuine concern on his face as the waves were lapping up the sand like candy outside. There were already palm trees rocking in the wind and you could see he was doing the best he could to contain the door from flying away from him.

"Uh, Shane?" Nick yelled over the howling wind.

"Hey buddy! You made it!" Shane screamed back, already holding a shot of some ungodly mixture he was calling the Ivan.

"Yeah, me and a couple of others. How many people did you invite?"

Shane, Clementine, Joy, and I rushed to the front windows that overlooked the beach and no matter which direction we looked, there were cars. There were girls in bikinis and guys wearing short shorts that defied gravity, all carrying cases of beer, and there were other folks carrying stacks of pizza boxes as high as their heads. This was suddenly a teen movie. The three of us slowly turned our heads in unison in the direction of Shane who had a shit-eating grin on his face and just shrugged an oops at us.

Within moments the entire dome was an official event. There was some dude playing DJ and a guy pouring shots and taking orders at the built-in bar. Someone had brought a ping pong table with him and people were playing beer pong. All three levels of the house were filled with bodies, alcohol, and music. The entire place took on a life of its own and we had, without question, lost control.

Some dude in the corner was playing "Wonderwall" to no one in particular.

As the winds outside began to howl and roar like a monstrous beast was about to consume us all, the music just roared and raged back louder. It was human innovation challenging God. We were Babel and Babylon. The entire place was throbbing with sex and drugs. There was no way to control it and so we just gave into the energy as it engulfed us. The music pulsated through every inch of our bodies and we released ourselves into its tantric indulgences. You weren't dancing with anyone, you were dancing with everyone.

The hive mind of humanity blended into a cohesive micro universe within our dome and everyone took their stances. Bartenders set up stations throughout the house to ration drinks and ice and make sure everyone was quenching their thirst. The pizza guys teamed up with the wing and sub guys and set up a cafeteria. They all had tip jars and money was flowing. We should have charged a door cover.

Unlike the movies, we actually knew all of these people. Maybe we didn't know them well or they weren't really friends, but by kin or legend we were all part of the same story of the circulating self-disparagement that flowed in the waters from the Mississippi to the Gulf of Mexico. There was James, the guy who played in some band each weekend at The Grind. I had never spoken to him, but I had made out with Jenny over there against the book cases in the corner while they played. I had just seen Mark walk by, he survived a suicide attempt and everyone at school had been glad he did but didn't know what to say. We all knew one another's stories, we had told them a thousand times, anecdotes of haphazard youths and failures to launch into college. Someone bumped into me and said, "How goes it?" and walked on. Wasn't that the girl with the weird name that ran away from home and put her baby up for adoption in California? Or maybe she took on a drug cartel in Mexico. I can't remember. These were our stories. We had been sharing them long before Twitter or Facebook. If you wanted to know what Jason did to Kat after their breakup, just head on over to the corner store for some bad pizza and to bum a cigarette. Now we all cloistered into this massive miniature Earth to seal our fates. A lot of people were about to become parents tonight.

Then, suddenly, it was dark.

There is no blackness this side of the earth's crust as dark as the sudden loss of all light as an angry sky is entirely covered by the hand of a wrathful god. We were Sodom and Gomorrah's ugly stepchild and challenging the creator to see if they really meant it when they said they would never flood the entire earth again. Bet? Maybe we would all be consumed into the belly of a massive wale. Honestly, I couldn't take three days off, but then again, I could have used the vacation. Within literal moments everyone's phones and lighters began to light the room with a robotic green hue. A noise rose up from within the crowd as every voice broke out in unison like a choir from hell and began to continue the music. Everyone was writhing like a rhythmic monolith. It was one of the most strange and beautiful sights I had ever seen. If God was going to strike us dead in this moment then we were going to bring the party straight to the pearly gates ready for our judgment day.

Out of the indiscernible number of hands and hips and thighs that were carnally gyrating to their own beat an arm extended through all the flesh and grabbed me by the collar and pulled me close. It was Nick.

"We are going to die!" he screamed.

"What!" I screamed right back.

"Look!" he said, pointing outside, and shoved a Maglite into my chest.

He pushed me through the piles of skin as we made our way to the front of the house and I flashed it on. Through all the rain and the chaos I could see that the sand and the roads were gone. Just as I was slowly processing this information I heard a loud scream behind me.

"My car!" someone shouted and the entire population of creation stormed the front of the building. I imaged this massive ball just coming un-wedged and us floating off into the consuming wilds of the waters as Tom Hanks screamed, "Wilson!" Just as this happened, we watched as one by one the cars began to float away in a chorus. Over the screeching winds there was a cacophony of metal scraping against metal as the cars joined us in a metallic orgy.

People began to panic and someone went for the door but was tackled before they opened it. I suddenly became afraid of where Joy and Clementine were. Like a true hero, Shane appeared out of the darkness and took my hand. We rushed around the room, with Nick in tow, as lights flickered and flashed from phones and rogue flashlights. We were looking in each and every direction. We found Clementine first.

"Where is Joy?" I screamed at the top of my lungs.

"I don't know!" Clementine yelled directly into my ear. "I lost her half an hour ago and then I just panicked and couldn't move."

We formed a human chain of the four of us as we all held each other tight. Nick was holding my hand so tightly. For all of our faults, we were family. This was family. No matter our disagreements or fights, when one of our kin was in trouble, this was how we responded. In a few days, a similar chain would be formed as the Cajun Navy would scour the muddy waters fighting gators and cottonmouths to search for survivors. Nick looked terrified as we searched the house looking for Joy. Eventually, we found her on the top floor. She was in the last room that was still alive with excitement. Someone had a battery powered boombox and had kept the party going. We grabbed her and the five of us huddled together. Just then, the entirety of downstairs screamed like a collective Jamie Lee Curtis. We rushed over to one of the windows as we watched the house on the western side of the building disintegrate into literal nothingness, consumed by a hungry Gulf.

From the best we could see the entire island was under water. We were at least a story up in the air but who knew how long the storm would last or what would happen if the waters breached the building. All I could imagine was the building falling apart and hundreds of us being rushed out to sea. This was a *Titanic*-level fuck-up and there wasn't enough room on the door for all of us.

"We need to pray!" Nick yelled.

"Fuck that, we need to sing!" Joy yelled.

At that moment she ran down the stairs and we all followed. People were running in every direction toward absolutely nothing. We were surrounded and there was nowhere to go. Buildings were crashing all around us and at any moment this building could be next. What had moments ago felt like a complete cohesion of the human spirit was quickly devolving into the worst parts of us. People were scared. There was a girl who had fallen on the floor and was in serious danger of being trampled.

This is how we die, I thought.

Joy had centered the five of us in the middle of the room.

"Just do what I do!" Joy screamed at us and we all circled back to back and holding hands. Honestly, if this was how we died, I couldn't have imagined a better way. Here we all were, entangled as we might be, holding one another closely. Heaven was welcome to take us or reject us, this was paradise. Finally, Joy lifted up her voice over the crowd and everyone stopped for just a moment in the middle of the chaos. "Every night in my dreams I see you, I feel you…"

Then, without hesitation, one by one everyone else joined in. "That is how I know you go on!"

The room began to calm. Lighters went up into the air and the crowd of hundreds of scantily clad twenty somethings began to sway back and forth in the storm. We may have been the ones they didn't build life rafts for but we weren't going to go out without our voices being heard. Joy's hand held me tightly as if to say, "I'll never let go, Jack." For nearly five minutes we all sang together as we swayed back and forth with the dance of the storm. Then the winds stopped raging, the waters calmed. We were in the eye of the hurricane. Everyone suddenly rushed outside and looked up at the stars as the sky opened to show the beauty right in the middle of the storm.

"Have you ever seen something so beautiful!" Joy exclaimed.

Yes, I thought. I couldn't even look up. Her eyes were the only stars I needed to see. Her face shone brighter than any moon. I was a fool in love.

It would be almost a week before us and our hundred closest friends were evacuated off the island. We rationed food and FEMA made an MRE drop. We all bathed in the salt water and did the best we could not to kill each other. The time after the storm was one of the most powerful experiences in humanity. It was a lesson in what it means to be a neighbor. No electricity, no cell phone service, just humans touching humans. We all had to step up and figure out how to make this impromptu community survive. After those days passed us by, we almost didn't want to reintegrate back into society. But they had to get us back off the island. The entire youth population was trapped in a singular location and these burgers weren't going to flip themselves.

***

Life is not that unlike a hurricane. You have limited time to prepare as the storm rolls in. There is never any telling which buildings will crumble under its weight or why certain structures are permitted to live on for a hundred years and watch all the destruction happen around them. I think it would be safe to say I struggled with a lot of survivor's guilt. All of it slowly ate away at my insides and crippled me from within. How come I was still standing amidst the storm while Shane and Clementine were washed away? It was enough to make you furious at existence. There were days when I would go without ever thinking about it and then, without warning, the howling winds of guilt would come rushing in like an unforgiving cloud of self-destruction.

If I were to analyze it with any level of honesty what I felt the most guilt over was that I was too afraid to live the life that I know they would have wanted me to. There are plenty of things I could pass blame off to and claim as circumstantial. But my inaction, that was my own and I could only blame myself.

But as the bitter bites of winter were finally fading away you could smell the salt air washing over from the island and toward downtown. We would soon be coated in a thick fog of humidity and possibility.

If spring break was the precursor to the wild abandon of the beach life, Memorial Day Weekend was the true jump off into the full chaos of summer. Whereas the rest of the country would be celebrating with Miller Lights, hot dogs, and American flags, the entirety of our little island would be taken over by over 20,000 LGBTQ+ travelers who were partaking in one of the longest lasting queer American traditions.

We were one of the many stops along a massive route of gay circuit parties held along many towns in the South from Atlanta to Miami and then making their way back up the coast and ending with Southern Decadence at the end of the summer in New Orleans. For one amazing weekend, the whole island became a powerhouse dance party. Drag performers from all over the country would fly in and there were parties from one end of the beach to the other and by now the party had spilled over into the city.

I had secured a full weekend pass because of all the parties and cultural events now advertising with our paper. Maybe I couldn't convince Joy to run off to Mexico with me but she might be interested in reliving our youth just a little bit and having a weekend we would never forget but could barely remember.

"I have VIP passes for all weekend next weekend. Want to be irresponsible?" I texted.

Later that day, I got a reply back. "You really know how to sweet talk a girl. Let's do it."

The worst part about having plans, for me, is that all of a sudden every single day is a miserable slow moving train of antici … pation. I wished I could have just gone to bed and slept until it was time for us to meet up. I spent the final minutes waiting for Joy to meet me at my office pacing outside smoking through one too many cigarettes. My phone buzzed in my pocket. "Running late. Dropping Clementyne off at my parents'. They will keep her the whole weekend! WHAT! Let's get fucked up."

In the entirety of our time together, Joy and I maybe only had two whole weekends with grandparents watching our kid. One of those weekends, we had to actually end things early because they got invited to some function. So really only one whole uninterrupted time to ourselves. This would be totally unique for us. After forty-five minutes, Joy arrived and she looked fantastic. She had gone completely all out and was ready to party. I knew this look. I had seen it a thousand times and had failed her at every point. Every birthday, anniversary, but this time was different: I was ready to actually let go.

The question became, "What to do first!"

We decided to start in town. We took in an amazing documentary downtown at the community theatre, which had been turned into a makeshift film festival. There was an improv group that was doing a performance at one of the bars and we had an amazing time. I even got called up on stage and completely participated my cold heart out. I wished in that moment that Clementine could see that I could do a dare every once in a while. Eventually, we decided we needed to get out to the beach or we might not be able to do. It took the better part half an hour to make our way to the hotel room that we had. It was comped by one of the parties the paper had agreed to promote. It was the most invaluable thing ever because parking was an absolute beast if you didn't have a reservation.

The second we got out of the car we were covered in rainbows and pride and the bass was beating deep down into our hearts. Joy looked at me with a "that's the party" look and we rushed across the street to one of the restaurants that had been turned into a nightclub for the weekend. As we made our way inside we were suddenly wearing far too much clothing. The party was a rhythmic ride of humanity.

"LEO!" I heard shouting from nowhere in particular. I looked around and then Alexandria jumped out of the crowd.

"Holy shit!" She gave me a big kiss. "I can't believe you are here! This is fantastic."

Just then Joy emerged from behind a group of dancers. Alexandria looked like she had just won the entire lottery. She leaned into my ear and pulled me close.

"Leo, don't fuck this up. Please, for me! That girl is looking at you some kind of different tonight. Don't let love flow away from you again, you deserve to be happy." She slapped me on the butt. "Don't! Just don't! It's our weekend, baby!"

Alexandria gave Joy a big kiss and sprinkled her with some glitter and disappeared into the crowd like the fae goddess that she is. For all the loss I have experienced in life, I cannot downplay the gains. Alexandria and Blake were angels that came into my life and lifted my broken soul up. I hoped that I had done the same for them too. Nothing can replace the things or people we have lost in our lives. But there is so much beauty out there in the world and it's so easy to let our hearts choke out and not let them open back up to new people and experiences. Our hurts can create ideologies and systems that prevent us from moving forward. That is a fate worse than death … to be alive but not living.

Joy grabbed my hand and said, "Dance with me."
And I said yes.

CHAPTER EIGHT

PARTICIPATION TROPHIES

I t takes a particular level of talent to be as profoundly bad at sports as I am. This did not prevent my parents from continuing to put me on sports ball teams in a vain attempt to coerce me into becoming "more manly." Of course, this didn't work. Instead, it resulted in me frequently crying in the dugout and desperately pining for a shaving Ken doll so that I would be able to play with Clementine and Joy when I was finally released from the Colosseum of screaming parents begging for the blood of adolescents to be spilt upon the diamond.

"Are you sure this is what you want for your birthday?" my mother asked, attempting desperately to be understanding.

"Yes!" I gleefully exclaimed, standing in the doll isle ogling the shaving Ken.

"Maybe we can give him to you after the party?" she inquired.

"Why? This is the coolest toy!"

The entire team was at my birthday party. I waited in anticipation, hoping, praying that inside that rectangular box was, in fact, that most perfect man I had ever seen. Could it be? As I tore through each present, I had a baseball glove and a new bat and some sunglasses. I saved what I hoped would be the best for last. As I grabbed the present, my father excused himself to go get another beer. I'll never understand why they sold beer and alcohol at Chuck-E-Cheese. Did they really hate being parents so much they couldn't even celebrate the reminder of our birth sober? I didn't care!

There was his amazing face, that so cool hoodie, and the razor. My God! I would no longer be segregated in my play with my friends. I wouldn't have to be Felicity anymore and disproportionately tower over the Barbies. No, my dreams had finally come true. Some of the guys on the team giggled. One muffled, "Faggot," under his breath. My dad agreed, without saying a word. Little did I know I had just damned myself to another year of sports. Maybe one more year of chasing other boys around with balls would straighten me out.

I once struck out playing t-ball.

After the entire crowd watched my spectacular failure at hand/eye coordination, I was encouraged to "take a walk" around the bases. The kids from the other team watched me as I passed each muddied white square as they scowled and stared. After my walk of shame past home plate, I took my place on the bench. We weren't given a point. I suppose the purpose of the exercise was to let me know how amazing it would feel to finally not suck. If I just tried a little harder, paid a little more attention, applied a little more focus, then I too could make a glorious run around this field of dreams and be declared a champion.

As each game would come to an end, we would line up facing the other team and take a long walk past each other, shaking hands, and liturgically saying, "Good game." This, of course, taught us sportsmanship. We were losers, but we weren't going to be sore losers. Then we would line up again as the ref would hand out small trophies to each of us so we could squint out smiles for a gratuitous photo to be hung in the office of whatever local joint happened to be sponsoring our team. We would take our miniature plastic gold tone statues and head out to get pizza.

What a bunch of stupid chubby kids we were just accepting these trophies on behalf of the entitlement of our parents. They weren't for us, they were for them. If we had had any level of foresight we would have returned them or burned them. How could we have known that years down the line these trophies would be used as weapons against us? Their little bodies would be boiled down into bullets to shoot our dreams with.

Every single trophy and plaque and silly little print out with gold stars on them would become kindling for a fire that would rage into a war on our entire generation. We wanted healthcare, not because our teeth were rotting out of our faces but because of trophies. If we just hadn't been handed these unearned rewards then we wouldn't want to receive due compensation for selling our time as line cooks and teachers and nurses. Now, this may just be the communism speaking, but is it possible that if they had actually taught us skills, how to do our taxes, science, and sex education in our schools, we wouldn't be wandering around lost in a world that we were never prepared for?

No, now we wanted to be paid consummate wages for our labor and it was all the fault of those trophies that we didn't ask for.

Not to be a socialist, Daddy, but maybe if you hadn't spent all that money shoving us into sports we weren't good at and instead put that money into a college fund for the children you chose to have then we wouldn't be drowning in student debt. It wasn't about being entitled to anything, it was about access. Last I checked, participation trophies, affirmative action, unions, matching

401Ks, those were all policies y'all fought for. Now we were being raked over the coals for wanting just a taste of some of the sweet nectar of opportunities that bought you that retirement home in Boca.

It was sure easy to get a little bitter about the whole thing when we watched not one but two presidential elections go to the second-place winner. The Electoral College, the second biggest participation trophy. It doesn't matter that more than half the country wanted someone else other than Bush or Trump; we had to line up against the other team and just smile and say, "Good game." Except there wasn't going to be any pizza party, just soup kitchen lines and a body count.

I suppose the secret to success might have been hidden under our desks and that's why we were told to spend so much time under them in school. But in real life, we didn't have the luxury of hiding from the bullets. Instead we had to take the punches and hope that we would die before our medical bills put us on the streets.

Just like the games we played in school, the awards weren't given out to the winners because the game was rigged. Purge the roles; make it against the rules to vote if you've been arrested for felonies; make healthcare inaccessible, also make drugs illegal. You can't snuff out the pain but you can't afford the legal drugs of the affluent. An intentional and systemic game of monopoly called life that was really just a poker hall on Wall Street.

They'll mock you for playing scratch offs while they live off dividends. The whole economy is one massive pyramid scheme and our parents are still dumb enough to think they'll get the pink Cadillac someday. Sorry, they gave it to Don Jr.

Not being shot by the police, having access to education, employment, healthcare, childcare, abortion, the ability to protest, journalism, marrying who you wish, housing, these aren't participation trophies. They are basic human rights. Saying we were entitled is the biggest gaslight of all time. Of course we are entitled! It's written into the very framework of everything we were taught as children. We are supposed to be able to have life, liberty, and the pursuit of happiness. But you can't very well do that with lead in your back. Yes, I am entitled. I am entitled to live; I am entitled to eat; I am entitled to have a roof over my head; I am entitled to see a doctor. Not because of some $3 trophy made by kids in China but because it's the right goddamn thing to do. Because it's what you got.

It was you who wanted the trophy, you're just mad that we wanted to take it with us when we moved out.

***

The proverbial they always say, "Scent is the sense most associated with memory." As I walked in through those doors, the smell of axe, stale delivery, and the lonely cum of five desperate men was not one I wanted forever etched in my memory. How was it possible, in my mid-thirties, I was back living here with these guys? This house was frozen in time, just waiting to welcome me back as the failure to launch that I truly was. After the breakup with Joy, it was back to this. On the weekends when I had Clementyne, we would stay at my office. This was my life. I was just doing the best I could with what was available to me. All of us were.

It turns out the bank doesn't give a shit how many trophies you got in middle school; they still won't give you a loan. No, our parents had short sold our futures. The subprime market now meant that we were a generation of pseudo-homeless vagabonds. These borrowed roofs over our heads paid for the vacations of our parents' friends.

My father liked to constantly remind me that he put himself through college, purchased his first house and a car for $500 with his weekend job. The way I figured it, by rate of inflation and hours worked, I should have been able to afford a mansion and a yacht by now. Somehow, the math wasn't working out like that. Maybe I was under my desk the day they taught that in school.

Nick seemed to always side with the parents over us. The noted exception was when he infiltrated the paper, or at least sold us out, whatever the case might be. He always leaned toward the side of the oppressor. I never understood that. He would rail about entitlement and trophy syndrome, but wasn't religion the original participation trophy? Say a prayer, eat a piece of bread, and sprinkle some water on your head and you get to go to Heaven. It doesn't matter what you did or how well you treated your neighbor.

It's almost like they couldn't see the disconnection between how angry they got at us for wanting the basic tools to survive and their own sense of entitlement. From Heaven to the White House, they demanded ultimate access! Yet, we were the villains for just wanting to be able to eat or have personal hygiene products.

Shane and the newly minted Father Nicholas once had it out about the whole concept.

"Don't you think it's odd that people want all these unearned rewards on the backs of someone else's labor?" Nick said as he took a chug of a light beer. He was the only light beer drinker amongst us. The lightest thing any of us drank was vodka.

Shane shook his head and couldn't contain his laughter. "Are you serious? You are preaching that people shouldn't have what you've got? You get hurt, what happens? Your insurance, paid by the diocese, covers it. You live in a free house, get regular vacations; your college was paid for by a diocesan scholarship for Christ's sake."

Nicholas shot him that, "lord's name in vain" look.

"All I'm saying is you get everything and it's all paid by a 10% tax you place on everyone for a place at the table of the Lord. And here I thought that one person paid the entire debt for the wrongs of the world, rich or poor, and you think people should suffer temporally in this life so that the richest institution in the world can afford to look humble on the backs of Mother-fucking-Teresa."

Nicholas never punched Shane, but I was always pretty sure he mentally added a couple of years to his sentence in purgatory. Nick would rail about all of the entitlements we already had and something about separation of Church and state just before he would excuse himself early so he could make it to the abortion clinic protest to raise funds to overturn Roe v. Wade.

As if the entitlement of our education had anything to do with being taught anything. No, we weren't sent to school to learn how to succeed, we were sent to school so our parents could go to work and then one day we could go to work. We were being assembly lined so that one day Jeff Bezos could buy another island and Elon Musk could go to Mars. We were told, of course, that these were the kids who didn't get handed trophies. They were the ones who fought really hard, knew the rules, and they won the bigger trophies fair and square. They built the businesses out of a one-car garage and with nothing more than a dream. One day, we too could ascend to such heights if we just applied ourselves.

I suppose the millions that Trump was given as a launching pad had nothing to do with it? It couldn't possibly have been the fact that he was able to avoid the draft while poor kids went off to fight yet another senseless war. No, just pure grit.

Some nights, when I'm hungry or unsure if the five of us will be able to scrape it together to pay the light bill, I wonder what would happen if I was given a million dollars and one of these billionaires was just thrown out to the streets to fend for themselves. One study argued that they would ultimately end up in the same place. That if everyone was put on a level playing field, the 1% would still end up top and we would all be scraping along.

I suppose that might be true, it isn't just access to wealth. Maybe in order to level the playing field accurately, you would need to spend decades lowering their self-esteem, telling them that they should be thankful for what they get, that they will never succeed, give them felony and a traumatic brain injury.

No second-place winners, just one big trophy for the champion and then everyone else can just slowly starve to death on the streets while they watch them eat McDonald's on fine china. That's a reality show I would watch. Just kidding, it's the one we are all starring in.

Chapter Nine

The Occupation

In the years following the death of our friends, the world seemed to just turn forward, completely indifferent to my own pain and suffering. The chaos from the economic crash still echoed well into the new decade. The struggle from the market collapse maneuvered its way from the top to the bottom. Trickle-down economics never led to the bottom half of the country ever seeing an increase in wealth, but it certainly resulted in them seeing an increase in poverty. As the rafters began to shake in the house that Wall Street built, golden parachutes were given out to the executives, and just like the *Titanic*, there weren't enough boats to save the poorest of us. Though many within the middle class began to feel the quakes rapidly, it would take years before the full-blown effects of the crash made their way into the poorest neighborhoods.

One of my professors in college said, "Sympathy is theory. It's the ability to share in someone's misfortune from afar. It isn't pricking your finger; it's flinching because someone else did. There is a danger of condescension within sympathy. Empathy is not theory but understanding. Empathy is knowing the pain because you've pricked your finger before; you don't have to imagine the pain … you've felt it. Both sympathy and empathy are dangerous, though, in that they are both a form of commiseration. It's just people feeling sorry for themselves and others. Revolution is born when the finger pricker knocks down your door with the needle."

We had all seen our neighbors suffer and we felt sympathy for them. We had all suffered in certain ways under the Great Recession, loss of tips, loss of wages, gas prices soaring, jobs disappearing. But it wasn't until those needle prickers showed up at my front door that I was fully aware of what it meant to want revolution.

Joy and I were deep in the throes of figuring out what it meant to be a family. It was a challenge full of poverty and diapers and uncertainty. One day in late August of 2011, a knock came on our door. The baby was crying in another room, refusing to go to sleep for her afternoon nap. She had just in that moment quieted when the disruptive thud hit the doorframe. The crying quickly began again and so Joy jumped off our secondhand couch and ran to the broom closet/nursery. I made my way toward the door and found a stout man in khakis and a button-up white shirt that hung out on one side. His belt was partially hidden under his belly. He was holding something in his hands.

"Listen, we aren't religious and aren't interested." I began to close the door.

"Sir, are you Mike Johnson?" he quickly squeaked in his confusion at my remark.

"No. That's my landlord," I said as I pulled the creaking door back open slightly.

"Do you have an address for him?" the man inquired.

"No, I don't. Is something wrong?"

"Well, I am here to serve a notice. He is more than three months behind on his mortgage and, well, I need to find Mr. Johnson." He handed me a piece of paper.

I stood there reading it for a long time. I scoured every single word trying to process in my mind what was going on. Joy came in holding our toddler in her arms. The man was looking at me intently like he wanted to sprint but was frozen. I was so very confused. We had been paying rent every single month. We were never even late once. Every single month we scraped it together. We had made tremendous sacrifices to make this work. We never bothered our landlord with small issues. When the dryer went out, we repaired it. The floor had a squeaky spot in the center and I did the research and found a way to lift it up using spray foam by drilling a small hole in between the panels. We were good tenants working hard to make sure that "our" home was in good repair. We owned nothing but took ownership of this space as if it was ours.

"Hold on," I said to the man, never even looking up to him, my eyes were glued to the piece of paper. He tried to say something and I just put one finger up to hush him and walked into the house. I looked in the junk drawer and around in the drawers of the computer desk. I finally found a little envelope that had all our receipts from paying rent. Every single month, Mike would drop by and we would pay him. He wrote on some little carbon receipt paper book and pulled out a little yellow slip for us. We had been renting there almost two years, we moved in just before Clementyne was born. Every receipt, thousands and thousands of dollars spent to pay someone else's mortgage, they were all right there. Proof that we had been doing the right thing.

I walked back to the door and handed the receipts to the guy.

"Here," I said as I put them toward him.

"Sir, I don't doubt that you've been paying." He looked upset for us. "I just… There is nothing I can do with these. That's not my job. I just need to know how to get a hold of Mike Johnson."

"Man, we met him here when we rented the place. He always just comes and picks up the rent. I don't have any info on him. What are we supposed to do?" I was desperate.

"I don't know."

"Do we have to move?"

"I don't know."

"How long do we have?"

"I don't know."

"Well, who fucking does know?"

The man made apologies as he slowly backed off of our stairs and scuttled off to his busted-ass car. Poor people tossing other poor people out because of other people's poor decisions. Was I even supposed to be mad at Mike? Every single one of us had been preyed upon in some way. Billionaires playing roulette with all our futures. They fucking bet against us, they hoped we failed. They made billions of dollars because we failed!

I sat alone on the couch and waited for Joy to return. The baby was quiet in the peace of her little sleep in her tiny little room. For the second time in our short lives together, I was handing Joy a piece of paper announcing we had to leave. Were any of us not homeless? Sure, we had roofs over our heads, but what was the difference? We didn't own anything. Just panhandling for tips so we could buy another beer and hope we had another night in some borrowed shelter until the cops come to tell us to move on. Just different tiers of the same crumbling cake. We silently wept in fear, not knowing what to do next, not knowing where to go. Neither of our parents would let us move back with them. We didn't have any sort of savings. Every single month we would overdraft at some point. We were broke. Mike was broke. The guy who was looking for Mike was broke. We couldn't stay but we couldn't go.

For the last few months, I had been working hard to resurrect the *Panhandle Free Press* but I was finding it hard to find stories I wanted to tell. There was no money in it, yet. It was just a dream. A hope to keep the memory of my friends and our ambition alive. Suddenly, just like my professor said, I found the words of revolution. I was ready to go on this journey. I was angry. *This is what my friends died for? This is what we were scrimping for? Working ourselves to the bone so that others could get rich and then gamble our livelihood and homes away?*

Fuck that.

On September 17th, a cry went up in New York City and it rang out so loud. It echoed from the bell towers and steeples and bounced around until it waved across the Great Lakes and the wind shuffled through the stalks of corn in the Midwest. The cry turned into a song and they started to sing it way out on the West Coast too. They put a beat behind it and sent it on over to Texas and they added a little twang and tossed it on over to Louisiana to add a little spice and a prayer to St. Ann Rice. Pretty soon we were singing it right here too. Drums were beating, we were all singing, we didn't know what we were doing, but we all knew what we had to do.

#OccupyWallStreet

September 17th

Bring Tent.

We were the 99% and we were all royally fucked. The last thing you want in the universe is for everyone who disagrees to find a way to look toward a common enemy. But with a million new people facing homelessness and us all forming lines at soup kitchens, we suddenly looked like photos we saw in history books at school. The only difference was these stories weren't going to be told as hindsight. We had Twitter, YouTube, and Facebook. We had zero intentions of this being told as some lesson in a class decades from now. No, we were posting them ourselves in real time. The revolution couldn't be televised; the same people stealing our homes owned the platforms telling us what to think. The revolution would be Tweeted. #VivaLaResistanceBitches! They, the preverbal they, were not telling our stories anymore. We were telling our story. This was writing history as it happened. The shocking, ugly, gritty, raw, and uncensored.

A small but boisterous occupation began in my own town. I walked the halls of this centralized organization of unorganized and disenfranchised people with one simple demand: listen.

It was here, walking through those open halls of a sudden shanty town, that I began to find my own voice. I was no longer trying to be something else, to just carry on the memory of voices cut down too soon. I was ready to scream from my own rooftop and tell the truth I was seeing unraveling around me.

Day and night I basically lived at the occupation camp. I sat in during the general assembly each morning and evening and devoured the words of the sidewalk scholars and lecturers. There was electricity flowing through the place. I was doing a ride-along with one of the unofficial leaders of the local general assembly meeting when he and another passenger panicked. I looked around and then I saw it too. A large black SUV was following us. We were on our way to the library. They were doing an open forum on the demands of the occupation and had decided to use one of the free meeting rooms there so that anyone who was too afraid to come to the camp could come out and learn. This vehicle followed them the entire way and then, as they pulled into the parking lot of the library, it vanished.

These kids were ready to take on the biggest financial establishment the world had ever seen. It seemed they were hitting a nerve. I was too. Suddenly, the stories I was writing and telling were finding an audience that was ready and willing to listen.

They would bust up a camp and then another would pop up. Where are you going to displace the displaced to? This wasn't Republicans vs. Democrats. This was everyone. There was a universal feeling of being just absolutely pissed and the time to listen was now. This was going to be the protest to end all protests. We wanted to face it all down. Reform the prison system. Reform Wall Street. Reform the banking system. End homelessness. End the war. End the criminalization of drugs. Free college. Free healthcare. Free market. We were truly the 99%. We were singing as one nation and we were a unified front. We were going to win this battle! What could they possibly do to divide us now?

***

The song that began in Zuccotti Park and raged across the nation begged the question: has justice been served and what would justice look like? In 1999, I was doing drills hiding under desks in case an active shooter ever overtook our school. By 2009, I was filled with the elixir of hope and change. Now, here I was in 2019 flying to Washington, DC to be given a prestigious writing award for the takedown I wrote of Barack Obama in 2012. Just a few short years after his time in office and I was being praised for pointing out that the polish was rubbing off the old hope and change mantra and all that existed underneath was the same bullshit in another package.

I still liked President Obama as a person. I'm not so sure there is ever such a thing as a good president, just less bad ones; that in and of itself is maybe the crux of the problem. In spite of the criticism I wrote, I still voted for him again in 2012. I still campaigned and donated what I could. It was kind of weird to be recognized for a piece of work that I kind of abhorred. I still believed every word of it but I hated how it had been used. The year that article came out, I felt like I had hit the nerve because both my liberal friends and conservative acquaintances praised me for it. It would take years to unpack that those conservatives only appreciated it because they looked at me as a scab, a strikebreaker. I was a tool to be used and misquoted and taken out of context.

Fuck me, I guess. This was going to be my legacy. Countless hours sitting in front of a screen and writing my heart out and I was being rewarded for something that was stale. Nothing more that fish wrapping. It seemed even stranger now in the age of Trump. What value does my criticism of a remarkably flawed president like Obama matter when we are now facing driving off the cliff into fascism? Was I allowed to say fascism in my acceptance speech? Who knows.

Justice is such a novel idea, isn't it? I had rarely seen it in my own life. I think in America justice is like a craving for a food you've never actually tried and so you order something that sounds similar to what you are salivating for and just shrug. "This is close enough." But you've never actually tasted it. You don't even know what it tastes like. It's a food served in restaurants that you don't have the right clothing to enter and you couldn't afford to eat there. Sometimes, people from the middle class save just enough to eat at that table on special occasions but they are too uncultured to know to order it. They are just content to be in the same establishment as everyone else who is chomping down on the sweetness. Or is that not justice? It's just privilege, which is justice's aborted nephew. Maybe justice isn't on the menu anywhere. Maybe it's the one spice we didn't rape and pillage from some other continent.

Hopefully, someone will make an imitation version at some point so we can all afford some.

When the trial finally rolled around for Shane's killers, I was told it was justice. One brother got life and the other got twenty years for being considered "the dumb one." We sat on benches and watched from our spectators' row as those who had torn a life away from us were only feet away recounting their recollections of events. I remember watching as Shane's mom took the hand of her ex-husband. I watched him as he sweated tears from his pores and rage built up inside of him. I wondered what it would look like if he jumped over that banister that separated us. Did he want to? I wanted to. Could he beat that smug man's face? What would his beaten face look like, smashed in by fists of rage by a father in mourning? Would his own mother be able to recognize him? Would they have to cremate him like we did with Shane? Would he become nothing more than ash blowing back into the endless void of the recycling of life? Could Shane's father have made it all the way or would he have been tackled by the police officer guarding our civility? Would Shane's dad have been tased or shot or killed to protect the system of justice? Is that justice?

What about these boys? Were they products of a forgotten South? As they wove their stories and attorneys painted pictures of failed men, did that in some way absolve them? Two brothers, identical in every way except intelligence. Raised by parents stuck in a generational poverty passed down from time and Reconstruction. Grandfathers just waiting for another chance to fight Gettysburg, just one little rematch. They had been practicing the scrimmages on an endless ghostly repeat in re-enactments. They would get everything right this time, if given a second chance, everything would be just, minus the cause or the intent. So that embittered rage would become transactional, passing from generation to generation. The eroding Southern drama of angry men fighting the establishment in any way they could, waving the battle flag of a defeated Virginian militia. They would fight against education and healthcare and housing and wages and defeat themselves once again. Were these broken trailer park sons of the Confederacy deprived of access and education receiving justice in this sentencing?

Probably not, but I'd fucking take it.

So we've now all become accustomed to settling for something that rhymes with justice. Stuck in an endless loop of the lesser of two evils and party lines. So by the time a real evil began to rise up out of the sea to consume everything we had attempted to fight against, we were too divided and too blind to see it. Our hyperbole had finally caught up with us and just at the goddamn moment we needed everyone to see the beast for what it was, fucking Godwin's Law crept up to bite us in the ass.

No president is good. They all make horrible decisions. I probably would have killed Shane's murderers that day. I probably would have killed Osama bin Laden myself, given the chance. Instead, we elect presidents and governors and appoint cops and judges to do our killing for us. The meat industry of justice. As long as I don't have to see it, as long as I don't have to clean the carcass, I'll eat it. We hide behind our leaders and scream for blood and cheaper gas and, sure, maybe a couple of dead Iraqi children have to be lumped in as collateral damage, but I went to a fucking protest against the Iraq war and I wrote a goddamn piece condemning the president so it's not my fucking fault. My hands are clean!

I consume, therefore I am.

So we scream at our collection agents when they call and never take the time to think about the fact that they are prisoners being outsourced by the prison industrial complex. Just poor people screaming at other poor people. I wonder if someday I'll get a call and I'll scream and tell them they are an idiot and that they are all a bunch of corporate pigs and really I'll just be yelling at Shane's murderer in a jumpsuit wondering how he got here but never having been given the opportunity to truly analyze any of those questions when it mattered. Is that justice?

Then every four years we vote for our next war criminal and hope to God that they never decide we are the enemy.

When I wrote my piece condemning Obama for his actions against the Occupy protestors, it seemed like the most egregious thing I could imagine. How could this man, a man who I supported, turn his back on these hurting people like this? Yes, he didn't create the problem. He was supposed to arrive just in time to clean up the mess of a broken war and a broken system and a broken president with eight years of scorched earth doctrine. Instead, those crying out for justice were told to be silent and their leaders were followed by black SUVs and put on no-fly lists and treated like the dredges. Mostly because they were the dredges and how fucking dare they, you know? Who the fuck did The People think they were anyways? Go flip a burger with your college degree and be happy with the scraps you can pull out of the trash, peasant! We kneel on necks, not in front of flags around here. God Bless America and pass the bacon.

But standing here on the other side of a Trump presidency with no end in sight, did my rebuke feel still worthy of its word count? Yes, Obama could have handled Occupy differently, but he wasn't calling on supporters at rallies to beat Black Lives Matter protestors, so kind of what the fuck was I complaining about anyway?

Maybe therein lay the problem I was beginning to grapple with. In light of the Trump presidency, we started to dig up the Bush administration and prop it up as not that bad. I mean, the guy paints puppies and faces of soldiers he sent off to die so that his daddy's oil company could be doing alright. I mean, that's kinda cute, right? So now, was I not doing the same thing? Absolving Obama of a genuine wrong in my mind because I was now being faced with such an evil that I was begging to go back to the oppression I had once begrudged. Please, put me back in the injustices of yesterday lest we face a different injustice today. Were we becoming so afraid of the injustices we feared might come that we would be willing to shackle ourselves yet again to the wrongs of yesterday because they didn't seem nearly as scary as the bogeyman of fascism that was dawning on the horizon?

So we acquit Andrew Jackson as the worst president and absolve FDR of his concentration camps and forgive Bush for misplacing weapons of mass destruction and Saint Obama because we face a greater evil. Will we ever be able to condemn a president after this and what power are we giving those future presidents if we are just grateful never to be ruled by someone quite like Trump again?

Is this justice? Maybe not, but I sure could settle for a little bit of not feeling like the entire Republic might crash around me in an apocalyptic evangelical self-fulfilling prophesy.

So we continue to crave that flavor we've never actually tasted and walk into the nearest McDonald's and order whatever politician feels most safe. Yum, almost justice! It tastes just like the meat I didn't have to think about, the carcass I didn't have to clean, and the kids I never had to bomb.

I'd like the Happy Meal, please.

CHAPTER TEN

DEARLY BELOVED

I was sitting in my newly rented office space and sort of soaking in the reality of the legitimacy. It didn't make me a dollar richer to be sitting here but it felt like the right room for a lot of different reasons. The *Panhandle Free Press* had found a way to make itself a little niche and folks in town were starting to take it seriously. We were writing the stories that fit in between the margins of what the big papers were willing to tell. I was telling national stories in a local context. We were focusing on the way in which Wall Street was affecting those right here on Main Street and the side streets and the neighborhoods that needed new streets. I had to learn how to divorce myself from how things would have gone if Shane was still there or if Clementine was still managing. I had to just go in the direction that made the most sense to me.

In the office, I had Shane's photo up on the wall with a little gold plaque that read, "First Editor in Chief." Sometimes, on really rough days, I would look over at him and hope he would be proud. On my desk was a picture of Joy and our baby and my mom. There was also one of Clementine. It was a beautiful shot that Joy had taken on one of those wind-up disposable cameras. Clementine was covered in paint from head to toe and wearing these old jean overalls. Her hair was pulled back into a curly mess and she was there in front of her easel painting a beautiful woman. She sat there on my desk frozen in time with that smile of genuine happiness and peace.

Even after all these years, my heart was still split in two. Now it was more fractured into a million pieces. It was broken by more than just love that was lost or friends that were returned to the earth. It was fractures of betrayals and disappointments and failures. Little pieces of indecision and almost and maybes.

My phone rang.

"Are you watching the news?" Joy said with excitement in her voice.

"No, hold on." I grabbed the clicker and turned on the small TV set that was awkwardly placed on a stack of unpacked boxes that depressingly didn't have beer or liquor in them as was implied by their packaging.

It was a commotion of information and it took me a moment to focus in on what was happening. Then, there it was, an eruption of rainbow flags and beautiful kisses and brides in dresses. The Supreme Court had finally and decisively legalized marriage equality. We were living in history and it was hard not to let the lump well up in your throat. Finally, I let the tears fall.

"It's beautiful, isn't it?" Joy broke the silence of my tears.

"It really is. Who could have imagined? And there it is."

I looked over at Clementine there on my desk. In moments like this, I couldn't help but wonder what she would think of the world that was being created. In just six years since she left us we had plus-size models on the sides of buses and she would be free to marry who she chose. The world wasn't perfect, it was far from it, but it was moving forward. I would have loved to have seen her that day and heard the excitement in her voice at the country she feared finally carving out a little bit of space where she fit. We were far from where we needed to be, but we were marching toward it, slowly, surely, determinedly.

There was a beep in my ear. "I'll call you later, Alexandria is calling in."

"You don't need to call me back; I've got plans with the boyfriend tonight," Joy said. "I just wanted to be the first to tell you."

We said our awkward goodbyes and Alexandria and I made plans to head out that night to Wonderland, our local queer bar in town. There was going to be an impromptu celebration.

I picked Alexandria up from her house around 8:00 PM and we made our way down to Wonderland and listened to NPR on the drive. The excitement wasn't lost on me but I wasn't exactly sure what letter in the equality alphabet I fit under. I don't think I really ever thought of myself in that context but others did, especially my parents. It would be the understatement of the year to say my father was more than displeased by me dating Alexandria. I lived somewhere safely in feeling like I was in a heterosexual relationship all the while the rest of the world certainly didn't view me that way. There was a lot of transformation yet to be made before we got to where we needed to be as a country, and within me as well.

But today was a good day.

The party felt like a perfectly irreverent wedding reception. The drag show featured performers from Mobile to New Orleans and a few local favorites. They were all dressed in white dresses and veils, with the notable exception of the master of ceremonies who was dressed as the Pope. They performed to such notable works as "White Wedding" and "Like a Virgin." It was absolutely everything this day deserved and more. A bunch of Southerners finally being able to shake their fist at the establishment that had pushed them down, persecuted them, and killed them for just wanting to be themselves. Now we were all able to marry whomever we loved without having to flee to NYC. The religious world no longer owned the institution of marriage, it was for the people. All people.

I was many things, but a dancer was not one of them. Alexandria loved to dance. She was tearing up the floor and just basking in the glory of freedom. Freedom to choose, freedom to be herself, freedom to marry, freedom not to marry. While she danced to the future, I took up residence at the place I felt most comfortable: the bar. I was nursing a drink that was notably less strong than I was accustomed to at the All Saints. I felt tulle rub against my shoulder and looked over to see one of the most stunning people I had ever seen. They were well over six feet tall and their skin shined like copper against the night sky. It was one of the performers from the earlier drag show and they were wearing a wedding dress that looked identical to what Ariel wore in *The Little Mermaid*.

"I'm sorry, baby. I didn't mean to knock you around. These sleeves have a mind of their own."

"It's perfect! I love it. What a wonderful night," I responded.

"Yes, honey, yes it is. I just hope we can keep this energy and ride it into the next battle. The fight ain't over yet, honey." They smiled big.

"When do you think it will be?" I inquired.

"Oh, honey, it'll never be over! That's the beauty of the battle. As soon as we win one fight, the next one is just waiting for us. Liberty isn't just going to just go marching on without us. The oppressors are already working on the next struggle, we just got to be ready to wave our flag high and march on until everyone is equal." Just then their sleeves knocked over my drink. "Oh, lord! Look at me. Let me get you another one."

I tried my best to avoid the avalanche of ice and liquor that was coming toward me. I jumped back and barely missed being doused.

"Bartender, baby! We need another one for my friend here!" And then they took me by the shoulder. "Where is your man? Am I about to get beat up?" they joked.

I pointed toward Alexandria. "That's my lady over there."

"Girl! She is beautiful. Good job." And then they leaned in close. "That's the next battle, honey. That is your battle to keep that beautiful girl safe. The world is rough for us, those of us that don't fit into the binary. You gotta do what you gotta do to make sure that every step she takes is wrapped in bubble wrap."

I looked down at my feet as I took my seat again. My new friend tilted their head at me and then crossed their arms. "Oh, oh no. You're about to break her heart, aren't you?"

"What?" I squeezed out and then quickly took a gulp of my new drink.

"I have a sense about these things. What isn't working, honey?" They sat down and took a confessional position. I suddenly felt like I was in church.

"It's complicated."

"Honey, I am a professional at complicated!"

"I just…" I suddenly felt like I was going to be far too honest with a stranger. "I'm just not sure where I fit. Just today, I was thinking about how my heart has been fractured into a million pieces. I've only ever loved two women in my life. One is the mother of my child and the other is someone I let get away. She was in love with me and her at the same time. I got scared and then I lost her… I lost her forever." I could feel the emotions welling up inside me.

"And what does that have to do with that sweet baby girl over there who's loving you from across the room?" they asked.

"I don't think I've worked it all out. And I'm afraid I'm not being fair. I don't want to lose Alexandria, but I don't want to lose Joy any more than I already have. And I'll never know what would have happened with Clementine. I just feel like…"

"Honey, you just got to be honest. That's all you got to do. You see that girl, your girl. She's known more fear and hurt in her life than you could imagine in a thousand lifetimes. You just got to be honest with yourself and you gotta be honest with her. Do you know how to do that?"

"How to be honest?" I took a big pause. "I don't know that I've ever really been honest when it comes to love."

"So you love her?" They took a judgmental sip of their drink and looked me straight in the eyes.

"I don't know."

"Well, that was the first honest thing you've said all night. Honey, that's the question you gotta answer and you are the only one who can do that. Just find your answer. If you learn to be honest with yourself and with others, you'll only lose the people who didn't matter and will hold tight to the ones that do. Trust me; being honest with myself about who I am, honey, I lost a lot but I've gained so much more."

The master of ceremonies walked back up onto the stage. "It's time for our second show!" The crowd went wild and the dance music came to an end. Alexandria waved at me and started to make her way back over to the seat my new friend had been warming.

"That's my cue, baby," they said and gave me a kiss on the hand and then patted it gently. "Just learn to be honest, and you'll never go wrong. But if you love her, even it's only as a friend, remember you have a responsibility to keep her safe. Always keep her safe. We are all family now!"

Just then, the master of ceremonies called out, "Let's welcome Christian to the stage!"

I reached out my hand. "I'm Leo."

"It's good to meet you, Leo."

My new friend danced off to the stage and took the microphone. The entire room erupted and I could feel the energy rising. Alexandria gave me a kiss and we sat there and pulled out our dollar bills to get ready for the big show. Christian took out a big rainbow flag, the crowd screamed some more. They pointed right at me and smiled. "This song goes out to my new sweet friend, Leo! They don't know where they fit in the world just yet, but there's no better place to figure that out than here, right honeys?"

Just then, the Beach Boys' "God Only Knows" began to play. As I listened to Christian's beautiful voice serenade the crowd, I knew what I had to do. I had to stop looking at love as a binary; I had to stop placing it into these neat little compartments. Loving Alexandria didn't steal from my love for Joy or Clementine or Shane. The lesson I needed to learn from today, the day that love was open to every single person, was that no one gets to define what love means to someone else. I just had to figure out what it meant to me.

***

I was late picking up Clementyne from Joy's house. You would think with as much as my ideologies had been stretched and bent and reformed that I would not completely cringe at the idea of having to see her living this happy other life with someone else. I should have been more evolved than this by now but I was profoundly not so. I was too cowardly to express my feelings and then jealous of the life she was choosing to live now. I was the problem.

That weekend we spent out on the beach for Memorial Day weekend was less than a month ago. Her boyfriend was working that weekend and so it wasn't even an issue for him. He was so much cooler than me. I hated that too. Even though it would not have gone against any of Joy's ethics at all for us to have slept together that weekend, we did not. We were perfectly platonic roommates, which, I might add, was remarkable in its own right. For all of the things that were wrong with our relationship, for all my failings and hers, we never had a problem in the sex department. We were very good at that. From the first time until the last. The last time we made love was many months after we had officially called it quits.

After we first consummated our relationship and had stepped over the threshold of being friends into being lovers, we couldn't keep our hands off each other. You would be hard pressed to find a dark place in this town that we had not, at some point or another, had some variant of sexual relations.

The swimming pool at that big hotel downtown, absolutely. The alley behind the pizza pub, more than once. The bathroom at the nightclub, also yes. The beach.

The bar. The reception hall at our friends' wedding. We were sneaky.

Joy loved living in the perfection of her dichotomy. I was terrified of commitment and the proverbial, "putting a ring on it." I had no qualms with the idea of monogamy or being a one-person man. Her, she loved the idea of love. She wanted to experience everything and everyone. A magical night by a bonfire could turn into a beautiful night in bed with a stranger and she would wake up the next morning and think nothing of it. It was a natural progression. Another note in a song. A conversation continuing beyond where words could take you. But in spite of her freedom to be free she also loved the idea of a white dress and a wedding ring and walking down the aisle to say, "I do." She just might also make out with the minister before the reception.

I pulled into the driveway and there she was with our beautiful little girl and the cooler guy. I exited my car and we did that thing. Shake hands, how are you. No, I didn't catch the game. Then I would drive away to spend the weekend with my favorite person in the world.

Today, it went a little differently than all that. Clementyne left her backpack inside and she and Joy went off into the house to look for it. So boyfriend and I were stuck there to shuffle our feet.

"Listen, I'm glad we have a couple of seconds alone," he said.

"Okay." I wasn't.

"You know Joy better than anyone in the world. I've got a question for you; I hope you can help me out."

"Okay."

He pulled a little box out of his pocket. I knew that box. I had one of those at home. It was sitting in my dresser collecting dust with all of my transcripts and my passport and other items I never used at the right time. I got stuck in a Hugh Grant level blinking stutter.

"Okay," I uttered again.

"I'm going to ask Joy to marry me this weekend. I think I've been listening, I think I know what she wants. What do you think?" And with that he popped open the box. It looked so different from the one sitting in my dresser. The one that used to burn a hole in my jacket pocket but never found its way out; never found its way onto her finger. As he pushed it closer to inspect, I suddenly wanted to hit one knee. I thought I was going to pass out.

"What do you think?" he said with such a genuine smile.

"I think she'll love it. If she loves you, then she'll love it."

Just then the girls rushed out of the house and he quickly hid it like a magician shoving the rabbit back in the hat. He gave me a thankful nod and I gave a smile that looked more like a Cool Hand Luke scowl.

I got Clementyne situated in the back of the car and we drove off to see a movie and get ice cream and do all those weekend dad things. Each day moved forward like burning ice against my skin. I couldn't sleep at night. *Is it happening now? What about now? Maybe now? It's definitely happening now. How did it end up like this? Now I'm falling asleep.*

I was the world's biggest idiot. What right did I have to be jealous? I had followed Christian's advice all those years ago; shortly after that night Alexandria and I broke up and morphed into the world's best friends. That was where she fit in love with me and I with her. I just hadn't followed their advice far enough. I fell short in my journey to honest by taking the further step of going to Joy and telling her I was sorry, telling her I loved her, telling her I was ready to grow up and let go and move on and jump on that plane and be one of the people she kissed under the Eiffel Tower. I panicked and let more years bury me under the sands of time. This weekend was a song I wrote.

What was I always so goddamn afraid of? Being second fiddle? Probably not anymore. And what was wrong with me that I could have loved her and Clementine but somehow I was too afraid to be one of the boys in her life? There was a lot to unpack in that. I wanted more time. But time is fleeting, a lesson I should have long learned by now but was still too stubborn to absorb.

Our weekend was coming to a sunset and so the dance began again. I placed my little girl back into the car and made the short journey across town. I pulled into the driveway. Shake hands, how are you. No, I didn't catch the game. Then I would drive away to spend the week alone.

I made my way back to my car and Joy yelled to me, "Hey, Leo."

I turned around, "Yeah." I bet he didn't say yeah. Cool guys don't say yeah.

"I said yes."

I walked away from the car. That car was somewhere we had also done it a lot. In a lot of different places. Parking lots and rest stops and that time we drove across Texas. We just sort of leaned there at the front of my car not saying a word until she broke the silence again.

"There's a problem though," she said with a grin.

"Okay." I really needed to retire this from my vocabulary. "What?"

"You know what." She smiled. "He pulled out that box and he got on one knee and … something wasn't right. It's not the ring I wanted. It just wasn't the right ring."

"Damn, I told him it was a good ring." I actually felt bad.

"It was a beautiful ring, for someone. It just wasn't the right ring for me."

"Well, just for my curiosity, what's the right ring? So I don't steer the next one in the wrong direction."

"That one you always kept in your jacket. That was the right ring, Leo. It was always the right ring."

She kissed me on the cheek and let me go. I drove away again. There were a million things I could have said right. I always felt that way. But maybe that was the problem. I always wanted to make everything perfect instead of being content. Joy was content. No matter where she was, who she was with, she was content. She was content to say no. She was content to say yes. In a romantic comedy, I would have driven to my house and dusted off that ring box and I would have driven back to her house. I would have dropped to one knee and asked her to be mine. But this isn't a romantic comedy. This is Southern Gothic. This is real life. This was full of complications and missteps and mistakes and snot accidentally blasting out of your nose when you sneeze. The truth is I wasn't even in competition with the boyfriend, well, fiancé (his name is Wyatt btw. I don't know why I always needed him to be nameless like that made it not real.) I wasn't trying to beat him. I just wanted to still fit somewhere.

I bellied up to the All Saints and Mikey looked at me. "The usual?"

Yeah, the usual. The same drink. The same bar. The same life. The same mistakes. No matter where I was, I was always there.

CHAPTER ELEVEN

THE JOKE

I often think about the concept of the butterfly effect; the concept of changing a singular event and suddenly setting everything into a delicate cloud of peace. Wouldn't that be wonderful? But where would you begin? After exhausting this mathematical impossibility for my own redemption I began to fetishize the concept within the world at large.

On election night 2016, as the rage and fear and resentment began to swell up from deep inside me, I couldn't help but think of another night altogether. A date that would live in infamy: April 29th, 2011. You probably don't know that date. It doesn't rush to the forefront of your brain like dates that won't ever be forgotten. You look at the wall calendar and see it's September 11th of whatever year and instantly you are watching those towers fall again. Mention April 20th and there you are a scared kid wondering if your school is next. But you probably don't give a shit about April 29th, 2011 even though it's the day that the detonator was placed on the ticking time bomb that would become the Trump Presidency.

Growing up, I was a nerd without any particular fandom to call home. At least the *Star Wars* nerds had each other and could hate the Trekki nerds. I was a jack-of-all-nerdom. I didn't hold a particular affection for any one universe and so I floated out there on my own. Bullies don't give a shit what brand or flavor of nerd you are, they are there to torment somewhat indiscriminately. I was just in a constant state of torture all through middle school. There was no reprieve from the lack of shame these guys felt in their need to demean and hurt others. It was a form of entertainment for them.

My parents used to give me the same advice echoed on every single after-school program. "They are angry. They are jealous. They are cowards. You just have to stand up to them."

This has been the pretty standard advice and I don't have any recollection of anyone ever stepping up and saying anything to the contrary. The only way to beat the bully at their own game was to challenge them, eye to eye, and stand up. So it was no shock to me that, at eleven years old, when a particularly vicious bully had taken me on as his current victim, my dad gave me this same tried and true sage advice. I arrived home to an empty house and went to my room to cry. When my parents got home from work, I told them I didn't want any dinner. I was too angry and hurt to do something as trivial as eat; didn't they know the extent of the cruelty I was facing? Eventually, my father entered my room and stood at the end of my bed.

"Boy, what are you going on about? Your mother has dinner downstairs," he said coldly.

"I just can't," I whimpered, "I can't go back to school. I don't want to. They are so mean and I just wish I hadn't been born."

"There isn't anything you can do about being born. You've got no choice and you better get up there and face these problems like a man. Do men cry?"

"No." I sniffled away at my nose with my wrist.

"Goddamn right they don't. Wash your face and get down to that table. You want to show them who's boss? You stand up to that punk and let him know you are a man. He will respect that."

That next morning, at school, I did exactly that. This punk walked up to me and started in about my pants and my hair and trying to make me feel smaller than I already was; I turned around, I didn't cry because boys don't do that, and I gave him some monologue channeling my inner Indiana Jones. I told him I wasn't scared of him and that he didn't have any power over me. He just stared at me and sort of tilted his head. I was winning, I thought. After giving him a resounding verbal lashing in front of everyone, I turned around and walked away. I mentally dusted off my shoulders and then suddenly I felt something warm on them. His meaty fingers had latched me by the shoulder and he spun me around. There we stood, nose to nose, David and Goliath stuck in the eternal battle of bully vs. dork.

Classic.

The blood came pouring down my cheek and I lifted my hand up to touch it and then inspect it on my fingertips. My entire head hurt and I had no memory of falling and hitting the ground. Everyone was having a good laugh. I jumped to my feet as fast as I could and I ran like lightning. I ran through the doors and down the hall and into the bathroom. I cried until the principal came in to tell me it was time to get to class. I emerged from the bathroom bloodied and swollen from the impact and the tears. The principal took me away, down to his office and called my parents. Neither of them came and I took the bus home.

That kid got suspended but he never served his full sentence. His mom came to his defense and talked about how it was really me that egged him on; that I was the one who started it by giving him a long threatening speech. I needed to learn my place. How dare I stand up to months of jeering?

The weeks and months leading up to the infamous day of April 29th, 2011 our president had been suffering endless bullying from a notable reality television star.

Why he was given any credibility will remain beyond me but he had the impassioned cheering on of his newfound interactive followers on Twitter. They laughed and they taunted like the entourage of my own bully. "Hit him again!" they would yell. They could not handle the concept of a Black man ascending so high. "It must not be true!" They foamed and raged. "How could this be allowed?" They began to search for any motive to tear him down from the desk that had been held by forty-three white men before him. Slave owners and slave apologists, some abolitionists and some who fought against injustice. All white and all looking back and telling Black folks to wait their turn; don't push too far, don't ask too much.

Then in walked Barack Hussein Obama, not asking any motherfuckers' opinions about a goddamn thing.

They screamed and howled and demanded something be done. Then, in a moment of insidious brilliance, Donald Trump began to bark up the tree. Here it was, here was the moment, question the very thing that will bite right at the root of their bigotry and feelings of supremacy: you don't belong here and you never belonged here. So the Donald questioned the legitimacy of the president's citizenship. This man isn't one of us! He isn't American; just look at him, just listen to his name. He must be Muslim, ignore him at church on Sunday; that is just a cover. He must have been born somewhere else, America doesn't look like this. He will let them jump the border; he will let them bomb your towers; he will destroy everything we stand for.

So this washed-up nobody took his minions of followers and questioned the ability of a Black man to even be from here. No, Black men belong on football teams, gangs, or in prison … it is the White House after all. "Thanks for building it, but you aren't welcome to inhabit it," was the clear message.

Then our nerd-in-chief took the advice every other nerd had ever been told his whole life, stand up to the bully. So on the night of the White House Correspondence Dinner, our president did just that. He began his remarks by showing the world his sense of humor and grace. He mocked the idea of his birth certificate conspiracy and handled it beautifully. The room was tickled pink over watching the bully being taken down. What a wonderful joke. And then, I watched as Barry made the same mistake I did that day before I got the shit kicked out of me. He put on his internal fedora and began to monologue.

Here is a transcript from the official Obama White House Archive:

"And I know just the guy to do it—Donald Trump is here tonight! (Laughter and applause.) Now, I know that he's taken some flak lately, but no one is happier, no one is prouder to put this birth certificate matter to rest than the Donald. (Laughter.) And that's because he can finally get back to focusing on the issues that matter—

like, did we fake the moon landing? (Laughter.) What really happened in Roswell? (Laughter.) And where are Biggie and Tupac? (Laughter and applause.)

"But all kidding aside, obviously, we all know about your credentials and breadth of experience. (Laughter.) For example—no, seriously, just recently, in an episode of *Celebrity Apprentice*—(laughter)—at the steakhouse, the men's cooking team did not impress the judges from Omaha Steaks. And there was a lot of blame to go around. But you, Mr. Trump, recognized that the real problem was a lack of leadership. And so ultimately, you didn't blame Lil' Jon or Meatloaf. (Laughter.) You fired Gary Busey. (Laughter.) And these are the kind of decisions that would keep me up at night. (Laughter and applause.) Well handled, sir. (Laughter.) Well handled.

"Say what you will about Mr. Trump, he certainly would bring some change to the White House. Let's see what we've got up there. (Laughter.)

(Screens show 'Trump White House Resort and Casino.')"

If you remove the notations of laughter and applause, the joke, which was likely written by an intern, was just over 200 words. He stood up to the bully; he humiliated him in front of the entire world. That is what nerds like me and Barry are told we were supposed to do. But underneath those tablecloths, Donald Trump was cracking his knuckles. His allies and historians agree that this was the moment Donald Trump decided to run for president:

April 29th, 2011.

On election night, it was all I could think about. I wondered what it would be like to travel through time and grab that Blackberry out of the hands of that intern penning those carefully crafted words into one big fuck-up.

"Don't do it, you idiot! You are dooming us all," I scream at some imaginary intern who lives in my head.

Your parents didn't tell you to stand up to the bully because they thought it would make them respect you. Our parents weren't telling us to stand up to the bully because they thought the bully was wrong. They thought we were weak, a pussy, a wimp, a pansy. They wanted you to get your ass kicked. Just like their wars, they were outsourcing the violence. They admired the bully more than you. They wished the bully was their son, not the sack of snot crying in front of them. They hoped that if you stood up to the bully, you would become the bully. They knew good and goddamn well that the bully was going to knock the shit out of you. Ask any of your friends; ask them what happened when they stood up. Busted lip. Cracked eyebrow. The total and systematic dismantling of democracy. Whatever.

***

It wasn't until we were well into Trump's first term as president that I realized I had been wrong about my assessment that he was the bully. I had always thought that is what my father found so admirable in him. He was the bully that he had always hoped I could be; he was the bully my father had hoped he could grow into. Oh, how bitterly wrong I was. They didn't vote for my bully on the school yard, they voted for his narcissistic sociopathic parent, the one that showed up to get the bully out of trouble with the school. The one who could twist the words just right, threaten a lawsuit, and turn it all around for them. The ultimate protector and enabler of their personal ideologies of arrogance and supremacy. We had been living with the bullies all along, they raised us and folded our socks and made us meatloaf. Don't cry. Do more. Try harder. Get an A. Shut up. Don't talk to me like that. As long as you are under my roof you will not think for yourself or have opinions or love differently than I can understand.

A political party made up of parents who opposed Roe v. Wade and then drove their children to suicide because they didn't really like the one they got. They opposed you making a choice about your own reproduction, but if you got out of line, suddenly they would push you to a super late-term abortion at the end of a razor blade they would place in your hand using the same techniques they told you to stand up to on the playground.

The worst fucking part about the whole miserable experience of living in this pre-dystopian empire that Trump was building is that you had to just keep on living in it.

"I gotta take a shit; I hope this isn't the moment that Trump drops the H-Bomb on Manhattan."

"I have a date tonight, I hope tonight isn't when he will have Hillary arrested."

"Should I watch reruns of *Dawson's Creek* or doom scroll the Nazi insurrection in Charlottesville on Facebook?"

I don't want to wait for my life to be over.

No, you had to just go on with your life and ignore the constant stream of destruction happening around you. I mean you couldn't totally ignore it because every day was a constant battle of tweet, protest, rally, sleep, tweet, protest, rally, drink.

We just had to go on living in the middle of it somehow. For me, on this day, that looked like doing something I should have done years ago… I was going on a date with Joy. I made my drive across town. I exited my car and we did that thing. Shake hands, how are you. No, I didn't catch the game. But this time I drove away with her with me. I wasn't putting my foot down or acting like I somehow owned her, even if I knew I had the better ring. It was enough to know I fit somewhere in her life, even if it didn't look the way that my parents or her parents thought made sense. I didn't have to answer to them, I was going to have to answer to me for my choices and answer to her for my lack of making good choices.

I felt the gravel under my wheels and we walked down that familiar hallway and took the turn at the neon light and into the room. We sat at the big round table and enjoyed a drink with the ghosts of our friends.

"Did you sleep with her, bro?" the specter of Shane whispers as Joy walks off to the restroom.

I shake my head.

"That's a yes; a denial is always a yes." His ghostly grin is just as I remembered. Because it's all just shadows of memories. He will always look the same. Never a grey hair or a wrinkle. But in the eyes of the world, though, I am now a decade his senior; I am no older, no more important, no more worthy of a place at the table. Just some stupid entitled millennial kid trying to get laid tonight.

I look back at the bathroom and wonder what Joy and the phantom of Clementine are discussing. Is she finally telling Joy that she loved her? Does she get the courage this time? Or is she stuck somewhere in the universe perpetually unable to find the love she so desperately always wanted? Is she there on the other side of the veil just waiting for the two of us to finally join her?

"Hey." Joy's whiskey voice beckons me to a game of darts.

Everything about this woman loves to reframe even the saddest night into a beautiful sunrise. Her least favorite pastime is to focus on any of the pain or misery that exists in the world. That was likely one of the reasons we struggled to succeed the first go around. I lived comfortably in that shadowy place of grief and despair and fear. Could I come out into the light with her, just a bit? Tonight, it seemed I would need to experiment a bit with being that sunrise, that beam of light. There was a cloud hanging over there unlike anything I had seen before.

"You doing alright?" I finally inquired after she missed yet another bull's-eye.

"I hate it when it's that obvious." She laughed.

"What's up?"

"I just wish this fucking impeachment stuff was over with. It's absolutely decimating my relationship with my father." She took another failed shot. "Everything is a hoax and a joke to him. In his mind, that monster could do nothing wrong. I can't comprehend how this is the same man who raised me. I don't even recognize him anymore."

Joy had a very different kind of relationship with her parents than I did with mine. They had the type of home where, in spite of their highly religious attitudes, they got out of the way a lot more of the time than mine did. I'm not sure it was any healthier of an environment than my home, it was just different.

I took my shot and busted. "Give me an example."

"I am not Nick and I will never be Nick. I think we've come to peace with that a long time ago. It really seemed like they were beginning to accept me for me. It's not like I didn't give them hurdles to climb. But it seemed like love was big enough. I just don't know how we are going to survive this, Leo."

She took another hit and a miss.

"I don't understand how these are the same people who took me to Mexico on a missions trip with our church and taught us that everyone on the other side of this invisible line are the same Church, the same family. Now they want to build a wall and think all those mothers and fathers we worked with are drug lords. When I was a kid, they would drag me to the abortion clinic to protest and say that children deserved a life. Now they are locking them in cages. My dad threw out a CD that Nick brought home one day because it had the n-word in it and dad heard Nick sing those words. He smacked him upside the head and said no son of his would use racist language in his house. Now he is sharing memes about lynching Colin Kaepernick because he knelt at a basketball game. Who are these people?"

This was dating in 2019, millennials commiserating over the existential crisis of their parents disintegrating into something we didn't recognize. Even my dad, who was a monster of a man, was becoming a version of himself that was terrifying. There were days when I was afraid he might shoot the mailman for being a communist living off the teat of the state. They were no longer content with hopefully being able to deny a gay couple a wedding cake or fantasizing about revoking their right to marry, they wanted to see them erased from existence.

Joy was dealing with something wholly different in that her parents were religious and so they had taught an ethical and moral ideology that she now saw them back-peddling on. As for me, I had grown up in a Trump-like household my whole life. My dad was exactly like Trump in every single way, minus the ability to make money. He was a perfect example of what my dad aspired to be: a crass egomaniac who could say anything he wanted without fear of consequences and was surrounded by women who would otherwise not pay him any mind. For Joy, she was watching this person who should otherwise repulse her family but instead was wooing them in with a yet untapped charisma. He had adopted the rhetoric of the Church and still got to keep his playboy mystique.

"It doesn't matter what I present to him," she continued as we moved on past our failed game of darts and instead decided to stick with something we were always good at: drinking. "No matter if I bring forward clear-cut evidence of wrong, it's all fake news."

Is it any wonder that we were a generation that constantly felt stuck somewhere as teenagers with receding hairlines and stretch marks and early onset arthritis? We were still having the same type of arguments with our parents. And now their leader had risen up to show them that no, you never have to retire, you never have to yield, you abandon the children who don't profit you, and the others will wait their turn patiently. Your kids don't exist for you to love them or for you to nurture them or for you to be a grandparent to their babies. No, they exist to prop you up and convert your Word documents to PDFs.

So here we sit and drink our drinks while my daughter's mother's fiancé babysits our little one so we can go on a date. Because we have to build a different type of community out of the rubble of the destruction our parents are creating. Something that looks wholly unlike the world they wanted to build in the image of the golden spires of Trump Tower. No, we were going to rewrite the whole goddamn narrative of what it means to be a family because whatever the fuck they exampled for us wasn't worth shit.

Mom and Dad, you're fired.

CHAPTER TWELVE

FOREVER YOUNG

I woke up in a cold sweat. I could feel the presence of someone, or something, in my room. I reached for my nightstand and turned on the light. There were three people sitting at the end of my bed and they were smiling. Instantly, I was no longer afraid. I knew these people so very well and I loved them and I knew they loved me. They didn't mean me any harm and my heart was suddenly filled with a sense of peace. I knew everything was going to be alright, even if I didn't know what was happening.

"Good morning, neighbor," he said with a smile.

"Uh, hi. What is this?" I asked the familiar figure. He was beaming and put his hand on my foot and gave it a little shake. His red cardigan was brighter in real life. For some reason I didn't question why he was sitting in my room or why I didn't seem alarmed by it. I imagine I should have been concerned that I was dead, but I guess maybe the dead aren't concerned with being dead. I wasn't really sure.

"Did you have a good night's sleep, Leo?"

"I did." And I stretched.

"What an exciting day you've got." he said. "It's the first day."

"The first day for what?" I inquired.

"Everything. Let me introduce you to my friends who came to be with us today. Would you like to meet them?" He asked so gently like I was actually able to say no if I wanted to, but I didn't want to. I nodded my head eagerly because I could see them coming through clearly now and I knew them too.

"Hello, mate! Oh boy, I am so excited for you! What a great day. It's the biggest day! You are going to catch it right by the tail and you are going to do great!" a man in cargo shorts happily yelled at me.

"Thanks!" I exclaimed.

"You betcha!"

Then the third figure appeared and walked over to my wall. Slowly he took out an easel and began to gently set everything up. He placed the paint pots delicately and counted them and checked their lids. He set out a little cup with paint brushes and inspected every single one. Finally, he turned to me and smiled.

"Hello, friend, I am so happy that you will be joining me today. Would you like to paint something beautiful?"

"Yes, I really would."

"Alright! Let's get started. The secret to doing anything is believing that you can do it. Anything that you believe you can do strongly enough, you can do. Anything. As long as you believe. Do you believe we can do that today, Leo?"

"Yes, I do. I really do."

"Okay, good. Then let's get started!"

"But..." I protested, "I don't know what we are painting."

The three of them looked at each other and smiled and laughed and then settled me back down. I looked around my room and it was full of joy. I was full of joy. Nothing hurt.

"We are going to build a beautiful neighborhood, where everyone is welcome," Fred sang.

"Oh boy! And a world too! We are going to make a beautiful world. It's going to be amazing and we are going to keep it safe. It's going to be great!" Steve was jumping with excitement.

"And it's going to have mistakes. Little mess-ups along the way. But that's going to be okay too. We can always turn those little mistakes into happy accidents." Bob put his hand on my shoulder and led me to the wall. Together we began to paint. At first I couldn't see what we were painting. It didn't make sense to me. But with each stroke it slowly took form. A couple of times I messed things up and Bob leaned over with a laugh and showed me another way to fix it. Steve was hyping me up the whole time. When it was done, I sang a song with Fred about how the world was a beautiful place and so was I. I reached for the door and it opened and I was whisked away through time.

I am standing in the house my parents owned before they had me. My dad is yelling at the television and the news anchor came on the television to announce that Jimmy Carter had won his second term as president of the United States. My dad is annoyed and throws a bit of a fit. He walked into the kitchen and got himself a beer and sat back down on the couch and my mother tells him it's going to be alright and he sighs a bit and admits it probably will be.

In this moment I realized that time wasn't holding on to me at all. All I had to do was think about an event and there I was. A bit selfishly I float from moment to moment. I sit in a director's chair and watch as Steven Spielberg directs Harrison Ford in *Indiana Jones*. It was a great day. Then I bounce around some more and watch fireworks flash across the sky at Disney World with no one in particular. I am not even sure how long I was there or anywhere else. I then flash back to my own life.

I watch as I participate in mundane things. I went to school and learned about things that mattered. I looked at the calendar: September 11ᵗʰ, 2001. I quickly look at the clock 8:46 AM. No one is running down the hallways. No televisions are rolled in. My teacher is writing on her dry erase board. I just wait there in that room and learn and soak it all in. When the day is done I walked out the doors and look around. No metal detectors, no resource officer. I look over at the school library door and a large poster with familiar characters reads in large letters, "Berenstein Bears."

Holy shit.

Joy grabs me around the waist and there are Shane and Clementine and Nick is picking us up. We drive away to live our lives. I don't know what the future holds, but I know it holds something different. Different than the outcomes we had been given. Bob's words gently move through my mind. "And it's going to have mistakes. Little mess-ups along the way. But that's going to be okay too. We can always turn those little mistakes into happy accidents." We drive on forward into the sunrise of our lives and I know we will make mistakes, maybe even a few failures, along the way. But they will be our mistakes and our failures and we will learn from them. They will be beautiful little accidents.

I wake up with the sun shining into my bedroom. I am alone. I did not travel through time and I didn't fix anything. But I still cherished the moments that I spent with those three spirits. Even though I could not fix the past and there were and are powers that try and push us down, I could still learn from the lessons of the visitors. There was still a future where I could correct course and make changes. It would be hard because, well, there were plenty of obstacle courses set up with the intention to make each of us fail. Some of us were set on courses even more treacherous than others. It was up to us all, collectively, as one big, beautiful neighborhood to remove the roadblocks and traffic stops and dismantle the systemic metrics designed to hold us back.

Time travel is real, I suppose, in the sense we are always spinning forward into time and it was now my turn to vote, and to change, and to make a difference. I couldn't spend any more time worrying about my losses but create gains for the next generation instead of just worrying about the fact that my own youth was bartered for the vampiric indulgences of our parents. It was time to build a shield around their grand-babies so that they could safely move into the unknown and blaze a bright new trail for themselves. Somehow, the sting of these bullets felt less bitter knowing we were now acting as a defense shield for our kids instead of just being target practice for the entertainment of the most bored generation known to humanity.

***

"Fuck," I yell as I jump out of bed. And then I realize I am late for nothing. I have absolutely nowhere to be. What an absolutely strange feeling. This is not a space I occupy all too often. I take a quick glance around the room to see if I may have accidentally cursed in front of one of my childhood heroes. No, it's still just a dream. A perfect dream. Today is a perfect day. It's one of two days out of the year that my parents will babysit. Tomorrow is the other day. But that doesn't really matter right now. The world is about to be reborn again. Nothing can go wrong. Trump has been impeached, it's heading to the Senate; the world is doing alright at this moment and it's my favorite day of the year.

New Year's Eve: 2019

In a perfect world I would tell you how I had made a plot to break into Nick's house that night and I was going to find that file with the words in red on them. Just as I pulled the files out to inspect them, he would walk in and monologue at me about how it was all a master plan. He had sold us out to the bishop, the mayor, and the sheriff. It was all part of the scheme. Sure, I had caught him, but that wasn't going to stop anything from moving forward. He would tell me that I should not have gone meddling in other people's business and then he would pick up a big brass crucifix that he was going to bash me over the head with. Just in that moment, I pull out my .38 Special and pew, pew, pew! The police will show up and off he goes screaming into a cop car. "And I would have gotten away with it too if it wasn't for you meddling kids!" I walk around with a detective explaining everything and still make it home in time for dinner and the town is now safe. Maybe justice will finally be served, cold.

A less violent approach is I could dust off that ring box that's sitting there in my dresser. I could place it in my jacket pocket and let it burn a hole in me all night. I can't hear or think and I'll just float around the world trying to enjoy the night. Just before the stroke of midnight, now it's my turn to monologue. I would jump up on the bar at the All Saints and talk about how much Joy has always meant to me. I'll admit the failures and mistakes I've made along the way. Just before the stroke of midnight, I drop to one knee and ask her to be my wife. She says yes, of course, and off we go to make love.

Even better, after my dream with the three specters of television wholesomeness, I wake up and it's all been a dream. It's basically *A Christmas Carol* and I didn't screw everything up. We make totally different decisions and everyone lives. I don't go through all this trauma and disappointment and Joy and I still end up together. After a long engagement we get married, today, of all days! Shane is my best man and Clementine is there. But does this work? In this narrative have I learned all my lessons enough that I learn how to deconstruct what it means to be a family enough to still make space for Clementine? Probably fucking not.

Instead, I am stuck here in this very real life where I have to figure all this shit out for myself and without the helpful guidance of Bob Saget coming in with John Stamos and Dave Coulier to tell me, "Steph, it's alright, here is how to be a grown-up and do taxes and stuff!" No, none of this is going to work out that way. I've got Rosanne Barr for parents and she's about to have a super racist Twitter meltdown: Trump 2020!

None of this was turning out the way I was told it was supposed to. We had all been hyped up for a future that doesn't look anything like the one we are living in. We were supposed to vote for the first Black president and end racism. Instead, we pulled the lid off of the ugliest parts of the American Nightmare and showed the genuine mess we had created. None of this was going to plan and yet whoever actually told us there was a plan? I'm pretty sure my parents were winging it the whole time. They were just better at hiding it all. They went to cocaine-infused orgies on the weekends and Halloween key parties and then woke us up in time to go to church on Sunday morning and told us not to fuck until we got married. They left out the part that they would fuck literally anyone and everyone as soon as they were married. Hell, I can't keep up.

So we do our best to blast the doors off the building and just expose ourselves, broken and raw. Here I am and what the fuck are you going to do about it? Ground me? Not let me get a mortgage? Cripple me with student debt? Make it impossible to afford a family but take away our access to birth control? Slowly watch us die out because we don't have access to healthcare? Well, the jokes on you; you'll have to finally watch your grandkids once we are dead.

I pick up Alexandria on my way to the restaurant we got reservations at. It's a super expensive tapas place but we are all going to split and make it work. Joy and Wyatt are going too. Blake is on his way but his date canceled and so he's finding a backup.

We are seated thirty minutes after our reservation and we don't complain to the manager. We discuss that we need to make sure we don't overspend so we can be sure to leave our waiter a great tip, they are slammed tonight. The six of us take our seats and laugh about the year and try really, really hard not to bring Trump up at all tonight. We do a pretty good job. None of us break into song or anything. There isn't a musical number about how we will all be friends for life and that nothing is going to keep us down, la vie boheme! But we enjoy our drinks and the food is amazing and we laugh.

I look around the table and I realize I have absolutely no idea what's going to happen from here. Will this be the last night I see one of these people I love? Will tonight change our lives for the better? Will Alexandria and I rekindle our romance? Will Blake and whoever the hell it is he found to come with him tonight drunkenly pass out at the bar? Who the fuck knows. Is there a goddamn thing I can do to change any of it? Would I really if I could? Joy leans in for a preview kiss with her fiancé. I'm genuinely happy.

I wouldn't miss this meal for the world.

We all pack into the back of an Uber and make our way to the gravel. Walkway. Door. Room. Bar. Drinks. Our new little family fills out that round table quite nicely.

Joy asks me for a cigarette. I pull out my phone and a pack. I look at the time; midnight is encroaching on us pretty quickly. Another year past. As brutal of a year as it has been, the unending deluge of news has been good for business. I am not comfortable, I am not doing alright, but I feel like I am going to be okay. Sure, the makeup of who was going to be kissing who tonight didn't hit the mark of where I wanted it to be by this point in life. Maybe by any point in life. But I was going to be okay.

Another round!

The clock is ticking down and there is nothing I can do to slow it down. Maybe this time I don't want to anymore. Could I be able to stop wishing I could control time and let go? Could I bask in the moment and be content with whatever direction it was choosing to take me? Lie upon my back and let the river just flow. Fuck the clock. Fuck the calendar. Time is racing and slowing and moving and going and I'm going to be okay.

Joy leans over. "Can I ask you a question?"

"Always."

"Is that ring in your pocket?"

Sure, I didn't have the balls to break into the bishop's apartment and steal some files and shoot him in a grand gesture. Absolutely, I didn't have the power to wake up a decade ago and reform my life. Those are silly notions of delusional fantasy, but I mean, yeah, I brought the ring. You never know what's going to happen in life, I've come to terms with that and the easiest way to just let life happen is to give it every single opportunity to do so. Just to step out of the way and be alright with whatever slugs and punches and kisses and hugs come your way. So yeah, I brought the fucking ring. Sue me.

"The superior ring?"

"No."

"The better ring?"

"No."

"What ring are you taking about, Joy?"

"The right ring."

I reached toward my jacket pocket to pull the ring box out and she grabs my wrist. I suddenly feel cold like my soul is leaving my entire body.

"Listen!" she says as the chorus begins.

Ten.

Nine.

Eight.

Seven.

Six.

Five.

Four.

Three.

Two.

One.

We kiss.

"Yes," she says. She extends her hand to me and here I am, finally, able to place it slowly down her tender finger. It clinks up against the other ring and then, suddenly, they look right. The perfect rings. It wasn't in the way, They complimented each other perfectly. One ring was ready to do everything I couldn't do and the ring I had was ready to be exactly what it was supposed to be.

Both?

Both.

Both is good!

That night we drink to our good health, we drink to our bad health, we drink to the future, to possibility, to friends we've lost, to the friends we have. We close the motherfucker down. The night rages on into possibility and we transport ourselves yet again from the All Saints to the only after-hours club that matters: the beach. We make a brief stop at the Waffle House and eat our weight in hash browns and eggs and sober up just enough to risk a cold brisk swim in those salty waters of our birth. The water is dark and unwelcoming, not a bad allegory for life. The six of us disrobe. The first story ever told was that Adam and Eve walked the earth like this and then they felt shame. We passed that shame from generation to generation as guilt. Everyone afraid of their bodies and their many parts and what they look like and what genitals they have and who does what with their genitals and with whom. Not us. Not today. You know why? Because Fred told me, "Your body's fancy and so is mine!" That's fucking why.

We dive into the cold waters of the Gulf and feel the icy waters revive us and the salt cleanse us.

We crash against the sand like a human wave and lie there watching as the waxing crescent slowly fades into the new sunrise. This is what Joy always wanted to show me, I think. It really is beautiful. As we all lie there exposed, I wonder will this stick? Who of us will be here next year? Have Joy and I really found what we have been longing for? Maybe I would finally pull one of the manuscripts out of my dresser and send it off. The six of us reached out our hands and held one another's palms and the new sun, of the first day, of the first moments, of the new dawn, of the new year, exposed every perfectly flawed inch of our skin. I doubt this is what the preachers meant when they said we should be born again, but this is exactly what it should feel like.

No, I don't know what the future holds. I'm letting go of attempting to control it. Our parents and senators and Wall Street long ago wrote the script. Fuck it. It's time for a complete rewrite. So as I looked out across our sandy bodies and uncertain future, it was a declaration of freedom. Of no longer being willing to be held back. We are going to fly to Paris; we are going to see that tower. We are no longer going to let our fears hold us back or be captive to the generation before us. We will break the shackles and run naked through the waters. This is the time to live, the time to breathe, the time to dance, to experience, to grow, to change. This is the moment we are going to finally be grown-ups and in charge and ready to take on the world before us. Even though we all knew it silently in the hopes of our hearts, we were all too afraid to say it, and then Joy, the eternal optimist, our lovely re-framer, jumped to her feet and lifted her hands to greet the new sun and let it all out in one explosive scream.

"2020 is going to be our year, y'all!"

Orgasmic.

ACT III
TWO THOUSAND TWENTY

Chapter One

Apocalypse

Well, you cool cats and kittens, I guess we really did get grounded from life. We are never going to financially recover from this.

ABOUT NATHAN MONK

Nathan Monk is a social justice advocate, dyslexic author and former Orthodox priest. He lives in East Tennessee with his partner Tashina, and their three children. He works with nonprofits and local governments to address issues associated with homelessness, poverty and social justice.

Nathan and his family spent much of his formative years living in Nashville, TN. After experiencing homelessness with his family as teenager, he has gone on to found numerous programs providing food, clothing, emergency resources, and shelter.

Currently, Nathan is the founder of the Charity Institute, a community growth program for nonprofits. Over his career, he has received notable awards, appointments, and national media for his accomplishments in the area of social justice and is an active public speaker, author, and guest lecturer at numerous universities.

Nathan is active on social media…
Follow
@FatherNathan
to get updates
facebook.com/FatherNathan
twitter.com/FatherNathan
instagram.com/FatherNathan
www.CharityInstitute.com

Manufactured by Amazon.ca
Bolton, ON